THE CHURCH

An addictive crime mystery full of twists

ROY LEWIS

Arnold Landon Mysteries Book 5

Originally published as
The Devil Is Dead

JOFFE BOOKS

Revised edition 2021
Joffe Books, London
www.joffebooks.com

First published in Great Britain in 1989
as *The Devil Is Dead*

ISBN: 978-1-78931-858-6

Hey-ho, the Devil is dead!
—*Old song*

NOTE TO THE READER

Please note this book is set in the 1980s in England, a time before mobile phones and ubiquitous CCTV, and when social attitudes were very different.

CHAPTER ONE

1

The moon was full but marked by high, drifting clouds. On the distant hill behind the churchyard an owl called, its screech echoing and re-echoing across the dark slopes of the valley, fading mistily in the distance but lending an eerie, elemental sharpness to the midnight cold. There were other predators on the hill, rustlings in the undergrowth, nocturnal movements in the long grass of the hillside, but in the churchyard itself everything seemed frozen to stillness as though the darkness was expectant, waiting for something to happen.

In the lee of the hill, on the edge of the village which had finally died, some fifteen years earlier, from the neglect of a century, the ruins of the old church seemed black in the moonlight. The faint glow of the embers, remains of the small fire that had been lit where the sacristy had once stood, were a reddish stain in the darkness. The lights from the shaded lanterns cast grotesque shadows against the old stone walls of the churchyard, patterns of dim movement, the rustling of dark cloaks shivering a backcloth of menace to the barely distinguishable forms that crouched against the ancient stones. As the clouds moved from the moon, the pale light sharpened, cast into black relief the tight circle in which the worshippers stood. The moonlight touched them, silvering the stones behind them, and at the touch they rose from their crouching positions to stand upright, heads still lowered, but eyes behind the hoods flickering sideways to their master.

The chanting began.

It was an old language, a cold language, words hauled out of a past dark with terror and viciousness, blood, sensuality and death. To the group the words were meaningless and yet full of meaning; they could not know what the chant signified but they were aware of its strength and its evil and its purpose. It was a thin noise, a controlled sound, touched by an undercurrent of fear but wary of the world beyond the gates of the church. It was a sound that faded among the tall, Gothic tombstones the early-Victorian mourners had erected to commemorate their dead a hundred and fifty years ago. But it was a sound that had existed for longer than those stones, a chant that had been heard for more than three hundred years.

The night had been still, in spite of the slow drift of clouds across the moon, but as though in response to the soft, cold chanting a breeze arose, whispering with the sound of rustling leaves through the long grass of the churchyard, touching the faces of the chanters with cool morning fingers. The chanting hesitated, died, and silence swept in about them as they looked expectantly towards the man who stood hooded, with his back to the wall.

He spoke, and again the words meant nothing and everything, but there was a cold passion in the tones, and the menace was communicated down to the victim, held within the circle, lying helpless, pinioned at their feet. The group looked down, hearing the words prickle the hairs at the back of their necks, seeing the terror in the eyes of the prisoner, and each of them experienced the same feeling, the sensation they had been told to expect. A surge of excitement, a realization of power, the dark forces released by the Master's words sharpening their senses, quickening their blood. They felt suddenly that they were as gods, masters of life and of destiny, creators of the most powerful of emotions, terror. They felt the taste of it on their tongues, and their heartbeats became a raging sound in their breasts as they watched, and waited, and saw the gleam of steel in the sharp moonlight.

Behind them, the last smoke of the ritual fire was fading away, drifting in the breeze, but the steel had been cleansed and the odour of the incense was still in their nostrils, cloying and sweet in intensity and richness. It was touched with corruption but it had cleansed the steel and now it was time.

The Master swept back his hood and the words seemed to come no longer from his mouth but from deep inside him, dragged out agonizingly in a more sonorous, purposeful chant, a call to the darkness, a raising of black storms from age-old visions and rages of ancient violence. His two gloved hands were black on the pommel, the Cross, raised above the glitter of the chased steel.

At their feet there was a whimpering sound, a sudden, brief struggling, but it was ineffectual. It raised no pity. The excitement was surging in them uncontrollably, a blood lust bringing heat to their eyes and a shivering excitement to their limbs. One man groaned as though in ecstasy and the glittering blade was poised, unwavering.

The Master raised his head, looked slowly around him at the tight gathering, the seven, the worshippers. His eyes seemed to glow, and the moonlight gave his head a silvery, haloed appearance, emphasizing an existence beyond reach of time, and they all knew they truly were in the presence of the Master, the Old One, the First One, born yet again in the flesh of the man who held the steel.

The silence and the moment held them, sickening in its expectancy, and they were unable to breathe as the tension took hold of their chests, squeezed at their hearts, formed a cold knot of expectation in their stomachs. Their eyes were fixed on the lethal shining blade. The moment seemed endless.

It glittered again, turning, and then it plunged with a solid, sickening thud. There was a howling, terrified sound, cut off by the severance from life, and the steel and the Cross of its pommel stood quivering, released from the fierce grip of the Master for that one moment before, tentatively, they all reached out and touched the haft, gently, with the tips of their fingers.

It was a frightening moment, a time of terror and fulfilment and dark dreams as they touched the steel and saw the victim at their feet, blood pulsing darkly in the moonlight. Then they stepped back and watched as, with the age-old ritual chant, the Master dragged out the steel and plunged it into the corpse again.

And again. And once more. Stiffly the believers ringed him while he used the steel, in the precise, ancient ritual that had been followed for three hundred years.

In the silent churchyard the Master's breath was a ragged, brutal sound.

2

Arnold Landon was not a member of the Literary and Philosophical Society of Newcastle-upon-Tyne. He was aware of its existence of course, and of its history, conscious that it was here that George Stephenson had first lectured on his invention, the miners' lamp, before Humphry Davy demonstrated his Cornish version and stole the northerner's thunder. It was odd in a sense that it was George's son, Robert, who had been honoured with a statue just outside the Lit and Phil building, but in Victorian eyes Robert had always been seen as a more worthy man than his father, for his engineering skills and, perhaps, his greater acceptance in polite society.

Although he knew about the Society, Arnold had never entered the building before. Ben Gibson met him just inside the entrance, at the foot of the handsome staircase, and took the opportunity to give Arnold a quick tour. It was Ben who had invited Arnold to attend with him the last of the midsummer evening lectures of the Society, and the little antiquarian bookseller had taken great pleasure in showing Arnold the delights of the idiosyncratic library, the subterranean reference rooms, the oil paintings and the busts, and called upon him to savour the old odours of the place.

Arnold had been impressed. In the library itself, with its solid oak tables and musty books, there had been the smell of coffee — Ben had explained the students and old men came to read and gossip in the mornings and enjoyed their coffee and biscuits. 'Best in Newcastle,' Ben had boasted. The iron staircase to the gallery had been ascended and the largely Victorian collection of volumes inspected, and Arnold had even been allowed to walk through the first-floor doorway that led along a small gallery to the large law library in the adjoining building, leased to the Newcastle Law Society. And if the place was a little short on volumes of quality on mediaeval architecture, well, that was to be expected. It was only in the esoteric university libraries that Arnold was normally able to find the kind of information in which he was personally interested.

Not that the lecture he had listened to was uninteresting. Professor Elliott Brandling, on Monastic Life. It hadn't sounded particularly stirring as a subject, and Arnold had told Ben so, but in fact Brandling had turned out to be an accomplished speaker, capable of interesting digressions, and as the historian wound up his lecture Arnold was pleased that Ben had invited him along.

'In summary,' Brandling was saying, 'I feel that if we are to understand a particular form of monastic life it's most helpful to know the setting in which it was lived, and the site of the monastery, the kind of enclosure, and the buildings with their dimensions, appearance and layout. Why then have historians of monasticism attached so little importance to such matters? Only the archaeologists study monasteries and then the history of their art. The picture of robed ascetics gliding along silent stone corridors has long been a romantic vision, but little effort has been made to set that cloistered existence against the background of the buildings which in fact sheltered them. I hope, this evening, I have been able to shed some light upon that monastic life, and perhaps fill in some of the gaps so shamefully neglected over the last hundred academic years.'

The Professor was sitting down, and there was a scattering of applause which swelled somewhat after a few seconds as the thirty-strong group came entirely to life, the several older gentlemen in the middle rows awakening from their torpor. Ben Gibson grinned at Arnold. 'Old stalwarts. Always turn up, whatever the lecture. Always go to sleep. Salt of the Society.'

Arnold nodded, smiling at the antiquarian bookseller. He was fond of Ben, in spite of the man's curious appearance. Ben Gibson reminded Arnold of nothing less than a battered little frog. His hooded eyes were set in a broad, squashy face and his back was bent. He suffered from arthritis and the joints of his hands were crippled but he handled old books with a soft tenderness and sensitivity that made light of his physical afflictions. He was well into his seventies now, a former watchmaker who had been forced to close his Tyneside business for lack of custom and who had moved to the Quayside to drink his Earl Grey tea in the tall-ceilinged rooms on the ground floor of one of the old commercial buildings on the waterfront. 'I enjoyed the lecture,' Arnold assured him. 'And I didn't go to sleep.'

'I did.'

'I noticed. But then, architecture is more my interest than yours,' Arnold conceded. He fell silent, as the speaker made himself available for questions.

The usual banalities occurred, inane questions that demonstrated the questioners' desire to hear their own voices and impress the audience rather than pick up serious points made by the historian. Arnold waited for what he guessed would come, and eventually it arrived, a question from a portly gentleman in a rusty black suit. It concerned one of Professor Brandling's entertaining digressions, and bore little relevance to the talk as a whole. But maybe that was why Brandling had included it — to lighten the general thrust of his lecture.

'Ah, Professor, I wonder if I could ask you about that . . . that Ragin' Wolf thing. Can't say I've ever heard of it myself.

Are you really saying there's a cult, and it still exists . . . based on the Templars, is that what you said?'

Arnold's glance turned to Professor Brandling, and for one surprising moment the historian's eyes held his, almost conspiratorially, as though they were sharing a secret. Then Brandling looked away, and smiled. 'I assure you, the cult exists, and has done so for hundreds of years.'

'I didn't quite understand its origins. Would you mind . . . ?'

Professor Brandling nodded indulgently. 'As I said, its origins lie in the persecution of heretics. But do remember, much mediaeval persecution was based upon the seizure of property — pure land greed. The Templars themselves were largely persecuted for this reason. They had a sinister reputation, of course, arising from the secret nature of their rituals. The charge against them was heresy, in the fourteenth century. The proof?' Brandling gave a short, barking laugh. 'Proof was easy enough to find.'

'Real proof?'

'Mediaeval proof. Every dark superstition, every fearful imagining of sorcery and Devil worship that was rooted deep in the mediaeval mind was hauled forth to confront the damned.'

He had already spoken of it in his lecture.

Arnold could remember the words used: suborned witnesses speaking of bestiality, idol worship, denial of the sacraments, adoring the Devil in the form of a cat, sodomy, intercourse with devils and succubi. Brandling repeated it now, for the benefit of the portly man who had already wriggled in barely controlled salacity at hearing it earlier.

'It would be sworn that their rituals called for initiates to deny God, Christ and the Virgin; to spit three times; to urinate and trample on the Cross; to give the "kiss of shame" to the Prior of the Order on the mouth, penis and buttocks. To strengthen their resolution in such circumstances, the initiates were said to be forced to drink a powder made from the ashes of dead members of the Society and of their own illegitimate children.'

'It all sounds impossible to believe,' rumbled a man in the front row.

'But you have to remember,' Brandling contended, 'that elements of sorcery and witchcraft were taken for granted in mediaeval life. Charges of dabbling in black magic were favoured, therefore, as a method of bringing down an enemy.'

Ben Gibson stirred himself and raised his head. 'And not just in mediaeval times,' he piped, in agreement. 'The Witches of Salem provide testimony to the mass hysteria that could murder innocents . . . and that was in the seventeenth century.'

'Quite so,' Brandling agreed. 'Four hundred years after the events I describe. But the recorded fact is, in March 1314 the Grand Master was taken to the stake. He proclaimed his innocence and cried to God to avenge him. He cursed his persecutors. The curse floated upward with the smoke of his funeral pyre in the red light of the setting sun, to hang like a deadly, mystic haze over men's minds in modern centuries.'

'Poetic,' Arnold murmured to Ben Gibson.

'But I thought you said the later cult had nothing to do with the Templar's curse,' the portly man persisted.

'That's so. The fact was, it became attached to a later event — the Templar's curse came to be attributed to the emergence of the "Raging Wolf" who was regarded as the elemental hand of the curse of the Templars.'

'Simon de Vieux Pont?'

'The very same,' Brandling agreed. 'Although a member of the chivalric order, de Vieux Pont rather went overboard in his passion for violence. Chivalry — however romantically later centuries came to regard it — was really nothing more than another word for force of arms, but in this man's case he used it as a raging wolf. He was a man of many scandals, obsessed with a lust for women, notorious, savage, even in a time of savagery. His private wars, fought largely for the purpose of increasing his inheritance and gaining lands, were fought with a single strategy. It was designed to ruin his enemy by killing the peasants and destroying crops, tools, barns, cattle and as many other possessions as possible. Men had eyes put out and feet cut off. The Devil was said to have aided him in pursuing a career of enmity and brigandage. He seized manors and convents, hung men by their testicles and, in the words of one scribe of the time, transformed his castles into nests of dragons and thieves.'

'Was he ever punished?'

'He was excommunicated, ungirdled of his knightly belt, and the anathema was ordered to be read against him in every church in the kingdom. It was from this that the cult began. On the other hand, it must be remembered he also married three times, founded an abbey in Yorkshire, and died in his bed. The Abbot Raoul thought him the wickedest man in Christendom. And on him was built a cult.'

The chairman of the meeting coughed, and fingered his clerical collar, obviously feeling that the discussion had little to do with the subject of the lecture, monastic life. Rather uncomfortably he cleared his throat. 'I think we should perhaps move on . . .'

They moved on. The questions were few and not particularly searching. Arnold barely listened, but took the opportunity to observe Professor Brandling, now rather more at ease than he had been while delivering his lecture.

He was a tall, spare man in a grey suit and pale-blue shirt, a neat dresser, a man to whom appearances were clearly important. His head was narrow, his features ascetic, his nose rather sharp and long. There was a quickness about his glance that suggested to Arnold the man had certain insecurities which he found difficulty in controlling, and while he generated an air of calm, he was unable to keep his hands still. When he spoke, his voice was carefully modulated, with just the hint of a suppressed Yorkshire accent. He smiled easily, but it was a smile developed to ward off difficulties and soften opinions that might offend. Elliott Brandling projected self-assurance, but the backcloth hid something else, deep, tremulous and wavering. Arnold's guess was that the man had become accustomed to public speaking through his sojourn at the university but there would have been a time when public performances of this kind would not have come easily to him.

The meeting was breaking up. The chairman with the clerical collar was giving a homily about how fortunate they all were that the eminent professor had taken time to visit the Lit and Phil and regale them with the result of his research. 'The one disappointment,' the chairman said unctuously, 'must be that he said little to us about *The Scribe of Odilo*, but that can only be the result of his own modesty . . .'

'What was that?' Arnold whispered to Ben Gibson.

The bookseller leaned sideways towards Arnold. 'A book. Brandling wrote *The Scribe of Odilo* as a piece of historical research, but oddly enough it took off with the lay public. It did very well indeed, in a market for which it wasn't intended, and then Hollywood latched on to it and made a perfectly ridiculous costume drama about it which was decently buried almost as soon as it was released. I think Brandling would have been happy to take the money they paid him, but wouldn't have enjoyed the result. I don't think it did his reputation at the university much good — and that wouldn't have pleased him either. I imagine that's why he won't be too happy about the chairman's reference to it now.'

Certainly, the smile on Brandling's thin lips seemed a trifle hard, and he made no response to the remark. The chairman was winding up, and a scattering of applause broke out when he asked the gathering to thank Professor Brandling 'in the usual manner'. In deference to the older members of the Lit and Phil, most of the group in the room retained their seats while the septuagenarians struggled out. Brandling was engaged in conversation with the chairman but his eyes were sharp, seeking escape. He caught sight of Ben Gibson and raised his hand, smiling. A swiftly murmured comment to the chairman and he was breaking away, walking across the room as Ben Gibson rose from his chair.

The Professor loomed over the little frog-like figure of the bookseller. Brandling scratched the side of his thin nose nervously, and muttered, 'God, I'm glad to see you, Gibson. I was about to be dragged out to supper, I fear, and an endless discourse on literature.'

'*The Scribe of Odilo*, you mean?' Gibson suggested mischievously.

'That was not literature, as you well know.' Brandling turned his head, glanced at Arnold and smiled vaguely.

'Ah, let me introduce you,' Gibson suggested. 'Professor Brandling, this is Arnold Landon.'

'I'm pleased to meet you,' Brandling said brusquely and held out his hand. His grip was firm and positive, fingers locking hard on Arnold's. 'Do you have any interest in mediaeval matters or have you just been dragged along by Ben Gibson?'

Out of the corner of his eye Arnold was aware of an involuntary movement on Ben Gibson's part, as though the little man was about to say something in protest. Arnold glanced at him, but Gibson was staring at Brandling, a vague surprise in his hooded eyes. Arnold smiled to himself: Ben Gibson knew all about Arnold's predilections and perhaps he thought that everyone else did too. 'I enjoyed your talk, Professor. I am quite interested in mediaeval matters, as it happens, and I was only too pleased to come along when Ben invited me.'

'Interested . . . as a layman?'

'Most certainly. I work as a planning officer in Northumberland, and although my work brings me into a degree of contact with old buildings I would still say my interest — my hobby, if you like — is not really concerned with my work.'

'You must surely have heard about Mr Landon,' Ben Gibson intervened. 'He has on occasions discomfited academic historians because of his close and wide-ranging knowledge of the history of stone and wood. He could probably tell you a thing or two, Brandling.'

There was an odd note in Ben Gibson's voice. A hint of mockery lay behind his words, and for a moment Arnold could not be certain that the bookseller was not baiting Brandling, or having a sly dig at Arnold himself. To cover the moment, and the momentary awkwardness he felt, Arnold blurted out, 'I doubt that it would be the case. Obviously, I have looked at monasteries because of the nature of the building and the light it all casts upon mediaeval architectural methods, but monastic life is something I have not touched upon. I would have to take a back seat on the matters you've been discussing tonight—'

'But you have an interest in the buildings themselves?' Brandling queried.

'Of a kind.'

'Of a kind,' Gibson snorted impatiently. 'He's an authority, Brandling. Don't let him confuse you with his modesty. Buildings, people, masons, architects . . . he knows all about them. Even if he is a planning officer. But then, you know that, so why lead him on?'

'We ought to get together sometime,' Brandling suggested. 'I've been doing some research into a monastic site near Jarrow, and while I think I've got the ground plans sorted out there are a number of things which confuse me. Perhaps you'd have time to look at them with me . . . Anyway, I'm dry as a bone after that talk. I'm dying for a drink.' He glanced back towards the clerical chairman, hovering in the background. 'He'll be offering me tea and conversation. Where's the nearest pub? Ben, if I say my farewells will you lead me to a watering-hole?'

Before Gibson could reply, the Professor had turned away and was walking towards his chairman. Ben glanced at Arnold apologetically. 'I'm sorry about this. I didn't intend . . . I wanted to offer you a cup of coffee on the Quayside, and show you a few old books I've picked up recently. But would you mind . . . ?'

'An early night would suit me,' Arnold suggested. 'I'll give you a ring in the week and maybe we can get together sometime again soon. Thanks anyway for the invitation this evening: I've enjoyed it.'

'Well, it wasn't entirely my idea—'

'You're not running out on us?' Professor Brandling was back, bearing down on them with a positive gleam in his eye. 'Come on, Landon, I intended you to be included in my invitation. Ben Gibson's not bright enough company by himself to seduce me to a session in a pub. Let's have some civilized, mediaeval conversation around his head.'

'Tall men always seem to have large egos,' Gibson said with a faint smile. He glanced at Arnold interrogatively. 'The Printer's Pie?'

Arnold hesitated, unsure whether he really wanted to go for a drink with Brandling. Then he capitulated, not wishing to appear stand-offish. 'The Printer's Pie will do fine.'

* * *

It was a short walk from the Lit and Phil, just across the busy street outside the railway station and along the narrow alley leading up the hill. The pub was busy, with a considerable number of students thronging the rooms below. Brandling sniffed something about 'bloody engineers' and led the way upstairs where they found a corner in the lounge bar somewhat less crowded than down below. Ben Gibson ordered a gin and tonic for himself. Arnold decided a half of lager would be enough, for he had to drive to Morpeth. Brandling asked for a double brandy. While Ben was getting the order, Brandling frowned, as if in some doubt about something.

'Landon . . .' He pursed his lips. 'Ben suggested I should know you. Now I *have* heard the name.'

Arnold shifted uncomfortably in his seat. He could guess what was coming.

Brandling was silent for a short while, staring at Arnold and yet not seeing him, turning something over in his brain. Then he nodded, decisively. 'That's it. Couple of years back. There was a television programme. You saw off that pompous ass over the matter of that Old Barn. Of course . . . mediaeval stuff . . . You're *that* Arnold Landon!'

'As if there was another,' Ben Gibson interjected as he placed the lager in front of Arnold and the brandy in Brandling's hand. When he returned with his own gin and tonic he added, 'I've told you before, Arnold has seen off more of you pseudo-academics than you'd believe. While you work at second-hand stuff, politically motivated writings, doubtfully authenticated white-washes of historical characters, he goes to the root of the matter. He looks at the truth on the ground. The wood. The stones. The realities.'

Somewhat embarrassed, Arnold laughed. 'You sound like my father, walking with me in the Yorkshire Dales.'

'He taught you a great deal?' Brandling asked.

Arnold nodded, a little reluctant to discuss the matter. The memories of his father and the walks they had taken in his childhood were matters of a personal nature. He was reluctant to discuss them in a pub with a stranger, or even with Ben. They were memories that concerned feelings and emotions, the glimpse of dead days and dead villages and crumbling stone; ancient woods and spreading trees; vistas along the fells and moorlands which had taught him as a child to believe in the past and to learn from it. From that early teaching he had developed his own understanding of wood and stone, and men too. It was not something he could discuss now, easily. He nodded. 'Yes,' he said. 'A great deal.'

There was a short silence. Arnold sipped his lager, aware that Elliott Brandling was staring at him, eyes sharp with interest.

Ben Gibson broke the silence. 'But it is Arnold himself who has chosen the path — and isn't it interesting, that the enthusiastic amateur can sometimes turn over stones ignored by the so-called experts! In my own small way, I have had the occasional excitements. A career as a watchmaker is not exactly the best grounding for book scholarship but there have been times when I have been able to assist. Indeed, one of your own research assistants approached me recently for help.'

Elliot Brandling raised one eyebrow. 'One of *my* students?' he inquired.

'That's right,' Ben Gibson confirmed. 'A young man called Cyril Robinson.'

'Cy . . .' Brandling murmured. He eyed the brandy in his glass and then finished it off in one gulp. 'So what did he want to see you for?'

Gibson shrugged. 'I'm not clear just what his research field is — I imagine you'll know more about that than I — but I guess it's connected with that. He just wanted my advice on mediaeval manuscripts — the sources I go to, the research libraries I have contact with, that sort of thing.'

Brandling rose to his feet, his empty glass in his hand. 'Another?'

Ben Gibson contemplated his barely touched gin and tonic. 'Not for me.' Arnold expressed the same sentiment and, after Brandling made his way to the bar, he glanced at the antiquarian bookseller.

Gibson grimaced. 'Don't worry — you'll never keep up with Brandling. He can really sink them at a pace.'

Brandling returned with another double brandy, topped up with soda water. 'Cy Robinson,' he said as he sat down. 'I'm a bit worried about that young man.'

'In what way? Overwork?' Gibson pursed his lips. 'He seemed a bit edgy, as though he had a lot on his mind when he came to see me, but he's a nice enough young man—'

'Not just work,' Brandling replied, shaking his head. 'He's got personal problems, and although he's not had a talk with me about them I can see he'll fall apart if things go on as they are. Still, it's not really any of my business . . . but let me know if he comes to see you again, hey? There's no point in his going overboard on his research . . . I should be able to give him some shortcuts and make sure he doesn't do unnecessary digging, you know, going over already well-documented ground.' His glance slipped back to Arnold. 'Anyway, we were talking about your interest in wood and stone. It fascinates me that you can identify in the way you have done, those facts that others like me have to dig out of musty old texts and manuscripts. You get out in the fresh air and do the same thing. I ought to enlist your help on the Raging Wolf cult.'

Arnold smiled vaguely. 'I don't list the occult among my general interests.'

Brandling shook his head vigorously. 'No, you misunderstand me. I'm not suggesting that I'm interested in the occult other than as an historical phenomenon. It's quite peripheral to my own research interests — as you'll have gathered from my talk, they tend in the direction of monasticism. But in researching in that field one inevitably has to deal with the heresies, and the cults that abounded in the Middle Ages tend to creep into the margins of my research with an irritating frequency. And these little annoying things intrude into one's subconscious mind. The balance of research can then be so easily upset if they're not removed, or the curiosity satisfied.'

'You have the curiosity,' Ben Gibson suggested.

'But not the time to satisfy it. I just wondered whether Landon here might look into it, rather than I.'

'Not exactly my cup of tea,' Arnold said.

'Pity. I have a theory . . . maybe a belief, that the cult is still practised. And at a church not too far from here.'

'A church?' Ben Gibson raised his hooded eyes. 'Surely a cult of the kind you suggest would hardly be practised on church premises.'

Brandling half-emptied his brandy glass.

He leaned forward, his sharp nose seeming to quest for an elusive scent. 'You'd think not. But Satanic cults, and similar, seem to be drawn to disused church premises. Give them some kind of extra kick, I suppose.'

'And the church?' Arnold asked, curious in spite of his reservations.

'St Michael's at Kentside. There are newspaper reports of some kind of Satanic activity practised there at the turn of the century . . . some sort of scandal affecting the priest . . . consecrated ground, all that sort of thing. But to hell with that. If you're interested in old foundations, perhaps you could turn your mind to helping me over my Jarrow investigation. Surely you'd be interested in helping me identify a Cluniac site?'

Arnold wriggled uncomfortably. He was being put on the spot. He knew little to nothing about monastic foundations, though he had read a certain amount about them.

'Might be an interesting exercise, Arnold,' Ben Gibson suggested.

'There are some ruins,' Brandling remarked. 'The Victorian antiquaries got it wrong as they so often did. They assigned them to a fourteenth-century manor house. But the foundations are much older, I'm sure, and I've got some papers . . .'

Arnold felt a prickle of interest. He was not particularly keen to get involved: he had received enough warnings from the Senior Planning Officer about his outside interests and activities, and the occasional publicity they gave rise to. But, on reflection, there seemed little harm that might arise from this kind of investigation, if he were to agree.

After all, to what could the Senior Planning Officer object if Arnold took a hand and helped Professor Brandling in his quest, to look at a few old ruins in Jarrow and help determine whether a Cluniac foundation had really existed on a site so badly described by the Victorians?

'A fourteenth-century manor house, you say . . .'

'You know how it is,' Brandling said easily. 'Enthusiastic amateurs in the eighteenth century did some digging, ruining a hell of a lot, then the Victorian passion for antiquities took over so that in the end it gets difficult to divide the reality from the romantic vision.'

'If there were a Cluniac foundation, the layout on the ground might help establish the fact. You've no written references?' Arnold asked.

'I thought you were the one who spurned written records,' Ben Gibson suggested mischievously. 'You always say the basic truths lie in the incontrovertible facts of stone and wood, rather than men's distortions of the truth on paper.

You know, Brandling, I often wonder whether Arnold actually despises me for my books, my repositories of learning.'

'You can't mean that,' Arnold protested. 'You know perfectly well I rely on the printed word—'

'Only when you can't get the proof on the ground,' the antiquarian bookseller insisted, smiling broadly.

Elliott Brandling waved his rapidly emptying glass excitedly. 'Be that as it may, Landon, how about it? Can you spare me the time to visit Jarrow, take a look at those old ruins and give me the benefit of your uncluttered advice?'

'I'm not so sure—'

Ben Gibson was grinning at Arnold wickedly. He knew Arnold as well as Arnold knew himself. He was aware that Arnold's interest had been raised, the challenge placed to his skills. He also knew Arnold was flattered by Brandling's request. There had been occasions in the past when Arnold had been snubbed by the educational establishment.

The Senior Planning Officer might have something to say about it, Arnold considered miserably, but there could be no real harm in helping the university professor a little. The decision must have shown in his face, for Brandling tapped the heel of his hand against the table in a decisive gesture. 'That's it, then. We'll take a look at the thing together.'

Arnold nodded slowly. He glanced at Ben Gibson and the little man winked at him. And yet, unbidden, something cold seemed to touch the back of Arnold's neck as though someone had opened a door behind him.

3

The major period in Cluniac history was, Arnold knew, the tenth, eleventh and twelfth centuries. At that time there was no doubt Cluny had been a major European institution, since the central Middle Ages had been marked by a noticeable religious movement. Monasticism had been one of the principal expressions and agents of that phenomenon.

Given the size and influence of the Cluniac movement and the international historical literature that it generated, it was perhaps surprising that there was no extant complete list of the houses affiliated to Cluny. While numbers ranging from 200 to 2000 had been quoted with confidence, there was apparently no historical basis for either figure. The term 'Cluniac' had been used loosely in the past, covering actual Cluniac foundations, houses that had adopted Cluniac customs, and foundations that had elected a Cluniac abbot. Even the sending of monks to Cluny for a time could lead to their home base being regarded as a Cluniac monastery. Arnold could guess at the nature of the problem facing Elliott Brandling in his investigations into the monastic past.

But whatever might be Elliott Brandling's problems, Arnold Landon had a few of his own. The Senior Planning Officer had clearly decided, having been warned by his disgraced predecessor, that the best way to have a quiet life and a low departmental profile was to ensure that Arnold was kept busy. The pile of paper on Arnold's desk testified to the Senior Planning Officer's commitment to the solution: there were at least three new files on his desk since he had last been in his office, and there were still several planning applications only half dealt with. Arnold was aware that he had papers on four compensation claims yet to be processed and one appeal against a compulsory purchase order.

Arnold sighed as he sat down behind his desk and began to pick his way gingerly through the new papers. The first he looked at made him groan aloud: a proposal to develop ten acres of land in the open countryside outside Morpeth for a model world, animal enclosures, picnic area, playground, parking, crazy golf and a restaurant. It was adjoining an area already designated as one of Outstanding Natural Beauty. The normally apoplectic Chairman of Planning would further empurple. Arnold wondered idly, and irrelevantly, who would be the man's successor if this application ever went to planning stage?

The second file in the pile was marked *Rafferty Common* and Arnold felt as if a little spider had crawled up his back. He could guess what the file contained. Sure enough, when he opened the manila cover to look inside, there was the scrawled note from the Senior Planning Officer. He had developed a reputation as a man who believed lengthy explanations could be self-incriminating so he always kept comments to a minimum. This one was headmasterly.

See me.

The peremptory tone was sufficiently unnerving to make Arnold rise to his feet at once, to make his way to the Senior Planning Officer's room. It was not that he feared the Senior Planning Officer; it was merely that he was aware what it cost the man, psychologically, to call anyone to his room. He disliked contact with his colleagues: conversations were a source of strain for him.

The likelihood was that he would have been sitting in his room dreading Arnold's arrival so the sooner the meeting took place the better, for both parties concerned. As it was, the Senior Planning Officer demonstrated considerable alarm when Arnold tapped on his door and looked in. It was almost as though he was expecting Arnold to ask him for a rise.

'Landon,' he barked nervously.

'You wanted to see me, sir.'

'I did?'

'About Rafferty Common.'

Confusion glazed the Senior Planning Officer's pale eyes. He placed his white-skinned, podgy hands on the file he had been perusing and frowned at them as though blaming them for his consternation. 'Rafferty Common.'

Arnold sighed. 'That's right, sir. You'll recall a considerable number of gipsies have been camping on the common. Local landowners have been complaining. The gipsies, unusually, have a spokesman who seems to know a little about the law and when we began squatters' proceedings to evict the gipsies, he claimed—'

'Who is he, this he?' the Senior Planning Officer interrupted irritably.

'Joe Connor, he calls himself.'

'Gipsy Joe.'

Surprised, Arnold nodded, previously unaware that the Senior Planning Officer had access to office gossip and nicknames. Vaguely worried that his senior might have heard some of the nicknames applied to himself, Arnold hurried on. 'That's right, sir, Gipsy Joe Connor. He claimed the authority was in breach of its duty to provide accommodation for gipsies under the 1968 Act. In the event, the possession order we obtained was set aside. We appealed against the decision.'

Light had returned to the Senior Planning Officer's countenance. 'Ah, yes, I remember. I sent you the file.'

'With a note to see you.'

'That's right. We've lost the appeal.'

'Ah.'

The Senior Planning Officer squinted suspiciously in Arnold's direction, but with his inherent inability to hold anyone's gaze for more than five seconds quickly found a steepling of his fingers more fascinating and less threatening to fix upon. He frowned, concentrating, as the silence grew about them. 'So what do you advise now, Landon?'

'I haven't really had time to read the file, sir, and—'

'We can't let things lie.'

'No, sir.' Arnold appreciated the reasons.

First and foremost, the landowners in the vicinity of Rafferty Common. They had powerful county friends. Secondly, the Senior Planning Officer's pride and sense of well-being. It was whispered that he had sleepless weekends if he lost planning appeals. Not that he took any positive part in their preparations: he merely saw such situations as an active governmental criticism of the efficiency of the office he ran so inefficiently.

'So what do you propose to do?' Carefully, Arnold suggested, 'I suppose we could make an application for a judicial review, on the ground that though the authority might have been in breach of its duty, its serving of the possession orders was an action that any authority would reasonably make.'

'Will that win the day?' the Senior Planning Officer questioned hopefully.

'I don't know, sir,' Arnold lied, being of the opinion it stood no chance whatsoever. 'But if you'll give me a little time to read the file — I have it here with me — and the chance to go out and talk to the complainants, and to Gipsy Joe himself, it may well be that I'll be able to make some more positive recommendations for your . . . ah . . . action in a week or so.'

Procrastination was an article of faith for the Senior Planning Officer and he understood its utility, even when practised by others. He nodded, demonstrating a decisiveness he tried to cultivate but could never summon up to order. 'All right, that'll have to do. A week then, Landon, and then we'll talk aga— then you can drop me a note,' he corrected himself hastily.

Arnold bobbed his head thankfully, and turned to escape from the presence. He was stopped by the Senior Planning Officer's command. 'One moment, Landon.'

Arnold's heart dropped. The Senior Planning Officer wanted company. That meant he had visitors coming, of the kind he disliked more than usual — he disliked all visitors but in varying degrees. 'Sir?'

'I have an appointment with a Mr Chaunter. You heard of him?'

'No, sir.'

'Unpleasant business. Man has to be told. I think it would be . . .' The Senior Planning Officer struggled with the word *useful* and finally settled for an alternative more to his liking. 'I think it would be *instructive* if you were to stay, and hear the matter out.' The telephone was already ringing. Escape was now impossible. Reluctantly, Arnold stood to one side while the Senior Planning Officer instructed reception to send Mr Chaunter along to his office. Then he waved Arnold to a chair, regally. He always felt happier if he had a colleague with him when awkward visitors with difficult planning arguments came to see him. A reference point, a saviour in difficult times, a minion to blame if things went wrong. Life could be so difficult, if one was not careful.

While they waited for Chaunter's arrival the Senior Planning Officer thought it best to pass the file in front of him over to Arnold, so that he would be relieved of the burden of answering direct questions from Mr Chaunter. His status demanded he be present, but it was often useful to maintain a dignified, magisterial silence while the colleague made any mistakes that were likely to be made. Knowing the score, Arnold hastily read the correspondence on the file.

The application had been for planning permission with regard to a site situated just over a mile from the centre of Birkbeck village. The permission requested had been in the name of Edward Chaunter; he wished to establish a meeting hall for religious purposes. Arnold just about managed to skim through the arguments before the door opened and Mr Chaunter appeared.

Edward Chaunter was a tall lean man, dressed carefully in a suit of clerical grey, a white shirt, and a grey tie. Everything about him seemed neat and ordered with deliberation; his movements were precise, his handshake applying just enough pressure, his skin dry and noncommittal to the touch. He had pale, grey-flecked eyes cold as an east wind and just as sharp; his mouth was thin-lipped and calculating, lacking humour lines at the corners and obviously quick to chide. He bore himself erect as though accustomed to command and when he looked at Arnold, on introduction, he clearly considered he was dealing with ranks other than his own. Arnold felt the man's religion would be a stern one. As for the Senior Planning Officer, he wriggled in his chair. He would be quailing inside, yet managed, in spite of the wriggle, to demonstrate the coolness that had so impressed the Appointments Committee when he had got the job. He waved Chaunter to a chair; the man accepted it gracefully and then fixed his glance upon the Senior Planning Officer.

'I've come for an explanation.'

'Ah yes.' The Senior Planning Officer waved a negligent hand in which the tremor could barely be seen. 'Mr Landon has the file.'

The glance which switched to Arnold was baleful. '*You* have the explanation?'

'Ah. Well.' Arnold fumbled desperately for the words. The file still lay on his knees; he stared at it, trying to remember the basic issues, and indulging in a secondary cursing of the Senior Planning Officer's cowardice. 'Your application related to the site at Birkbeck.'

'Correct.'

'For the meeting hall . . . for religious purposes.'

'Correct.'

'It was rejected by the Planning Committee.'

'I know. I've been told. I want an explanation.'

'I—'

'Is the council against the spreading of the Word of God?'

'I don't think—'

'Does it assume that it is only the organized church that has a direct link with the Almighty?'

'I hardly believe—'

'Are there interests on that council who consider that the paths that lead to Salvation are trod only by those who are members of the established Church?'

'Mr Chaunter,' Arnold said firmly, 'I'm quite prepared to give you the explanation that is demonstrated in this file. I personally did not handle this application—' He glanced towards the Senior Planning Officer but was presented with a chiselled, unmoved profile. 'But in any case, I can assure you it would have been dealt with on its merits, not against a background of established Church interests. Your sect . . .'

'The Vicars of Jehovah. We prefer to discard and reject the word "sect". We consider ourselves to be on the True Path. Our aims are Righteous; our motives Pure; our strength is truly as the Strength of Ten, as is the magic number of our Circle—'

The Senior Planning Officer had allowed his lower jaw to drop slightly; he had clearly never heard anyone speak in capital letters before. Arnold had. In his childhood he had been taken by his father to listen to an itinerant Welsh preacher of the fire and brimstone type. Impressed at the time, he had been less impressed later to hear that the man had been arrested in Swaledale for exposing himself to the local vicar's wife in an attempt to convert her to the true religion.

'However you describe yourself, Mr Chaunter,' Arnold interrupted, 'the facts as disclosed in this report would seem to be based upon one central issue. The site you seek to use as a meeting hall is already scheduled in council policy documents as one suitable for holiday and associated leisure purposes. It is a flat and open site and—'

'Are you aware I have made three previous applications for a meeting hall at the village? And that *all* have been refused?'

Arnold stumbled mentally; he hadn't seen that in the file and he needed to proceed with care. 'I'm not sure it is relevant to discuss—'

'I would contend we have here a vendetta, and in such circumstances, before I decide upon what further action to take, I need to know the full details of the reasons for this later rejection. It is not enough to hold up council policy to me. Besides, I countered the argument.'

Hurriedly, Arnold scanned the file again. 'Ah yes, I see, you argue that the proposed activity of people attending your meeting hall—'

'In their leisure time—'

'—is not unrelated to people attending a meeting in a conference centre.' Arnold sighed. 'It's stretching it a bit, Mr Chaunter. If you were able to show that the site was particularly suitable, or contributed to the economic well-being of Birkbeck, or that there was a large area of land available for holiday purposes otherwise—'

'You know there isn't!' Chaunter snapped.

He glared at Arnold, who felt suddenly as though Chaunter had taken a personal dislike to him. Moreover, the coldness of Chaunter's eyes seemed to have increased; their ice chilled Arnold, and he was uncomfortably aware that fanatics could be dangerous men.

'The findings of the committee, as shown in this file, would suggest you haven't made out a case, Mr Chaunter,' Arnold said quietly. 'It's not for me to make one out for you.'

Chaunter seemed to grow taller; he sat more erect in the chair and his thin lips were pursed slightly as though sourness had touched them. 'You're called Landon,' he said.

'That's right.'

'I will remember the name.'

There was a frosty menace in the air. All three men sat silently for several seconds, the Senior Planning Officer seemingly riveted in his seat. Then Chaunter rose. He seemed to tower above them, and there was a malignity in his presence that made him appear more massive, more powerful than his lean frame would suggest.

'I will remember the name,' he said again, sonorously and menacingly, and then he walked swiftly out of the room.

There was a short silence. The Senior Planning Officer was staring at his hands again. He cleared his throat after a little while. 'I thought we handled that reasonably well, Landon . . . You can hang on to that file for the time being. No need for me to see Mr Chaunter again, if he wants another interview.'

* * *

Arnold made his way back to his office in a despondent frame of mind. It was not that he was overly disturbed by the cold ferocity of Chaunter's eyes or the belief that the man's veiled threat was anything other than the fury of disappointment; rather, it was based upon the difficulty of having to work with the Senior Planning Officer. His predecessor had been bad enough, but this one was so lacking in the human touch, so isolated and indifferent to the problems that faced his staff that professional life in the Planning Department could be depressing.

A solution to his despondency might be a hot cup of coffee. He obtained a disappointingly warm one from the vending machine in the corridor and then walked up the stairs to the Department of Administration, past the filed rows of law books and along to the desk near the window, occupied by Ned Keeton.

'So how is it, ancient of days?'

'Three weeks to go, so how should it be? Not so bloody bad, I'll tell you.'

Ned Keeton, about to take early retirement, raised his shaggy eyebrows and inspected Arnold. They had known each other a long time and a mutual respect had grown between them, enhanced, oddly enough, by the activities Arnold indulged in outside the office. Ned Keeton had no interest in archaeology, but he loved seeing Senior Planning Officers get impotently over-excited at Arnold Landon's innocent penchant for getting into trouble. 'You look down,' he said.

'In a planning office you have to keep saying no to people.'

'When the politicians take the decisions.'

'Which we have to defend.' Arnold sighed. 'Still, it's a job.'

Keeton smiled a tobacco-stained smile. 'Rather be out and about in the fields, hey? At least you've got an excuse to do that. Me, I've had thirty years in this bloody office. You could do worse. But I can't believe you came up here for cheery conversation. And the coffee here's no better than the muck you've got there. What abstruse point of law are you seeking to pump out of me?'

Arnold smiled, and shook his head. 'Not law, really. You live near Rafferty Common, don't you?'

'Not far. Why?'

'I've had the file on the squatters order dumped on my desk.'

'Good luck,' Keeton growled feelingly. 'It's a bitch, that one.'

'I'm not too conversant with the situation.'

'Situation, you call it? In not too long a time it could turn into something like a shooting war!'

'As serious as that?'

'Isn't it always? Once folks get excited about things like rights and principles, logic goes out of the window, rumour takes over and lies become standard truths. The fact is, gipsies are here to stay — after all, they have been for a thousand years. The Romanies are travelling people but they have to stop a while occasionally, and the State insists they educate their kids anyway. But where do they stop? I don't want them on my door, of course, but when everyone says that, where do they stop?'

'The 1968 Act—'

'Is a bloody dead letter, isn't it? How many authorities are fulfilling their duties under the Act?'

'And Rafferty Common?' Arnold asked.

'Is a flashpoint. Tempers are beginning to flare, and harsh words used. I pick up plenty of local gossip. I just hope it gets sorted out in the next few weeks — I want a quiet retirement up there near the Common, not a modern Vietnam!'

'You're exaggerating, Ned.'

'Or Gipsy Joe Connor is.'

'Is he the one to see first of all?'

'Him, or others. But if you take my advice, talk to Marcus Gullick first.'

'He owns Gullick Farm.'

'That's the one. But talking of seeing people, I had a phone call ten minutes ago. They were checking at the switchboard; didn't know where you were.'

'I was with the Senior Planning Officer.'

'Nice.' Keeton grinned. 'Anyway, there's someone waiting to see you, name of Robinson.'

'Why didn't you tell me earlier?'

'And spoil your coffee and the opportunity for good company?'

* * *

Cy Robinson was perhaps twenty-two years of age. He was of middle height, slim, dressed in jeans and a lumpy sweater. His features were small and regular but his brown eyes displayed a basic vulnerability that would appeal to women, particularly the mothering kind. He gave the impression of appearing to need protection, perhaps from his own enthusiasms as much as anything else. Arnold warmed to him as soon as they met in Arnold's cramped office. Robinson stuck out an eager hand.

'I'm Cy Robinson.'

'Arnold Landon.'

'Yes. Mr Brandling has told me all about you.' When he spoke it, Robinson handled Elliott Brandling's name with reverence.

'You're a research student with Mr Brandling, I gather.'

'That's right,' Robinson enthused. 'I was extremely fortunate to be able to be taken on by him. In fact, I had joined Professor Fredericks and we had decided upon the basis for my thesis and it was submitted and approved by senate and all that sort of thing, but then Professor Fredericks moved on to Lancaster and, in a sense, I was left hanging out to dry, so to speak. That's when it was decided that Professor Brandling should take over as my supervisor. I don't think he was too pleased at first . . . as far as I can understand, he and Professor Fredericks didn't exactly see eye to eye over a number of things.' Robinson paused, his warm brown eyes becoming anxious. 'Maybe I shouldn't say it, but I think Professor Fredericks was a bit . . . well, jealous of Professor Brandling. Anyway, Elliott Brandling took me on, reluctantly, like I said, but we get on very well, in fact, and he displays a great deal of interest in my work, more than I should expect, really. But it is a field in which he's interested, of course.'

'What is it you're researching into?'

'The Albigensian heresies in the thirteenth century. Oddly enough, it's sort of a wheel turning full circle in that Professor Brandling's own mentor years ago had built his reputation upon a study of the heresies. I'm finding his work particularly useful in my own research.'

'Is that so?' Arnold felt he should find some way of stopping the young man's rush of words but hadn't yet found a suitably polite phrase.

'Yes, indeed. One of the problems is that David Loxton — that's Professor Loxton, Professor Brandling's mentor — he didn't publish all that much before he died some years ago. What I mean is, he researched, but he had no great interest in publishing, and as a result he didn't have much to do with the standard houses, but some of his work has been produced by quite minor publishers whose stock has gone out of print, so I've had to chase around for quite obscure titles—'

'Which is why you went to Ben Gibson,' Arnold suggested desperately.

'That's right,' Robinson hurried on. 'I came across a most interesting reference, strictly speaking not so much to do with my own research but rather of interest to Professor Brandling . . . Have you read *The Scribe of Odilo*, Mr Landon?'

'No, I haven't.'

'Marvellous work. A piece of publishing history in a way, in that it was written as a scholarly thesis but caught the public imagination and became a bestseller. No one expected that, of course, least of all Professor Brandling, but it made him a deserved reputation, and although some people have carped at his reputation, such as Professor Fredericks, and though some have suggested that there are certain quantum leaps in his thesis that are perhaps unsubstantiated . . . which makes it all the more interesting for me, if Mr Gibson can find that reference for me—'

'Mr Robinson,' Arnold interrupted urgently, 'is this why you've come to see me?'

Cy Robinson's vulnerable brown eyes widened in astonishment, then clouded over rapidly with chagrin. 'See you? No, of course not. I'm terribly sorry, Mr Landon. I'm wasting your time. The trouble is, when I start talking about my research interests I tend to get carried away, and now I've found an overlap with *The Scribe of Odilo* it's all very exciting . . . oh hell, I'm starting again.' He smiled, brightly, and thrust out a small package. 'These are from Professor Brandling, Mr Landon.'

Brandling was clearly wasting no time in recruiting Arnold to the cause of his research. The half-promise extracted in the Printer's Pie was being acted upon. Arnold began to open the package. It seemed to contain a number of documents: some photocopies of original material, some typed sheets, a few handwritten notes.

'Do you know what these are, Mr Robinson?'

'Not specifically,' the young man admitted. 'He did mention to me they're something to do with the research he's carrying out at the moment on a possible Cluniac foundation. But precisely what the papers are I don't really know.'

Arnold began to sift through them, his eye running swiftly over the contents. 'There seems to be a certain amount of material here which relates to the cult of de Vieux Pont.'

'The Raging Wolf?'

'Ah. You've heard of it.'

Cy Robinson shrugged and smiled in a self-deprecating manner. 'Heard of it, yes. I can't say I know very much about it, however. Professor Brandling has mentioned it to me a couple of times, though not in much detail. There've also been a few rumours—'

'Rumours?'

'That's right.' Robinson shrugged again, his warm brown eyes serious and thoughtful. 'You know, suggestions that the cult has been revived in the north of England and that local places up here have been used to practise the cult, a sort of Devil worship.'

'Do you believe this?' Arnold asked.

'I don't know, sir. I mean, I've come across no evidence, but that's not to say. I suppose . . .' He hesitated. 'Well, what I mean is, if Professor Brandling thinks seriously enough about it to consider it's worth looking into, then I suppose there must be some evidence . . .'

'But all you've heard is rumour. Where do the rumours come from?'

'I really can't say, Mr Landon. One . . . hears things,' Robinson said vaguely. 'I believe there have been one or two items, news reports in the papers, church desecrations, that sort of thing—'

'Usually the kind of thing done by young vandals rather than Devil-worshippers,' Arnold suggested mildly.

'That may be, Mr Landon. But I really don't know. And as I say . . .' Robinson hesitated for a moment and then glanced at his watch as though remembering something. 'Oh, hell, I hadn't realized the time. Waiting for you—'

'I'm sorry, do you have another appointment?'

'No, it's OK, it's just that Professor Brandling asked me to drop these papers off, and I didn't think it would take long, and I sort of said I'd be out before now, so I'd better be away. I'm . . . I'm expecting a lift, you see.'

Oddly enough, the young man had flushed.

In his early twenties, he could hardly still be capable of embarrassment of the kind Arnold suspected might be affecting him, but embarrassed he certainly was. Arnold smiled and began to repack the documents. 'Well, give my compliments to Professor Brandling and tell him I'll take a close look at these and then later I'll be in touch with him.'

'That's fine, Mr Landon. It's been good to meet you and talk to you.' Cy Robinson smiled warmly and put out his hand to seize Arnold's. 'I look forward to meeting you again. Er . . . what's the best way out of here?'

Arnold glanced at his watch. The afternoon was well advanced, he was on flexitime, and he suddenly had a yearning to get back to his cottage and sit in the late-afternoon sunshine for an hour or so, forgetting the Senior Planning Officer and gipsies and Mr Chaunter and everything else. 'I'll see you out and off the premises, Mr Robinson. It's time I knocked off, anyway.'

The research student was lavish in his thanks. Arnold led him towards the lift and they got out at the ground floor to take the back entrance to the car park. Arnold's car was parked there and in the visitors' parking area there were three cars waiting. One of them was occupied by a young woman. When Robinson caught sight of her he waved, involuntarily, and then looked vaguely sheepish as he realized Arnold had noticed. 'It's my lift,' he explained. 'I'll say goodbye, now, Mr Landon.'

Robinson hurried across to the waiting car.

The woman in the driving seat smiled tensely up at him, said something and glanced at her watch and then opened the passenger door for the young man. She was wearing a white blouse with short sleeves; she had short blonde hair and a pert, upturned nose. Arnold gained the impression she was somewhat older than her young passenger. He watched vaguely from the door of his own car as she drove out of the car park. In a few moments they had turned out into the main street and were lost in the traffic making its way home over the bridge into the town.

Arnold placed the Brandling package on the back seat of his car and got in behind the wheel. He started the engine and then sat there for a few minutes, belatedly irritated at the thought of the Senior Planning Officer and the manner in which he always seemed to place burdens upon other officers while accepting none of his own. And now Arnold had to deal with the gipsy matter as well.

He slipped the car into gear and drove out of the car park. The traffic was fairly heavy and he had to wait a while before he could edge his way out into the traffic stream. After a few moments Arnold became aware there was a man standing on the pavement some ten yards away from the car park entrance. He was of medium height, dressed in a dark jacket and slacks, middle-aged, thin-featured, but stockily built, barrel-chested. He seemed to be staring fixedly at Arnold's car, and for a moment Arnold wondered whether the man had noticed a flat tyre or some other oddity about the car.

Then their eyes met.

There was something familiar about the glance, a coldly remembered sensation that caused a prickling of the short hairs at the back of Arnold's neck. He stared back at the man, vaguely aware of beetling eyebrows and the fixity of the eyes below them. Then he jerked his attention away, dragging his eyes back to concentrate upon the traffic, yet still uncomfortable at the thought of the man's eyes boring into him.

At the first break in the traffic Arnold pulled out. As he drove away he glanced back in the mirror. The man with the black, heavy eyebrows had stepped forward and was staring after Arnold's car. Uncomfortably, Arnold thought he might be making a mental note of the number plate of the vehicle. Arnold accelerated nervously, driving rather faster than traffic conditions allowed and meeting a few angry glances from other drivers as he made his way along the High Street.

But it was only later, when he had poured himself a cold beer and was sitting in the sun in his back garden, that he realized what was familiar about the man outside the car park. It was his eyes.

Cold, chilly, they had held the same committed malignancy Arnold had already seen earlier that afternoon.

In the glance of one of the Vicars of Jehovah; in the eyes of Edward Chaunter.

CHAPTER TWO

1

Arnold Landon respected Ned Keeton's judgement. He had found in the past that Ned's advice was usually sound, and if it was his view on this occasion that Arnold should first talk to Marcus Gullick before he went any further with the Rafferty Common matter, it was a view that Arnold was inclined to go along with.

Consequently, the following morning Arnold rang the owner of Gullick Farm and fixed an appointment to see him the next day. Gullick announced he would be able to see Arnold when he returned in mid-morning from his lower fields, so Arnold took the opportunity to set off early at eight o'clock. It would give him the opportunity to enjoy a leisurely drive in the morning sunshine into the Northumberland countryside.

Arnold did not entirely approve of the efforts of the Northumbria Tourist Board. He could understand that a drive for tourism would be of benefit to many in the area, and create more jobs in rural communities, but he was selfish enough to feel that one of the major attractions of Northumberland was its emptiness. It was not that Arnold disliked people: it was merely that he found them hard to take in large numbers. The beauty of the rolling hills and harsh crags of the northern landscape was enhanced by their loneliness; the harsh rattle of the black grouse and the solitary cry of the curlew were calls that could be lost in some areas if there was a considerable influx of visitors. The climate would always keep many away, of course, though on a sunny morning like this Arnold could hardly recall the bleakness of the upper moorland as it appeared in the autumn months.

The road took him up into Coquetdale, and as he followed the winding of the river past Rothbury he caught the glitter of its waters, tumbling over dark rocks to his left. The road rose, climbing over steepening gradients and the hillsides opened out ahead of him, sparsely covered, shining in the sun. Then he was cutting off to the left, descending again towards the river, and in a few miles he would come to the contentious area, the outskirts of the village and the common land that was in dispute: Rafferty Common.

Arnold stopped the car near a small copse crowning the hillside. He got out and felt the fresh, warm breeze on his face, carrying the hint of brine from the distant coast. There was the murmurous sound of bees about him as he left the car and began to climb the hill, through the copse, until he came out at its head, emerging from the rustling undergrowth of the trees to enjoy the vista that spread out before him.

He could see for some twenty miles. The cluster of buildings at Morpeth were hidden, blocked off by the rolling hills, but the panorama took in the Cheviot, dark-crowned and somehow almost menacing in its shadowed form under the morning sun. Eastwards, he could pick up the glitter of the sea, an indeterminate horizon, but closer at hand he could see clearly the spread of the village, the clumps of trees that fringed it and the open land that was Rafferty Common. From this height, and this distance, the gipsy caravans, some still hand-painted and horse-drawn, but mostly now modern vehicular caravans, rendered the common gay with splashes of bright colour, lending an air of excitement and movement to the scene. The reality, Arnold knew, was more grubby, with litter, waste, the scars of fires and a general air of poverty among the majority of the site users — though some of the larger caravans boasted amenities which suggested a creative use of unemployment benefit or some hidden and unrecorded means of support.

He sat there for an hour or longer, as the sun rose higher in the sharp blue sky, musing, thinking about the Yorkshire Dales and his father, and the interest Arnold had since developed in the manner in which people had carved their histories and left their mark on the landscape in wood and stone. He thought of Elliott Brandling: the man wasn't the usual kind of academic Arnold had come across. He lacked the intellectual arrogance of many of his breed; he seemed more amenable to suggestion and help, and, in his reading of the papers sent to him by Brandling, Arnold had detected a basic love of research of the kind he himself could appreciate. In reading those papers Arnold had warmed to Elliott Brandling: there were uncertainties and insecurities in the man that were demonstrated by the manner in which he seemed to pick his way through the facts before him, gingerly, wary, not yet observing the distant vista, waiting until the footholds were secure before he raised his eyes to the horizon.

It was an attitude Arnold understood. After a while, recalling his duties, Arnold rose from the craggy rock on which he had seated himself. It was with reluctance. He had a premonition that his meeting with Marcus Gullick would be unsettling.

* * *

He arrived at Gullick Farm within fifteen minutes of leaving the crag. He left the main road at a side turning some half-mile from Rafferty Common itself, turned right at the sign which announced the road to the farm and found himself driving down a bumpy twisting track that ran past tall lime trees, a stand of beech and over a narrow pack bridge whose walls had clearly been in conflict with a heavy vehicle. The lichen-marked dry stone wall that crowned the hill swung left abruptly. Arnold crossed a cattle grid and saw the farm itself, nestling in a hollow, sheltered by the slope of the hill and a clump of trees, the corrugated iron barn contrasting oddly and harshly with the soft sandstone of the farmhouse itself.

It was old.

Arnold parked some fifty yards away from the house at the main gate. He got out of the car and looked at the farmhouse appreciatively. It was built with two narrow wings, so that the main part of the house faced upon a small untended courtyard flagged with old stone grey-green with lichen, but warm and protected by the wings from the harsh winter winds. There had been a small garden to one side but it was ill-tended, dismissed by the owner as a frippery, Arnold guessed. The house had not been constructed of local stone; the original builders clearly had gone to some expense to bring in a material that warmed their hearts and minds and eyes. It was soft and glowing, perhaps not entirely practical, for it had worn and pitted under the harshness of the Northumberland winters, but the pride of the yeoman farmer who had picked out his initials and those of his wife — GNC — was clear, a proclamation to the world that he had been here and lived here and worked here. The date was also picked out in brick, forming an ornamental pattern above the doorway: 1696.

There was a battered Land Rover parked to one side of the house, at the left wing where there would have been a servants' entrance in the old days, with access to the kitchen area that looked out over a kitchen garden and a gently sloping area leading down to a winding stream. Near those old oaks, Arnold guessed, the house's midden would have stood two hundred years ago. Near the kitchen entrance stood a Jaguar, sleek, of recent vintage, and muddy. Arnold hesitated, not certain which door he should attempt, the narrow, low door that had served as a front entrance for more than two hundred and fifty years or the side entry beside the parked Jaguar. The problem was resolved for him as the front door opened and a man stood framed in the entrance.

He was perhaps five feet six inches tall, broad-shouldered, deep-chested, clad in a worn, patched leather jacket and jeans, with heavy boots scarred and muddy from the fields. His features were coarse, cheeks roughened by wind and sun, a thick-lipped, opinionated mouth, and eyes that would have seemed mean-spirited even before they had become narrowed by the seaming and wrinkling of years squinting against the glare of sun on the hills. His hair was reddish, greying; it sprouted belligerently from his scalp, thinning at the temples, badly cropped and uncared for. Both hands were clenched into fists, as though perpetually prepared for trouble. He did not seem pleased to see Arnold, but that could have been an habitual expression, developed over his forty-odd years.

'Landon?'

His voice was low, growling, and aggressive.

'That's right. Are you Mr Gullick?'

'Who else?'

Marcus Gullick stood in the doorway as his ancestors had done before him, fitting the door, his height accommodated neatly by the low lintel. He seemed to hesitate, as though considering whether he should demonstrate the normal hospitality of the countryside by inviting his visitor indoors; then he decided against it, deeming a planning officer from Morpeth unworthy of such consideration. He stepped out into the courtyard, his boots ringing on the stone flagging.

'Can't spare you much time. Need to get to Morpeth within the hour.'

'That's all right, Mr Gullick. I merely wanted to have a few minutes with you to discuss Rafferty Common, as I explained on the phone. We have a certain situation developing—'

'Bloody vagabonds!'

The vehemence surprised Arnold and stopped him in his tracks. Gullick had almost spat out the words with a controlled viciousness that denoted a considerable depth of feeling. He glared at Arnold as the silence suddenly lengthened around them, and then his mean, red-stained eyes wandered around the courtyard, picked up the distant line of hills, the meadows about him, the winding track, back up to the main road.

'You been down to Rafferty Common yet?'

Arnold shook his head. 'I was there some years ago, when trouble arose over an encampment. This present situation, I've not been dealing with the file and—'

'The reality is out here, dammit, not in your bloody office! It's all very well for you people to sit there in Morpeth deciding what to do in the safety of your centrally heated hideaways, but it's out here it's happening, and it's out here that the filth is coming in and the robbery and the theft and—'

'Mr Gullick, I assure you—'

'Assure me of nothing!' For all of Gullick's rough appearance, his accent was only slightly marked with bucolic Northumberland, and he had clearly been well educated, probably in Morpeth, for the farm itself was a prosperous one and always had been. Perhaps his parents had paid for a boarding-school. Be that as it may, the education had not taken the rough edge off his language. 'Those bastards down there are the scum of the earth. Oh, I know what counts in government and in bloody Morpeth! There'll be much talk of the duty society holds towards that rabble. There'll be some emotional pleading, some romanticist standing up and proclaiming about the heritage of the Romanies, the thousand years they've wandered this land. But look at that—' He turned, and stabbed his finger in the air, indicating the wall behind him.

Arnold stared at the doorway and the lintel: GNC-1696.

'Nicholas Gullick built this house in 1696 and he put his name and his wife's name — Clarissa — up there to demonstrate this was a yeoman farmhouse, and owned by a family who go back five hundred years. My family lived on this land, worked it, built it up, kept it going through pestilence and war as well as good times. So don't talk to me about

Romany heritage; don't give me that muck about having to look after people who have chosen a wandering life.'

'I don't intend—'

'If the sods want to wander, well, let them. But stop them sitting on the bloody common! Move them on, as they've always been moved on!'

'They have to stop somewhere,' Arnold argued gently.

'Why here?' Gullick made a growling sound deep in his throat. 'I remember how it was when I was a kid, and my grandfather was alive. He had no truck with that kind. He knew them for what they were. He used to go down after three days with a shotgun and three dogs. That's all it took: a shotgun, and three dogs. They would go then, within twenty-four hours. He didn't have to say much; just stand there, and look. They got the message; they knew the old man.'

'The 1968 Act—'

'Don't talk to me about bloody Acts of Parliament. I'm telling you the reality is here!' Gullick was considerably shorter than Arnold and he squinted up at him now, fists still clenched, angry, committed and vicious in his self-righteousness.

'You bastards at the council offices have to recognize what's going to happen here if things don't get sorted out. There're enough of us now who feel the same way about things. You can't get away from the fact that those bloody gipsies are breaking the law—'

'Mr Gullick, I understand that, but the council does have a duty to provide accommodation by way of sites under the 1968 Act and at the moment there's an appeal pending since the gipsies have argued that Rafferty Common is the only place where they—'

'I'm not talking about the legality or not of their staying on Rafferty Common. I'm talking about the fact that since those scummy thugs have moved into the area the same things are occurring that always happen when they're around. Quite apart from the fact that they constitute a bloody nuisance with the scattering of filth and rubbish and their generally disgusting personal habits, there's the general matter of theft to take into account. Chickens are taken regularly — and if they say it's foxes they're bloody liars. How come foxes suddenly proliferate when the Romanies are on the common?'

'Mr Gullick—'

'I've started losing lambs, naturally enough. That's par for the course and nothing new in the general situation. But in the past we've all been prepared to accept that. My grandfather even — he'd accept it for a few days. But after two or three lambs had been taken, then he'd be down at the site with his gun and dogs, and the message got across. But no longer.'

Feebly, Arnold attempted to break into the flow. 'I understand precisely the problem you feel you're facing, Mr Gullick, but in a sense our hands are tied. While the families refuse to move, and in a situation where the appeal—'

'I think you understand sod-all,' Gullick insisted. His eyes seemed to have reddened even further, dark blood of anger surging up as his contempt for the workings of bureaucracy sharpened. He thumped his fists on to his hips and stood foursquare, glaring at Arnold. 'I think you'd better get something quite clear. We've had enough up here. I'm not alone — though maybe I'll admit to being the rowdiest. But that's because I've got the guts to stand up, say my piece, and then do what I've said I'll do. Listen to this, Mr bloody Landon. I want those damned Romanies moved off Rafferty Common. I've had my fill of their thieving and filth. They wander on to my land, poach, steal, damage and destroy — grown-ups and kids, they have no respect for property. The next time I catch any of them on my land I'll whale the living daylights out of them, so they'll never want to come back again. But more than that: if you idiots at County Hall don't get this Common thing sorted out pretty damned well sharp, there'll be vigilante activity starting on Rafferty Common that'll make the Ku Klux Klan look like a tea party in a bloody beauty parlour!'

There was a short silence between the two men, Gullick squinting up belligerently in the sunshine at Arnold, and the planning officer standing tense and quiet.

'Mr Gullick, I have to make it clear,' Arnold said seriously. 'There can be no swift action on this matter. Our hands are tied at Morpeth, and we have to go through the necessary procedures—'

'My grandfather knew all about procedures,' Gullick snarled unpleasantly. 'And our hands are not tied up with red tape. You came up here to find out what local landowners felt, Landon. Well, now you know. If you clowns at County Hall don't sort things out, and soon, we up here will sort things out for ourselves. And to hell with the consequences!'

'They could be serious, Mr Gullick.'

The narrow, angry eyes glared at Arnold. 'You can still stuff the consequences, Landon, and stuff them where it hurts!'

* * *

Arnold got back to his car and drove away from Gullick Farm. Once on the main road, he hesitated; he switched off the engine and parked for a while and a few minutes later he heard the sound of a car coming up the track. It was the Jaguar; Marcus Gullick on his way to Morpeth. He gave no sign of recognition as he swept past Arnold in his small Ford.

There was an unpleasant taste in Arnold's mouth. The anger in Gullick had affected him. Ned Keeton had been right to suggest to Arnold that a visit to Gullick would be instructive. Arnold had not realized the strength of feeling that the presence of the gipsies on Rafferty Common had aroused. If Gullick was typical of the local farmers, they could expect trouble.

Strictly speaking, the threats uttered by Gullick were hardly Arnold's problem: it would be a police matter if violence visited Rafferty Common. Nevertheless, Arnold felt vaguely responsible for the situation. It was a planning matter, and the gipsies had a point. There was no appropriate site available for them in the locality, designated by the authority, so they were in a sense making a stand for their legal rights. On the other hand, Arnold could respect Gullick's views, even if he could not approve of their consequences or the man's manner of expressing them. It was a difficult situation.

And it was time Arnold took a closer look at the site itself.

* * *

The common lay west of the village, fringed by a bank of ancient oaks and beech, with a stretch of scrub and alder crowding the banks of the small stream that meandered down a steep-sided gully at the near end of the common. The stream lay between the village and the common. Arnold stopped the car and got out to look down into the gully. The stream was in a filthy condition, blocked with rusting iron bedsteads, cans and the detritus of modern living. A vaguely unpleasant smell of decay and sewerage arose from the stream; the bedsteads could hardly be blamed on the gipsies, Arnold concluded, but everyone was familiar with the curious mentality that made people drive out from the environs of Morpeth and Newcastle to dump unwanted items in streams rather than use officially designated dumping sites.

Arnold got back into his car and drove over the narrow stone bridge that crossed the gully, and parked at the edge of Rafferty Common. He got out, locking the car as an afterthought, and began to walk across the common towards the sprawl of caravans that were drawn up on the east side of the area.

The grass was scarred with wheel tracks and litter; paper scudding along lightly in the breeze, rustling through the lengthening grass. There was an odd odour in the air, a strangely rich mixture of the smells of cooking and kerosene and garbage. Near to Arnold were the larger caravans, white and blue, cream and red, motorized vehicles that would have cost thousands of pounds and on which had been lavished, by way of decoration, further large sums of money. They bristled with television aerials and in the open doorway of one of the vans sat a young, bold, brown-legged girl of perhaps seventeen years, watching Arnold with careless eyes.

Beyond the expensive caravans was a huddle of the older kind: curved, brilliantly painted roofs, ornate sides, open at the rear with traditional cooking pots suspended above open fires near to the vehicles. Some twenty ponies grazed near the stand of oaks; small, lithe, muscular, they seemed contented enough and well cared for, which was the difference that Arnold's town eye discerned between them and the scattering of children who lounged or played about the encampment.

They were uniformly dirty. Their clothes were patched and occasionally ragged, and the dark colour of their faces was due not only to the sun. They had sharp knowing glances for the intruder, but they made no approach to him, as though they had become indifferent in their knowledge that officialdom was failing to move them on and, therefore, impotent in attempts to affect their lives.

There were few adults about. A small number of women had congregated near one of the far wagons, but they made no attempt to approach him: there was a sullen hostility in the way they presented their shawled backs to him. An old man sat near the ponies, hunkered down against one of the gnarled oaks, smoking a pipe, but he also paid no obvious attention to Arnold. It was as though Arnold barely existed in their consciousness; the only evidence of their hostility was a prickling of his skin as he walked about the site. Even the dogs seemed to have become accustomed to the visits of men from County Hall; they scratched themselves and yawned vacuously, apart from one pair that were making a desultory attempt to mate.

Dispirited, Arnold completed his brief tour of the encampment and turned to make his way back to the car. He was still some distance away from it when he realized there was a man standing beside the passenger seat. Warily,

Arnold walked forward, his stomach muscles beginning to tense as he saw the man, arms folded along the top of the car, leaning on the roof casually as he observed the planning officer who had invaded the encampment.

Alone.

Arnold approached the car. The man made no attempt to move, or take his arms from their resting place on the car roof. He was a big man, in his early thirties. His hair was black, tight with small curls that clustered thickly to his head, bristling low along his jawline. He was clean-shaven, his skin tanned dark. He had a wild, handsome air about him, a sensuous mouth that could easily turn ugly and eyes that were deep and brown, exciting to a woman, dangerous to an enemy, supportive to a friend.

Arnold had no doubt in which category he would fall. He paused, inserting the key in the lock of the car door. 'Good afternoon.'

'And to you. Seen enough?'

Arnold hesitated. 'I think so.'

'And what was it you'd be looking for?' There was a slight Irish brogue in the voice, probably picked up from an Irish tinker parentage.

'Nothing in particular.'

'And it's nothing in particular you found, then, is it?' The bantering tone was not entirely sincere; it held an edge of menace, the timbre of the voice low and controlled.

'My name is Landon. I'm a planning officer at Morpeth.'

'Now is that the truth!'

'I've taken over the file on Rafferty Common.'

'So we have a file on us,' the gipsy mocked. 'Now, that's grand!'

Stiffly, Arnold went on, 'I thought I'd better visit the site, to familiarize myself with the situation—'

'Situation? What's that, the situation? In my book, it's all over and done with, ink dried, book closed. Isn't that the way of it, Mr . . . Landon? Isn't it the truth that the county's got blood on its nose, and we're in the right, the poor bloody Romanies are in the right, after all?'

'The planning appeal—'

'Has been turned down. So we're in the right. Isn't that the way of it? So what is it you'd be doing here, Mr Landon?'

Arnold stared at the dark-haired man facing him. Slowly, he said, 'You're Joe Connor.'

'The very same.' The gipsy seemed amused at being recognized by Landon. 'It seems fame has reached out to touch me, hey, when a planning officer can pick me out of a crowd!' He glanced about him, smiling slightly. 'Even if there's no crowd around us.'

In fact the only person who seemed at all interested in their presence together was the brown-legged girl Arnold had noticed as he entered the encampment. She was now standing some small distance away, watching them with a curious intensity, as though she would dearly have loved to hear what they were saying but lacked the courage to approach nearer.

Connor caught Arnold's glance and looked at the girl. A slight frown crossed his features, then he turned back to Arnold. 'So, let's have it, my friend. Just what kind of report will you be making back at Morpeth? What did you hope to discover here today?'

'I wasn't looking for anything in particular. Merely trying to familiarize myself with the situation, talk to a few people—'

'Talk?' Connor's eyes were fixed suspiciously on Arnold. 'Talk to whom?'

Arnold was slightly flustered. 'Well, you—'

'I didn't know you were coming. You didn't know I'd be here. Who've you been talking to, Mr Landon?' Connor waited, then as the silence grew around them he gave vent to a short barking laugh. 'Landowners, that's who, is my guess. Am I right, Landon? Landowners!'

Arnold made no reply. From the corner of his eye he saw the brown-legged girl edging closer, almost casually. Connor took a deep breath. 'Or maybe not even landowners, not any of them but just one. It's not that you'll have been talking to a man called Gullick, is it? After which you thought it'd be a good idea to come down and see how the pigs live, to confirm what Gullick's been saying.'

'Mr Connor—'

'*Mister*, is it?' Connor sneered unpleasantly. 'I think I've hit the iron all right. You've been talking to that bastard Gullick. All right, let's get a few things clear, Landon. To begin with, the council's tried to throw us off this land. But I'm not so stupid as Gullick might think all Romanies are. I can read, believe it or not. And I know the law. The council's got to provide us with camp sites. It isn't doing that. You tried to throw us off this site. You got a possession order. That's been thrown out of court. You've appealed. And you've lost. But that doesn't suit friend Gullick, does it? He's got other ideas. Like if the law won't help him, he'll help himself. Well, there's two can play at that game.'

Arnold took a deep breath. 'I'm not taking sides in any dispute or unpleasantness between you. Yes, I've spoken to Marcus Gullick. I was advised to do so in order to test the strength of local opinion.'

'And now you're testing the strength of local opinion on this site. That's fair enough, Mr Planning Officer.' Connor bared his teeth in a parody of a smile. They were very white, even, strong teeth and they contrasted with the darkness of his skin. The girl had moved closer, but Connor ignored her. 'We're local people while we're here, and we have a point of view. It's this. We got a right to stay here: the court's said so. It's your people up at County Hall who have the problem, not us. But if Gullick thinks he can take the law into his own hands that's all right by me. He's a man out of his time, is Gullick. He thinks he can behave the way his grandfather behaved fifty years ago. Don't get misled into believing Gullick's myths — it wasn't the old man who moved the Romanies on. They went of their own accord; it's their way of life. It pleased old Gullick to think he had the power. But it's a bad mistake for Marcus Gullick to think he can ride roughshod over the families. We'll stay as long as we like, and we'll move on when it suits us.'

'Mr Gullick—'

'*Mister* Gullick can go to hell. And let me tell you this, Landon. If Gullick thinks he can stir up trouble, just let him start. He'll get more than he'll bargain for.' His voice had dropped, a lower, menacing tone creeping into it. 'There are dark nights, my friend, and things can happen on dark nights, unseen, and blood can flow. We're superstitious people, Landon, and we know the powers of darkness, and of the knife, and of evil. Any man can be evil; maybe he has it born in him, like they say. Gullick is evil — his views are evil. A Romany can match that, and more — we've had a thousand years' practice, since the ancient days of Egypt. So, if you have any influence over that swine Gullick, warn him, Landon — or he'll not wake up one morning when dawn comes bright.'

Arnold stood facing the younger man indeterminately. He wasn't sure how to respond. The gipsy clearly hated Gullick in the way Gullick hated all Romanies on Rafferty Common. But this was all nothing to do with Arnold. It was a political matter that the members at County Hall would have to take into account in determining their policy over the appeal. There was no way in which Arnold wanted to be drawn into a conflict of this kind; although it seemed that he inevitably would be, as the man in the front line, standing between the two parties.

'So you'll have got the picture now, Mr Landon?'

Arnold began to say something but thought better of it. He nodded, and opened the car door. Connor removed his arms from the roof and stepped back, staring down at Arnold as he got into the driver's seat. 'Don't come back too often, Mr Landon. We're an easy-going race, but we don't care for people snooping around too much. You were ignored today. Maybe next time some of them up there—' he gestured back towards the caravans — 'maybe they'll want to talk to you next time, put forward a point of view.'

The message was clear in his tone. Putting a point of view forward would not be verbal. Arnold started the car and

Connor smiled contemptuously and moved away, turning his back.

Arnold reversed the car to make the turn back to the entrance to the common. As he did so, he slipped off the track and his rear wheels encountered a soft patch of ground. In his nervousness he revved the engine and the wheels spun madly, whining as they failed to get sufficient purchase to thrust the car forward. Arnold cursed mentally. He glanced in his mirror. Gipsy Joe Connor was looking back at the car, uninterested, then he continued to walk away. The girl was standing in front of him; she put a hand on his arm, saying something to him.

Arnold pressed the accelerator again, but the whining increased. He stopped, telling himself to calm down. He waited for several seconds, then gently rocked the car, changing gears from reverse to forward several times, moving the car gently out of the churning earth. He finally felt the wheels gripping and slowly he moved forward, turning as he did so until he managed to manoeuvre the car on to the dirt track leading back to the main road.

As he drove away he was sweating. He glanced sideways to where Connor and the girl had been standing. They had been joined now by an older man, spare, elderly, with a seamed face and thin grey hair. He seemed angry; he was shouting something at Connor and waving his arms, while the girl walked away, back towards the caravan where Arnold had first seen her.

Arnold grimaced.

It would seem there were other matters in contention at Rafferty Common apart from the clash between Marcus Gullick and Gipsy Joe Connor.

2

It was the weekend before Arnold found the opportunity to relax and deal with the matters that were closer to his heart than planning applications over gipsy encampments. He had been feeling slightly guilty about the fact he had done nothing with Elliott Brandling's notes, so on the Saturday morning he sat down with the package that Cy Robinson had brought him and began to read the material closely.

A brief letter was enclosed from Brandling.

Dear Mr Landon,

I'm grateful for your assistance. You'll see that I'm a bit confused about the Jarrow site. I have some documentation which seems to refer to it, but the measurements don't tally, and maybe your practised eye can pick up something I've missed.

Sincerely,

Elliott Brandling

Arnold turned to the sheets that were attached to the letter. They were in Elliott Brandling's handwriting and they consisted of notes relating to the Jarrow site. The first was headed FARFA CUSTOMARY.

Arnold read it swiftly.

The length of the church is 140 feet, its height is 43 feet and it has 59 glazed windows. The chapter house is 45-feet long by 34-feet wide. The parlour is 30-feet long, the camera 90 feet. The bathroom is 70 feet by 23 feet and contains 30 lavatories. The monastic kitchen is 30-feet long by 25-feet broad and the kitchen for the lay folk is of the same dimensions . . .

As Arnold read on he realized that the Customary notes must have been copied by Brandling from a manuscript held in a religious library, probably a Vatican manuscript transcription since most monastic records were now kept in Rome. The material described the layout and construction of a monastery, that was clear: it also gave some insight into the life of the time and the way in which the monastery was used: customaries normally described the manners, rules and customs of a locality or country, hence the name.

Close to the Galilee a guest house 135-feet long by 30-feet wide for the reception of people who arrive at the monastery on horseback . . . A central position in the guest-house tables similar to those in the refectory is arranged where men and women may take meals together . . . Accommodation is provided for all the tailors and their sewing assistants to sit and work at whatever the chamberlain orders them to do . . . a cemetery for lay folk . . . stables for horses . . . accommodation for people travelling on foot, in which they can receive an appropriate gift of food and drink . . . goldsmiths, gem-setters and glaziers may ply their crafts . . .

Arnold read on, picking up some additional scrawled notes which Brandling had added later in the margins, and as he worked through the papers, and looked at the roughly scrawled plan of the monastery that Brandling had added, his interest was kindled. Brandling was no artist, but the sketch was clear enough. It looked an interesting situation.

Arnold decided it might make a pleasant excursion for his Saturday afternoon, so he made some sandwiches and a flask of coffee and set out for the North Road.

He drove to Morpeth, passed through the big gate and headed south on the A1 before cutting through to North Shields and through the Tyne Tunnel. The road to Jarrow was signposted and he knew generally where he needed to be from the directions Brandling had noted in the sheets provided.

The site was a grassy one, bordered by a housing estate on one side, Jarrow Slake on the other, and a ruined chapel on the sloping ground. Arnold nodded thoughtfully: it was a curiosity that as religions came and went, as new churches arose and old decayed, the place for worship never seemed to move far. There had always been a tradition that one cult used the site another had chosen earlier . . .

The lines Brandling had drawn were, on the ground, marked by scattered stones embedded in the earth and grassy ridges underneath which, Arnold presumed, some of the building's foundations would lie. There was little evidence of excavation other than of the most desultory kind. Few other than Brandling would have displayed much interest in this site, and yet, as he stared at the ground, Arnold was left with the feeling that Brandling could well be right. If the details given in the Customary matched some of the measurements to be made on the ground, there could be sufficient evidence to argue for the existence of a monastery on this site.

And a very old monastery, at that. Arnold spent the long, sunny afternoon, measuring and pacing out the boundaries of the old site, marking the stones and the ridges and comparing them to the rough sketch Brandling had made. He began his own rough drawing, relying partly upon experience and partly upon his own imagination. He applied the rules of monastic building that he was aware of and gradually a picture that excited him began to emerge.

In his view, Brandling was right. As the sketch built up on paper and in his mind, he began to see that this site could have held a nave divided into seven bays by three round and four square pillars opening on to a broad transept. Six small chapels . . . a sanctuary . . . a main apse marking its end. It was the classic Benedictine layout.

He was able to find the bases for five of the ancient pillars, and then south of the cloister he found signs of the calefactory and the refectory. The fifteen-feet wide passage that would have led through them was swallowed up by the grassy edge of the site, and the ruined chapel buildings. The fountain that would have been used for ablutions was probably situated on the east side of the cloister.

Arnold worked on, oblivious of the time, pausing only in the late afternoon to eat his sandwiches and drink his coffee. Even then his mind was active, his eyes scanning the ground for further signs that might provide clues to the link between the Customary statement and the evidence on the ground.

It was eight in the evening before he finally finished, if finished was the word. He was stiff from crouching, and his neck ached, and there were still ideas buzzing around in his head as he began to wonder what stone had been used in the building after the original wooden structure had fallen. He could not know at what period the monastery had gone into decline. Perhaps Brandling would have that answer. Certainly, it must have disappeared long before the dissolution of the monasteries or otherwise its presence would have been recorded in that great rape of the Church by the Crown. These were not questions he could ever attempt to answer. Brandling's own research would have to confirm that, based on documentary evidence. As far as Arnold was concerned, there was a strong case to argue that the Customary did indeed refer to the Jarrow site; or alternatively, that the Jarrow site had been built in a fashion similar to that described in the Customary. Either way, it pointed to the existence of a monastery on this area.

Arnold would be able to lend some support to Brandling's theory. The thought pleased him, not only that he could lend support, but that he had been asked to help in the first instance.

He was as open to flattery as any man, he thought wryly to himself.

Arnold collected up his notes, put them into some semblance of order, tucked them in behind Brandling's own notes and sketch-map and returned to his car. He did not like the way two young urchins were leaning against a low brick wall nearby, gazing idly in his direction, and suspiciously Arnold checked that all four of his wheels were intact and the tyres had not been deflated. Satisfied, he smiled at the lads and unlocked his car. They seemed surprised.

He checked his watch. If he drove through the Tyne Tunnel again it should be quiet enough and then a leisurely drive through the countryside away from Morpeth would be longer, to get him home, but it would be more pleasant than the main road and would take him through some splendid scenery. He started the car and drove away, leaving the huddle of Jarrow behind him.

North of the Tyne he stopped at a hotel and obtained a modest meal in the restaurant there. It was fairly quiet, with just a scattering of commercial travellers and a small group of teenagers, clearly out for the first time to a restaurant meal. The lads were out to impress and the girls were giggly. Somehow, watching them made Arnold feel a little sad, and lonely.

It was nine before he left the restaurant and went on his way. The sun was low in the heavens, dipping below the hills ahead of him, but the sky itself was a pale blue with no hint of cloud to mark the red staining in the west. The countryside was green and quiet; there was little traffic and Arnold felt at peace with himself. He had gained a certain satisfaction puzzling out the Jarrow ruins, and he now felt he had something to contribute to Elliott Brandling's research.

The name KENTSIDE on the signpost leaped out at him as he was still thinking about the Jarrow monastery.

Arnold braked, slowing, not quite certain why the name of the village should impinge so sharply upon his consciousness. The car came to a halt, and Arnold frowned, staring at the sign. Then he remembered. Elliott Brandling; he had spoken of St Michael's Church at Kentside.

Arnold glanced at his watch. He was in no hurry to get home and it would be a matter of driving only a few miles out of his way. And he felt a twinge of curiosity. Brandling had suggested they might visit St Michael's together sometime, but Arnold preferred to reach his own judgements about places, and he was certainly stirred by a certain scepticism regarding Brandling's story about the church.

Satanic rites? The cult of the Raging Wolf? Arnold smiled to himself, put the car into gear and drove slowly into the bend, taking the narrow road to Kentside. He had the feeling he had been through the village years ago, but he now had no recollection of what it was like. Perhaps it was high time he renewed his acquaintance with the place.

In many ways it was a disappointment. The road twisted and turned for about three miles past high hedgerows, grey stone walls and over a hill banked with a scattering of ancient oaks and majestic lime trees. Then it dipped towards the village itself, but Kentside was little more than a huddle of nondescript stone houses, some derelict cottages, rather unkempt gardens, a small general store that was firmly locked, presenting out-of-date display material, and at the far end of the village, down a narrow side street, the church itself.

St Michael's, Kentside.

It must have lost its congregation years ago, for it presented an appearance as unkempt as the village itself. Most of the villages in Northumberland seemed to retain a sense of pride, however far they were from the major centres like Newcastle, Morpeth or Berwick. But Kentside was different: its population had clearly decreased — Arnold had paid due note to the derelict cottages — and the church was obviously no longer a centre for the community. It bore every appearance of disuse, and it was possible that lack of support over the years would have meant that services would be held there no more than once a month, under the control of a reluctant and itinerant vicar.

Arnold parked his car in the lane and got out somewhat despondently. He was not certain now why he had bothered to come; there would be little of interest here. The gate squealed rustily as he entered the churchyard. The tombstones were badly overgrown and marked with lichen. He peered at one that leaned drunkenly beside the pathway. He made out a date, 1756, but no name. He looked around, guessing that there would be older stones here, buried in the long grass and creeping tendrils of weed and the small bank of rosebay willow herb. He walked up to the lichgate, and the dilapidated porch. Arnold had been wrong. The notice proclaimed that there would be no services until further notice.

The villagers had abandoned the church, and now so had the church authorities.

Arnold shivered, inexplicably. He looked about him. The sun had gone now, and dusk was approaching, slowly, with a light touch, and he knew that the sky would soon turn from pale blue to a darker, more intense shade. There was no breeze and he could not account for the sudden shiver that had affected him. He looked up at the dark stone of the church itself and almost unconsciously applied what he knew about such buildings to this decaying structure at Kentside.

The keynote for the church itself was the central tower. It was flanked with transepts of no great length. He began to walk around the building. On the eastward side was a short chancel; on the westward side a narrow nave. Larger churches than this had a standard pattern, aisled in four or five bays. Without going inside the boarded-up church Arnold could guess that this would be one of the aisle-less class, usually described as being on a six-square plan, with two squares representing the nave, and the others occupied by tower, chancel and transepts.

Arnold frowned, thoughtfully. What was it he had read somewhere . . . ? The semi-circular apse of the early Christian architecture of Rome was never suited to the English plan of nave and chancel as it always made the chancel too short . . .

Arnold puzzled about the quotation. Why had it sprung to his mind? He shook his head, and as the evening began to darken about him he paced his way around the building, half stumbling where the pathway had become overgrown or littered with fallen masonry and broken tombstones, picking his way with care where the path disappeared altogether.

At the back of the church, where a six-feet-high stone wall in a reasonable state of preservation kept vandals out from the churchyard, the dilapidated state of the graves was even more marked. The grass was three-feet-high in places, and in one corner of the area against the wall a pile of builders' rubble seemed to have been deposited. The far end of the churchyard seemed more level, where a dark rose hedge had crept over and engulfed the wall itself with a splash of deep green and pink.

Arnold turned back to the church. English apses were nearly always apsidal-ended chancels, in fact. In ancient Mercia a form of apse had appeared — Arnold had seen an example in Buckinghamshire. French influences in the eleventh century had brought about a revival of the semi-circular apse in south-eastern England, but this far north it had never been popular. And there was something slightly puzzling about St Michael's, something he could not put his finger on.

Anglo-Saxon masons, he knew, had reached a high standard of building in the Middle Ages but there had still been a vast amount of construction that had perpetuated the traditional timber style. Perhaps that was the key to the matter that was bothering him here — the existence of a break in the pattern of building, something that offended his eye in terms of approved style, a leaning perhaps towards principles that had been laid down in wood long before the decision to build in stone had been taken.

His skin tingled.

Irritation struck at him suddenly; the church was affecting him in a peculiar way, not in an aesthetic, intellectual manner but physically. It was a feeling he neither understood nor enjoyed. He felt cold even though there was no breeze;

he felt irritated even though he could find no cause for irritation. And an indeterminate unease made his skin tingle and prickle.

Annoyed, he glared at the darkening walls of the building. He was too close to it to make out its lines in a correct manner; perhaps if he moved across towards the wall and the rose hedge he would be able to get some clearer clue to the history of the church. It was not old, after all — even if some of the tombstones predated its building.

He glanced behind him, then backed off through the long grass, squinting up to the central tower, taking rough measurements with his eye. He stumbled, felt a crunching beneath his foot, as though he had stepped on fragile, decaying bone, and he kicked the material aside, nervously, but did not look down.

The wall was at his back, the stone cold to his touch. He stared ahead, picking out the structure and the layout of St Michael's Church, black against the sky. There was something wrong about its proportions, something disturbing, but he could not come to grips with the problem. He would have to go home, think about it, maybe go to Newcastle Library and look up some tomes on mediaeval church architecture.

But this church was not a mediaeval structure.

Arnold scowled. His brain seemed thick, heavy, turgid in thought processes. It was as though he was drugged, unable to think clearly and distinguish one problem from another, one possible solution from an alternative. So turgid, in fact, that he could not even define the problem in the first place. He felt dissatisfied, irritated, and still . . . cold.

There was something else.

It was offensive. It attacked his senses but, in the confusion of mind that seemed to affect him, it was several seconds before he was even able to decide which of his senses was offended. He looked about him in the gathering darkness and saw the dark green mass of the rose hedge, scattered with light pink splashes of flower. He could smell the roses, a cloying, sweet, heavy smell but one that he had never associated with wild rose before. He walked towards the hedge, almost dizzily, his brain swimming, his eyes almost out of focus, and the odour became stronger, richer until he knew it was not wild rose but something based on decay and horror, rather than life.

Arnold stopped, the smell strong in his nostrils. He stood facing the rose hedge, undecided. Then he turned, looked about him in the long grass. The winds of winter had broken dead branches from the sycamore tree which had seeded itself many years ago near the wall; they lay unregarded in the grass. Arnold picked up a dead branch and turned back to the rose hedge.

The rich, decayed smell was still strong in his nostrils.

Arnold pushed the branch into the lower reaches of the hedge, pushing the briars apart, spreading them, thrusting the end of the stick down into the undergrowth. He struck something soft, it gave with a slight sucking sound and a faint, then stronger whiff of something unpleasant reached up for him.

Bile rose in his throat, making him gag. He prodded again, felt the soft give of decayed flesh, and then he could make out a heavy mass of flesh, large, putrescent in the undergrowth, concealed by the fall of the rose hedge. He stepped back, disgusted, not wanting to know more, barely able to control the thick, unpleasant taste in his mouth. He threw the stick aside, turned, and walked back quickly to his car.

He had forgotten the problems he had been dwelling on. His mind was numb as he drove, and he was hardly aware of the route he took, driving almost instinctively. But as he made his way north through the twisting lanes, heading for the warmth and comforting security of his home, the decaying, death-like odour was still in his nostrils.

And he was still conscious of a cold in his bones, an inexplicable prickling of his skin, a lifting of the hairs along the back of his neck.

CHAPTER THREE

1

The following Monday started badly.

In the first instance, Arnold had trouble with his car so he was late arriving at Morpeth. As a result, he missed an early morning meeting of some importance with the architects; the atmosphere was distinctly chilly when he finally arrived. Then there was the notification that the pay rise that had been claimed by the union was hitting heavy weather with employers and government: as a single, unattached man, Arnold did not find it difficult to live within his means, but there were others in the department with greater commitments and over coffee a number of wild, angry statements were being made, even suggesting strike action.

The thought was anathema to Arnold. Then there was the Senior Planning Officer.

That particular gentleman had already used Arnold once to fend off Edward Chaunter and his planning application for the meeting hall for religious purposes at Birkbeck. Arnold still recalled with a shiver the baleful glance of the leader of the Vicars of Jehovah and the manner in which he had taken his leave of Arnold.

I will remember the name.

Consequently, it was with a sinking heart that Arnold read the note left on his desk by the Senior Planning Officer. For that carefully insecure gentleman, it was quite verbose.

> *Landon:*
> *Mr Chaunter wishes to have a further interview. I thought we had dealt with the matter quite satisfactorily on the first occasion, but it seems he wishes to discuss it further. I'm sure you can handle it without my assistance. Please do so. I have agreed he can see you on Monday at 11. Your diary would seem to be relatively light at that time.*

Arnold scowled, screwed the note into a ball and hurled it into the wastepaper-basket. The last thing he wanted was another discussion with the unpleasant Mr Chaunter. Reluctantly, he drew out the file he had been given on Chaunter's application. He sat staring at its cover for several minutes without opening it to refresh his memory.

His advice to Chaunter had been to sharpen up the arguments Chaunter wished to raise. The Vicars of Jehovah needed to demonstrate more positively that their proposed activity would bring acceptable results to the area. On the other hand, advice was cheap: Arnold could not for the life of him determine what additional arguments Chaunter could raise, not see what purpose might be served by Chaunter having a further discussion in the Planning Department.

The Senior Planning Officer should have had the courage to refuse Chaunter any further meetings — but perhaps that was not sound policy for a self-effacing servant of the community. Arnold sighed, and waited despondently for the clock hands to turn to eleven.

Chaunter was prompt, at least. But he was not alone. The tall, lean man with the grey-flecked eyes came in first, but was closely followed by two companions. The first was of medium height, balding badly apart from strips of dirty grey hair above his ears, and sporting a thin moustache that was startlingly different in colour from his hair. The dark pencil line emphasized rather than disguised the weakness of his soft mouth, and there was a lurking unease in the man's eyes that made him seem to be constantly searching for enemies — or men who knew the truth about him, Arnold considered.

Bustling in his wake came another tall man, lean like Chaunter, equally cold-eyed, but with a nervous energy that he found difficulty in containing. He seemed to want to push himself forward but lacked the confidence to do so when Chaunter was in the room, and he watched the military-like bearing of his leader like a hypnotized bird in front of a snake.

'Landon. I thought,' Edward Chaunter intoned, 'it would be useful after our last unsatisfactory interview, if I brought along two of my colleagues to sit in on our discussion. I have wasted much time and money over the Birkbeck application. I would not wish to replicate the experience. I am seeking advice, Landon, and the advice you give will be recorded by my colleagues so there can be no later misunderstanding, and a true record of the conversation will be kept.'

He clearly expected hostility and was preparing for it. Arnold wriggled uncomfortably in his seat. He shrugged. 'As you wish, Mr Chaunter. But I'm not clear what advice you think I can give you. On the last occasion—'

'This is Mr Santana,' Chaunter said icily, as though Arnold had not spoken. The tall, nervous man nodded in Arnold's direction. 'And this is Mr Daniels.'

'Nick Daniels,' the short man with the soft mouth added. He managed a weak, uncertain smile. 'Three's better than one on business like this.'

Chaunter glared at Daniels balefully for several seconds. The man seemed to wilt under the force of the displeasure. Arnold was left in no doubt that Edward Chaunter saw himself as very much in charge of this operation, whatever its objective might be.

'May we sit down?'

Arnold had hoped they wouldn't be staying long enough to do so. He rose to get another chair from the room next door so that all three men could be accommodated; his office was really too small for meetings of this kind, but he was reluctant to take them to a formal interview room: it might have the effect of prolonging the meeting.

'Well,' Arnold began when they were all settled, 'I have the file here, and I really feel there is little, if anything, I can add to what I told you last time, Mr Chaunter. Any advice I can offer—'

'We had better clarify the situation immediately,' Chaunter interrupted with a stiff smile. 'You can . . . dispose of that file whenever you wish. We have no further interest in it.'

'I don't understand—'

'The site at Birkbeck no longer interests our group. I have found a buyer for the property who is more interested in serving Mammon in the manner in which your council prefers. The religious instruction that we would have carried on there will now be superseded by a bingo hall or suchlike.'

Bewildered, Arnold said, 'I don't think the outline planning permission covers bingo—'

'A figure of speech,' Chaunter interrupted coldly. 'I have no knowledge and no desire to know for what purposes the purchaser of our property has decided to use it. It is enough that we have decided to sell, and he to buy. The planning application regarding Birkbeck can, therefore, be closed. The reason why we are here now is that we have placed an offer for another property — but the Vicars of Jehovah want to be certain that no further petty tyrannies will be visited upon them by minions of the Planning Department here at Morpeth.'

'Another property?'

Chaunter's pale eyes narrowed and he sat very upright in his chair. He gazed at Arnold intently. 'That is so. We intend to purchase a building large enough for our purposes on the outskirts of Denton Gap. As far as I've been able to ascertain, it's been empty for some time, and indeed is in a state of dilapidation.'

'Denton Gap—'

'The village is somewhat isolated for our purposes, but no matter. Peace, and the ability to do God's work, is all we seek. But before we go ahead with the purchase it seems wise, in view of our previous experience at the hands of the Planning Department, that we should ascertain whether there is any . . . blight that might be put upon our plans.'

Denton Gap. Arnold thought hard for a few moments; he should know the village, he was sure he had passed near it recently. His eyes strayed towards the map of Northumberland pinned to the wall. Chaunter caught the glance. 'Denton Gap,' he offered superciliously, 'is on the north side of Rafferty Common.'

Inwardly, Arnold groaned. He could foresee the possibility of two problems arising in the vicinity of Rafferty Common. He cleared his throat: Chaunter's icy stare made him feel nervous. 'What sort of building is it you're intending to buy?'

'A Methodist chapel. Disused.'

Arnold blinked. The Vicars of Jehovah, an obscure sect, using a Methodist chapel. Surprising, bearing in mind the sensitivities of all religious parties when the matter of their buildings was at issue, but on the other hand . . . 'I presume you'll wish to use it for the kinds of purposes mentioned in your planning application for Birkbeck, Mr Chaunter?'

'Precisely.' Chaunter's severe mouth seemed to thin and he sniffed. 'I imagine there can be no objection to our using for religious purposes a property that was specifically built for such purposes.'

'If the Methodists don't mind,' Arnold remarked facetiously, 'I don't see how the Planning Department can object.'

'So there will be no block put on our so using it?'

'I wouldn't have thought so.' Arnold hesitated for a moment. 'Will you be carrying out any structural alterations?'

The man called Daniels wriggled on his seat, and Santana turned his head slightly to fix his gaze upon Arnold, as though he had uttered some obscenity. The atmosphere was suddenly icy, for reasons Arnold could not comprehend.

'Alterations?' Chaunter queried. 'What sort of alterations do you mean?'

Arnold shrugged. 'Well, there's the possibility the chapel is a listed building. It's unlikely, but once you identify the property I could do a quick check and let you know. If it is a listed building there'd be the possibility of problems if you wished to carry out external alterations. You'd have to submit plans to the authority and the Planning Committee would—'

'The Vicars of Jehovah have travelled that road,' Chaunter cut in. 'They have no wish to travel it again. There will be no external alterations.'

Arnold hesitated. 'Internal?'

There was a short silence. The tension had risen in the room, inexplicably, but it largely emanated from Chaunter's two companions. Chaunter himself seemed completely in control, cold as ever, his pale grey-flecked eyes unmoved. 'It is quite likely that we will need to make certain internal . . . rearrangements. The pulpit—'

'Edward—' The interruption came from Santana. His tone was low and urgent, pressing for care. He was sweating lightly, his nervousness communicated to his companion. Chaunter barely turned his head. He lifted his right hand, two fingers raised as though in admonition at Santana's failure to realize Edward Chaunter did not need guidance on private matters.

'Some internal rearrangements will be necessary,' Chaunter continued. 'The pulpit is in an unsatisfactory position and will be removed: we will be building a dais there, and there will be certain other decorative matters that might involve some restructuring. But I hardly imagine they will need your . . . supervision.'

Arnold shrugged. 'We only get interested if there's a change of use, or if the external appearance of the building is changed. From what you say—'

'There will be no external visual impact,' Chaunter announced firmly. In the sudden silence that followed,

Daniels snickered. It was an incongruous sound, occasioned by what would seem to be a private joke between the three men. Chaunter's hand was raised again, and the snicker was cut off. The silence grew around them.

At last, uncomfortably, Arnold said, 'Is that the only advice you wanted from me?' He paused, but Chaunter made no reply. 'I can't give you assurances until I've investigated the listed-status possibility but I think it's unlikely that will arise as an issue. The age of Methodist chapels generally—'

'We want only one essential thing from you,' Chaunter interrupted. 'We want to be left alone.'

'I can assure you—'

'Any assurances must be made before my colleagues. There must be no doubt. We want no prying, no official bumbling around our premises. Our religion is a closed one but the God we serve can be a terrible one in His vengeance. Landon, let's be clear. I give you the location of the chapel. I assure you there will be no external work. You must assure me — and my followers — that we will then enjoy privacy.'

'It's not part of my brief—'

'The location, as I've told you, is Denton Gap. The chapel itself will not be difficult to find. The land on which the chapel is situated backs on to the common. I would be grateful if you would carry out whatever search you deem necessary, visit the site and so on, and advise whether there are likely to be any problems. I want the purchase completed quickly.'

Arnold hesitated. He glanced again at the wall map. 'There may well be one small problem, strictly none of our business, of course, but you are aware of the trouble that's been bubbling around Rafferty Common?'

'The Sons of Belial,' Chaunter said grimly.

'I beg your pardon?'

Santana leaned forward, his narrowed eyes glinting with malice. 'Gipsies, Romanies, the Egyptian wanderers. Yes, we know about their presence on the common. We know also they will not stay.'

'Well, of course, we're doing all we can to make sure that—'

'They will not stay,' Santana insisted. 'Whatever you might do, we have our own ways.'

'Zeke,' Chaunter interrupted, showing signs of urgency for the first time and allowing his cold reserve to be shaken. 'The way in which we will deal with any problems from the Romanies is our affair.'

Santana seemed disappointed at losing the opportunity to suggest methods by which the gipsies could be persuaded to leave Rafferty Common. 'I was only going to mention that when we are installed at Denton Gap, our own powers are such that we will overcome the ribaldry and the insults of that rabble and that there are ways—'

'Zeke! Enough.' Chaunter turned his cold gaze back to Arnold. 'You do what is necessary, Landon, but don't worry about us. The proximity to that kind of problem does not disturb us. For your part, remember the one thing. We will demand of them what we demand of you.' He rose slowly, seeming almost to uncoil himself from his chair. A dry, cold snake of a man. 'Privacy, Landon, that's what we want. And that's what we insist upon.'

The others rose with him and followed him as he swept regally from the room. Santana glanced back as he was leaving, and Arnold detected a wolfishness in his eyes that gave him pause. His mouth was suddenly dry. It seemed to him then that the obvious person to sit with for a while was Ned Keeton. Arnold made his way to Keeton's office.

* * *

Keeton seemed amused by Arnold's reaction to his visitors. He heard Arnold tell the story of the brief meeting, and the bewilderment he felt about it all and then he shrugged, grinned, waved his pipe vaguely as though to take in mankind in general and said, 'The world's full of queer folks, Arnold.'

'But the visit seemed so pointless.'

'Not to friend Chaunter. Whether he gives you the shivers or not, he's a careful guy, seems to me. He was just checking on whether you're going to give him trouble.'

'I'm not in the business of creating trouble,' Arnold said peevishly.

'You're a Planning Officer, for God's sake! Next to lawyers and social workers, you're one of the most despised of earthly creatures! All right, Arnold, don't sulk . . . I was just joking. But tell me again about this remark concerning Rafferty Common.'

Arnold shrugged vaguely. 'Chaunter and his . . . acolytes seemed aware of the problems that are current on the common.'

'I know the old chapel,' Keeton mused. 'Used to take the dog up there for a walk, years ago. Been in a pretty dilapidated state for a few years now. Dog's been dead three years, after all. But it's not all that secure, you know. And if, as you suggest, there's some kind of feeling about Romanies in this Vicars of Jehovah cult—'

'I can't be positive about it, but it's certainly an impression I gained,' Arnold said.

'Well, if that is the case, old Bible-puncher Chaunter might be biting off more than he can chew. The wall at the back of the property, backing on to the common, is in a pretty sad state. If they get to singing hymns on Saturday nights I can see some of the young rowdies from the camp slinging stones to say the least.'

Arnold shook his head thoughtfully. 'I don't actually see Chaunter as a Bible-puncher, somehow. And my guess is that hymn-singing is out.'

'I thought you said he was religious?'

'He denies the word sect. He doesn't subscribe to standard organized religion. They call themselves the Vicars of Jehovah but I've never heard of them before. I get the feeling it really all revolves around our friend Mr Chaunter himself . . . and he's the kind that can give you the creeps.'

'You make the man sound almost interesting,' Keeton considered. 'Myself, I've never been turned on too much by religious maniacs.'

'That may not be an inaccurate way to describe him. All I can say is, he scares the hell out of me when he gives me one of his cold-fish glances.'

Ned Keeton grinned. 'Ah, but then, you always were a sensitive young flower, weren't you, Mr Landon?'

2

It was a full week before Arnold had the opportunity to visit Ben Gibson. He tried to call in at Gibson's house on a fairly regular basis: he liked the old antiquarian bookseller, and Gibson had few callers. The trouble was, Arnold's job took him to Newcastle only rarely, and he was sometimes reluctant to break into weekends that were precious to him, spent as they were wandering in Northumberland, on the fells and along the narrow river valleys, inspecting sites, looking at old buildings and musing in deserted villages.

On this occasion it had to be a Saturday. The weather had turned cold and a mackerel-grey sky threatened rain, so late in the afternoon Arnold drove to Newcastle, intending to arrive at Gibson's little shop before it closed. As it was, the traffic moving along the North Road was heavy and he was somewhat delayed; consequently, the amount of browsing time he would have before Ben shut up his shop was limited. Not that Ben minded him staying on; it was simply that Arnold had no desire to keep the old man from his refreshing Earl Grey tea at the end of a working day.

'Don't worry about it, Arnold,' the little frog-like man said. 'I'm expecting a caller anyway, so I'm going to keep the shop open a while longer. I promised him the book today and he rang to say he couldn't get in from Berwick until late this afternoon.'

'The traffic's heavy today, Ben.'

'Aye, I guess that's why he'll be late.' Gibson eyed Arnold speculatively. 'You're looking for something yourself? I mean, it's not just a social call?'

'There's a lot of the Scot in you,' Arnold said, and smiled. 'I come here to help a lonely old man while away his time and all you think about is selling me books!'

'Time will be when you buy one,' Gibson said in a mock-grumpy tone.

'What I am looking for is a Customary.'

'Tall order . . . and an expensive one.'

'Well, I don't mean an original. But there must be some reprints, or extracts.'

'Anyone in particular?' Gibson asked, his hooded eyes becoming more animated as his interest was kindled.

'The Farfa Customary.'

'Oh, yes . . .' Ben Gibson frowned. He turned, shuffling back among the musty shelves of the narrow shop. 'If I have anything connected with that — which I doubt — you'll find it buried somewhere along those shelves up there. You can use the steps. My old bones are getting too brittle for dangerous heights like that. Farfa Customary . . . What's your interest in that? Monastic history isn't really your line.'

Arnold looked up to the shelves above them. They were lined with faded, leather-bound books filmed with a light layer of dust. He pulled the shaky wooden steps across to the shelves. 'It's your fault, really. You introduced me to Elliott Brandling. He asked me to do the checking for him at Jarrow. I went out there, with the papers he gave me. Interesting . . . Anyway, the notes that he had used, and which he gave me, were based on the Farfa Customary, so I thought I'd like to check the references, add a few of the dimensions before I talk to him about what I found.'

Staring up at Arnold as he climbed, Ben Gibson put one hand on the frame of the steps to prevent it shaking too violently. 'What did you discover at Jarrow?'

'Brandling may well be right. I think there's a strong case to be made out for the existence of a monastic order there. I'm just looking at the evidence on the ground, of course; he'll have to produce the real learning to back up the theory.'

Ben Gibson grunted. 'Aye. That's as may be.' He paused, wrinkling his brow, and chewed his pendulous lower lip ruminatively. 'What do you make of Professor Brandling?'

'Make of him?' Arnold steadied himself with one hand on the shelf and scanned the titles of the books in front of him. 'I can't say I've thought too much about it, really. What do you mean?'

'I'm not certain. He seems to me to be . . . strained.'

'I don't follow you.'

'I don't know that I can explain it myself,' Ben Gibson admitted. 'He's a successful, well-respected university figure, he's doing what he wants to do in life. I would have thought he has all he wants . . . and yet he seems nervous about something, insecure. It's as though he's still trying to prove himself.'

Arnold moved on to check the next line of books. 'There's insecurity in all of us, Ben.'

'But we don't try to drown our insecurities in drink.'

Arnold glanced down, surprised by the sudden waspishness in the bookseller's tone. 'Is that what he does?'

'You saw the way he sank those brandies at the Printer's Pie.'

'Yes, but—'

'Oh, all right, maybe I'm reading too much into it. And maybe there's something I don't quite like about the man. It's a feeling I have, a sound maybe.'

Arnold grinned. 'A sound?'

Ben Gibson grinned in response, a trace shamefacedly. 'You know what I mean. Solid gold has a different ring from dross.'

Arnold shook his head, laughing. 'Is that how you spend your time, going around knocking seven bells out of golden goblets?'

'I wish it were so. Anyway, all I'm saying is there's something . . . and I wouldn't advise getting too much involved with him.'

'I'm only helping him out, after you put me on the spot.'

Ben Gibson frowned. 'Aye, that's the funny thing. I meant to tell you before but — oh, damn!'

The bell on the front entrance of the shop had pealed, signifying someone had entered. Ben Gibson had no view of the shop, and there was always the possibility of urchins coming down from Dog Leap Stairs, making a nuisance of themselves along the Quayside and then running into the antiquarian bookshop to steal volumes which they'd later throw into the Tyne. Ben bustled away to check, and a moment later Arnold heard him greeting someone in the shop.

Arnold turned back to the books.

The shelf above had carried a few volumes of interest, but little on monastic history, and the next shelf down produced nothing that would be of assistance. As always when he was browsing in this manner, he found himself becoming sidetracked, reading a paper on Cruck Construction in a volume of Mediaeval Archaeology — with which he disagreed — and spending a little time learning that the building of Salisbury Cathedral had suffered badly from distortions in the crossing piers which had caused a drift of all the arcades towards them. Now he thought of it, the drift could still be seen: he recalled noticing the way in which they all seemed to lean inwards . . .

'Mr Landon, how are you?'

Arnold started. In his reverie, he had not heard anyone approaching. He looked down. At the foot of the stepladder was a slim young man in a sports jacket and jeans. His brown hair had been recently washed, and was falling forward, boyishly, into his eyes. He smiled eagerly.

'I'm not sure—'

'Cy Robinson. You remember. Professor Brandling's assistant.'

The young man who had brought the Farfa Customary papers to Arnold. Arnold nodded, 'Ah yes, I'm sorry, Mr Robinson, I was in another world . . . How are you?'

'I'm fine. I've been up to Berwick, and I was late getting back. Had to call in to get this book that Mr Gibson's managed to obtain for me.' The young man glanced eagerly past Arnold to the shelves. 'I gather you're following something up for Professor Brandling.'

'Sort of,' Arnold said sheepishly. 'I went out to Jarrow for him, and I thought I'd just do some checking.'

'He's pretty thorough,' Robinson averred. 'I doubt he'll have missed anything. That was one of the great things about *The Scribe of Odilo*. It was the detail; the kind of detail that amazingly made it a bestseller.'

Arnold glanced reluctantly back to the shelves. 'Well, I don't think Ben Gibson has anything here that will help, anyway.' He began to climb down the stepladder. 'How is your own research going?'

'Into the Albigensians?' Robinson smiled wryly. 'Well enough, I guess. Somehow, I don't seem to be able to put the time in as I should . . .' The smile faded, and he frowned briefly before his natural effusiveness returned. 'Still, I might even manage to make a shortcut, the way all scholars like Professor Brandling seem to be able to do — make the quantum leap, as they say. The book Mr Gibson's obtained for me, it's a real find. I think I was telling you the last time we met, it's been out of print for years and it was only a privately printed volume anyway, by Professor Loxton, and I just have this gut feeling that I'll find some basic research references in it which will help me slice through some of the secrecies that tended to build up around these heresies. It was the effect of the Inquisition, you see . . .'

He was launched. From his admittedly brief experience of talking with Robinson, Arnold was yet convinced that if he failed to move, draw the young researcher away from the confining shelves and into the main area of the shop, he would be pinned there long after Earl Grey time. As Cy Robinson continued to chatter about his theories on the Albigensian heresies Arnold gently edged away, nodding and smiling, but only half listening, more concerned to gain the safety of the shop entrance and the presence of Ben Gibson.

When he caught sight of the bookseller, Gibson was grinning, aware of Arnold's problem. He chuckled. 'Well then, Mr Robinson, do you think I could start shutting up my premises?'

Cy Robinson turned his head, saw Gibson grinning and blushed. 'Ah, I'm sorry, Mr Landon, forgive me, I kind of get carried away—'

'That's all right,' Arnold soothed. 'It's always interesting listening to an enthusiast—'

'But Mr Landon only really visits my bookshop to cadge some of my tea on a Saturday afternoon,' Gibson interposed wickedly.

'I really must apologize,' Robinson said hurriedly. 'I was late after all, and—'

'Here, young man,' Ben Gibson said firmly. 'Your parcel is all wrapped up.'

'Payment—'

'There's a bill in the parcel. Let me have a cheque next week. I hope to see you again, young man.'

Cy Robinson was propelled gently towards the door, nodding, still apologizing. As the door closed behind him, Ben Gibson slipped the bolt, and sighed. 'The eagerness of youth . . . Just a few moments, Arnold, while I tidy up, then we can sit over a cup of tea and have a chat.'

He shuffled away to straighten some papers on the old-fashioned desk behind which he kept vigil in the shop. Arnold walked across to the window and looked out over the Quayside. Late on the Saturday afternoon there were few cars parked now along the waterfront. Saturday shoppers in Newcastle were streaming across the Tyne Bridge in a constant flow, but at the Quayside itself it was relatively quiet. On the Gateshead bank a grey frigate was moored: the Royal Navy paid regular courtesy visits to Newcastle, not least because it was recognized as a place for a good night out for matelots.

Cy Robinson was crossing the road to a car parked near the moorings. It was the same car that had picked him up outside Arnold's office the first time they'd met. There was a woman in the driver's seat, probably the same one who had driven Robinson away on that last occasion. She was turning her face up to the young research student and her blonde hair was lifted by the breeze as he leaned forward and kissed her lightly, before walking around to the passenger side and joining her in the car.

Arnold could see them clearly as they drove past. They were laughing. They seemed happy.

Young love.

'Right.' Ben Gibson announced. 'I'm finished. Shall we get the kettle on, my friend?'

* * *

It was seven in the evening before Arnold left the bookseller. Ben Gibson had pressed him to stay on for a meal, but Arnold did not wish to impose upon his hospitality, having arrived without warning. He was also oddly tense. It might have been the unsettling effect of browsing along those shelves and finding nothing to assist him at a time when his mind was still active with thoughts of the monastic foundation at Jarrow. Or it could possibly have been that Ben Gibson's return to the subject of Elliott Brandling had upset Arnold.

'He's unmarried, you know,' Gibson had announced as he sipped his tea.

'Brandling? So am I . . . and so are you. What's the problem?'

'You don't understand me,' Gibson had snorted. 'I'd be the last to argue that marriage is a panacea, or even a settling influence. But you and I, we're of a kind. We have a major interest in our lives which fills our waking hours with unexpected delights. For me, it's my old books; for you, it's wood and stone—'

'So what's different about Brandling?' Arnold questioned, a little aggressively. 'He has his Cluniac theorizing, his monasteries, and his sidelines about esoteric cult figures—'

'He's different,' Gibson insisted.

'How?'

'He's . . . obsessed.'

Arnold sighed. 'Maybe we are all three tarred with that brush. The Senior Planning Officer certainly thinks so in my case.'

'Brandling is a lonely man.'

'How can you know that?'

Gibson sidestepped the question. 'Obsession in a lonely man can be dangerous. It can lead to losing perspective, becoming too closely involved in the matters that interest you. I don't want to see you get like that, Arnold. You have balance. Don't lose it. Don't get like Brandling.'

'Why should I? You're talking nonsense, Ben.'

The conversation had irritated Arnold, unreasonably. He did not particularly care for Brandling, he hardly knew him, in fact, but something about Ben Gibson's attack on the man nettled him. It was as though he could detect in Gibson the lack of balance that the little man claimed was the case with Brandling, and the thought that Ben could be mean in his assessment of people was disturbing to Arnold. It called into question, subconsciously, the relationship that Ben and Arnold themselves enjoyed.

As a result, Arnold decided not to stay, yet felt unhappy about not staying, feeling he had disappointed the antiquarian bookseller he called his friend. He left the shop but did not immediately return to his car. He walked along the Quayside, gazing at the freighter moored near the Custom House, listening to the black water lapping on the hull, against the muted roar of the southbound traffic on the Tyne Bridge.

A second freighter was coming up river, and Arnold watched as the Swing Bridge moved slowly to accommodate it; the slow, stately movement of the bridge was soothing, and yet Arnold could not understand why he was in a disturbed state. Perhaps he was tired: the Rafferty Common dispute still seethed among his papers, a meeting had been arranged and scheduled for next week with villagers and farmers in the vicinity, and it was not an occasion Arnold was looking forward to.

But there was something else.

It was a compounding of the feelings he had experienced several times recently — at St Michael's Church in Kentside; when facing the Vicars of Jehovah and Edward Chaunter's cold eyes in his office; and that day when Cy Robinson had left Morpeth and Arnold had been aware of the man with the beetling eyebrows, staring after him as he had pulled away from the car park.

And yet it was different. The hairs on his neck prickled again; he felt he was being watched, observed silently and secretly and his skin was cold, his nerves on edge.

Slowly, Arnold turned. The Quayside was quiet. A deck-hand on the freighter was leaning on the rail, gazing upriver; muted voices came from the frigate on the Gateshead side; a young couple walked arm in arm towards Dog Leap Stairs; a tiny knot of anglers fished silently and hopelessly for the salmon that were said to be returning to the Tyne.

He felt eyes upon him still, and yet he could detect no one, no watcher. Arnold shivered. Suddenly, he felt the need for company. He turned, looked back towards Ben Gibson's shop, hesitated. Having refused Ben's company; he could hardly go back now.

There were restaurants along the side streets from the Quayside, but they would provide no one he could talk to, or would even want to. Arnold's were peculiar interests: they were not material for small talk and casual conversation with strangers.

Perhaps Ben had really been talking about Arnold Landon when he spoke of loneliness.

He saw the telephone box and walked towards it. It had been vandalized; there was no telephone directory inside and the windows had been smashed. Arnold walked up the hill towards Grey Street. The hairs still prickled on his neck, but he did not look back. He walked into the Lambton Arms and asked the barman for a directory. He found the number quickly enough, and dialled at the public phone in the corridor beyond the bar.

'Professor Brandling? Arnold Landon . . . I wondered . . . I've been down to Jarrow. It was interesting. I thought we could meet and . . . tonight? Yes, that's fine. I'm in Newcastle now and if you don't mind, since I live further north . . .'

Professor Brandling would regard it as no problem. He would drive from his home on the banks of the Wear and would meet Arnold in Newcastle, at the Fisherman's Wharf, shortly after eight o'clock.

Arnold was left with the vague feeling that in some way he had been disloyal to Ben Gibson.

3

It was as well that Arnold went straight into the Fisherman's Wharf after phoning Brandling and making the arrangements to meet, because he had not counted on the fact that the restaurant was a popular one and Saturday nights tended to attract a considerable clientele. Arriving shortly after it opened, however, he was able to book one of the few tables left and he walked through into the bar area to wait for Brandling. He ordered a lime and soda to begin with, aware that he had a longish drive ahead of him after dinner, and settled down to wait for the Durham professor.

The Fisherman's Wharf was a pleasant restaurant; he had visited it a few times before, during the week, and enjoyed both its atmosphere and its menu. On this occasion — the first Saturday evening he had spent there — the clientele tended to be rather younger than he had experienced previously, and certainly noisier.

One group was celebrating a birthday and they were clearly determined to enjoy themselves: it was reflected in the amount they had to drink before dinner and the insistence with which they pressed a drink upon Arnold. He was forced to capitulate, reluctantly, to avoid a scene; as it was, the whisky and soda was larger than he cared to accommodate. They watched him with eagle eyes while he struggled with it.

He was relieved when Brandling arrived, just as the party was going in to the room across the corridor to dine.

'Got a start on then, have you?' Brandling remarked as he entered and greeted Arnold.

'Birthday party,' Arnold explained grumpily.

'I'll drink to that,' Brandling replied cheerfully, ordered himself a double brandy and, when Arnold refused a drink, settled down in the chair beside him. 'This is a pleasant surprise.'

'I was in Newcastle,' Arnold said defensively. 'If I was going to talk about Jarrow with you sometime, it might have meant a long drive for one of us. This way—'

'I approve,' Brandling boomed. 'I was doing nothing special anyway. Had decided to do some work, but it's more convivial, hey, on a Saturday night to get out and have a meal with a like-minded soul.'

Arnold thought of Ben Gibson, alone in his Quayside house, and wriggled uncomfortably. He looked at Elliott Brandling, trying to weigh up the man against Ben's view of him. Brandling was dressed rather more casually than when they had first met at the Lit and Phil. He wore a white shirt with a discreet red-and-blue stripe, and an expensive, pale-blue sweater. His slacks were well cut, his shoes light, real leather and clearly obtained from one of the more exclusive shops. He seemed in a relaxed frame of mind and there was little of the quickness of glance Arnold had observed on their first acquaintance. He always seemed to project self-assurance, but this time it seemed more genuine, with few of the dark, lurking insecurities to shadow it.

Brandling sipped his brandy with every sign of enjoyment. 'So, you've been to Jarrow. You got my notes, of course?'

'Cy Robinson duly delivered them. I was interested to read the details you'd culled from the Farfa Customary.'

'I was lucky to find them.'

'I checked to see if Ben Gibson had any information. He didn't.'

'No.' Brandling chuckled easily. 'One of the advantages of working at the University. You can get all sorts of stuff sent through to you. Particularly if you're on the tenured staff. Anyway, did you find anything interesting there?'

Arnold was not built to dissimulate or hold out on a story. He nodded. 'Yes. I think you're right. I believe there was a monastic order based there, on that site.'

Brandling expelled his breath in slow, measured surprise. 'You can say it . . . just like that.' He took a draught of brandy, and shook his head. 'On what evidence do you base your view?'

Arnold toyed with the whisky glass for a few moments before answering. 'Well, clearly, I was influenced by the notes you'd made, but when I came to check them on the ground it was clear that the similarities are so great . . . and the Cluniac monasteries were built on generally traditional lines . . .'

'So tell me.'

Arnold settled down to explain. He commented upon the general layout as shown in the Farfa Customary and described the relationship with the foundations as far as he had been able to ascertain them. Brandling questioned him on points of detail as he went on but was generally prepared to listen as Arnold put forward his own views.

They broke off briefly to place orders from the menu, and when they were called in to dine Arnold was discussing the layout that had possibly been established at the eastern end of the site.

'I think it would have been an infirmary, at an oblique angle to the other buildings. There would have been four cells for the sick, one being used for the "maundy"—'

'The washing of the feet.'

'That's right. But there's another possibility. I'm no scholar, Professor Brandling, but the translation of your Customary suggests "Let worn-out brothers come here for changing" . . .'

'So?'

Arnold hesitated. 'The Latin would be *illi fratres qui exusti sunt ad mutandum*. But you see, in view of the proximity of the cells for sick brethren, this might suggest bloodletting. If that were the situation it might be the Latin *exusti* was really *exuti*.'

'In which case . . .' Brandling mused.

'We can assume the room would have been used for the laying out of dead monks. It would then follow that, nearby, there will be a calefactory and very probably a burial place, possibly around the hollow inner court.'

'And such a construction should not be too difficult to unearth.'

Brandling looked keenly at Arnold. 'That's a most interesting supposition, Landon . . . and one I appreciate for the possibilities it raises. It deserves a good wine, by way of celebration.'

He chose a Sancerre with their first course, and ordered a Bergerac to follow. Arnold began to glow; he had to admit to himself that he rather enjoyed putting forward proposals to a university don, and having them accepted so readily. In his experience such people had been dismissive of his ideas.

They continued to discuss the Cluniac site, and the bottle of Sancerre soon vanished. The Bergerac arrived early and Brandling worked his way through it, while Arnold contented himself with one glass. Brandling clearly had an astonishing capacity for alcohol; he was in a state of subdued excitement and his lean features were flushed, his eyes bright, but there was no trace of slurring in his speech as they continued to dwell on the possibilities of the site.

'So, if we are to summarize,' Brandling said expansively, 'we have here the possibility of a house not excessively large but sufficiently elaborate; harmonious proportions; characteristic in its main Cluniac features: order, just measure and equilibrium. It was Conant who remarked about Cluny, I recall: wise in its restraint, elegant in the living grace of its proportions, and built to last.'

The thought suddenly silenced them both.

Built to last, and yet now at Jarrow there was only the scattering of stone, ridges in the grass, and the suppositions of two modern men. They were untalkative for a while, Arnold teasing his steak with his fork, Brandling staring at the red wine in his glass. The bottle was finished. Brandling ordered another, and when it came he poured Arnold another glass before he could protest. Arnold thought it polite to drink it.

The glow returned in a little while, and with it the confidence that drink inspired. 'After I left Jarrow,' Arnold confided, 'I went to another site that you're interested in.'

'Oh?' Brandling's sharp nose was raised above his glass, as though sniffing at the wind. 'What site are you talking about?'

'I went up to Kentside. To St Michael's Church.'

Brandling seemed hardly to have heard; certainly, he displayed no curiosity. He took a long pull at his Bergerac and thoughtfully topped the glass to the brim again, staring at it unwinkingly.

'It's an odd place,' Arnold offered.

'In what way?' Brandling asked carelessly.

'There's something funny about it.' There was a short silence, and then suddenly Brandling looked up. If he had seemed uninterested before, he had now changed; there was a light deep in his eyes and he was no longer smiling.

'Funny? No. You mean something else.'

'I do?'

'You mean evil.'

Arnold's brain felt hazy; he was unable to think straight for a few moments. Then it was as though the haze was clearing, as he remembered the last few minutes he had spent in the darkening churchyard. 'Yes,' he agreed dazedly. 'That's right. You're right. Evil . . .'

Brandling was silent, contemplating his glass. Somewhat bemused, and suddenly reluctant to talk of the way in which his emotions had affected him that evening, Arnold turned aside from the thought. 'But the church itself, I took a good long look at it, and there's something odd about it.'

'You already said—'

'No, no,' Arnold interrupted hurriedly. 'Apart from the feeling of the place. Look, let me try to explain.' He thought for a few moments, sipped at his wine, and then went on carefully. 'It's necessary to understand how early mediaeval building went on. In the absence of building stone, or even good rubble, fine timber was used, and this was common in the twelfth century.'

'St Michael's is nineteenth-century.'

'Please . . . Wooden pyramidal structures comprised many of the early churches. Some of them were preserved in stone later, the same lines followed, with just the wooden tower being retained as a bell tower in many instances. Now if you carry out a close examination of these structures you can sometimes work out their dates, but it can be an unreliable guide, because timber buildings were easily taken to pieces, transported to another site and re-erected.'

'I don't see what this has to do with—'

'A moment, please. Let's jump forward to the fifteenth century. This was the period of the wool boom. Space and size became viable. Bishops and abbots concentrated on the construction of huge presbyteries; but the designers of parish churches went for spacious naves which were intended to hold large congregations, gathered together as closely as possible to the chancel.'

Elliott Brandling was frowning. 'St Michael's is derelict now. It never had much of a history; it was never popular, according to the records. My own theory is that what you felt up there, what I've felt . . . the touch of evil . . . it's an old feeling, one which has remained and left congregations uneasy, so they never came in large numbers. But I'm not clear on what you're trying to say . . .'

'I've walked around that church. The central tower is nondescript, and is flanked by two small transepts. The chancel to the east is short; the nave on the west is narrow. It's built on a six-square plan. When I was there, a thought struck me, a quotation . . . it puzzled me. I've thought about it since.

The semi-circular apse of the early Christian architecture of Rome—'

'You're losing me, Landon,' Brandling objected.

Arnold took a deep breath. The ideas that were a tumbling over in his head now, confused by the wine and yet also in a curious way released to flow uninhibited, were a summation of the half-formed ideas he had been dwelling on, almost subconsciously, since his visit to St Michael's. 'I've looked at the Mercian apse. I've taken French influences into account; but the key to this puzzle at Kentside is wood.'

'Wood?'

'There's a break in the pattern, something wrong, for a modern, nineteenth-century church. I think it's older.' He paused. 'Much older.'

'The records show it was built in the nineteenth century—'

'Not the present church. The foundation. It dates way back. In my view, the original church that was placed there was built upon an axial plan.'

'What's that?'

'Let me show you.' Arnold took a pen from his pocket, smoothed out his paper table napkin and made a rough sketch to show to Brandling.

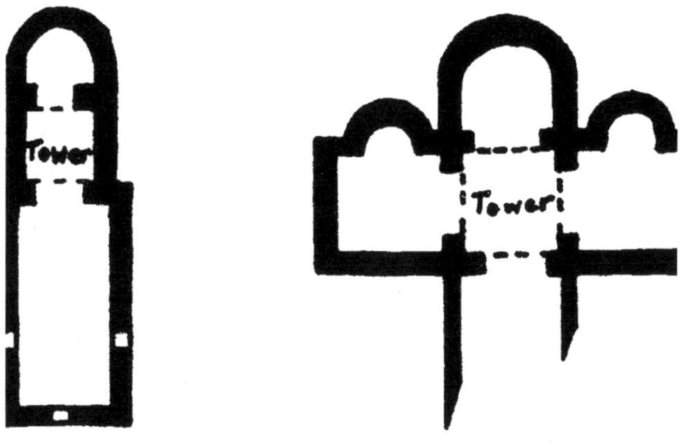

'The sketch on the left is the simple axial plan. An aisleless nave and chancel separated by a simple lantern tower. Scores of these churches were built in England — but they represented the English architects' representations of a Holy Land church plan.'

Brandling's eyes widened. 'Holy Land? You mean the Crusades?'

Arnold nodded. 'The Crusaders were faced with a standardized form of provincial church in the Byzantine Empire; they adapted it and founded such churches throughout the Holy Land. The Crusader churches were later Romanised, but generally, at a later date, all this developed into the English cruciform church. I've sketched an example: it's the one on the right.'

Brandling stared fixedly at the two drawings. He nodded. 'I'm beginning to see what you're driving at. St Michael's is based on a classic axial form.'

'Not generally used in the nineteenth century.'

'Unless built on an older foundation.'

'A much older foundation. It should have been erected on an old cruciform pattern. It wasn't. That suggests a very old foundation.' Brandling nodded thoughtfully. He paused. 'How far back, in your estimation, Landon?'

Arnold shook his head. 'I can't say. Only old records . . . or excavation, would tell us. But I would certainly guess it could go back as far as the twelfth century.'

'The time of blood . . .' Brandling said quietly, and drained his glass slowly.

The waiter arrived to clear their dishes. Neither man wanted another course. They ordered coffee, and a brandy for the Professor, and then huddled over the table like two conspirators, nursing a secret knowledge. Brandling toyed with his drink, his lean features set in a serious frown. 'The fact is, of course, if you're right, there's another possibility we should also take into account.'

'What's that?'

'The Augustine practice.'

'You mean, of encouraging the building of churches where earlier religious sites had flourished?'

'Let's make the assumption,' Brandling suggested. 'You say St Michael's is a sham; its nineteenth-century shell was actually built on foundations that were much older, dictated by the axial plan of the twelfth century. But what if that twelfth-century church had itself been built on something even older?'

Arnold agreed it was perfectly possible. He also had the feeling he was becoming a little light-headed. He took another glass of wine to overcome the effect.

'One might even suppose,' Brandling said slowly, 'that the original church could have been built on a pagan site.'

'It has been known,' Arnold said owlishly.

'Do you believe that evil flourishes where it had taken root over centuries?'

After three or four glasses of wine Arnold was prepared to believe anything.

'Well,' Brandling said seriously, 'let me suggest to you that therein lies the solution to what you've felt at Kentside, and what I certainly have experienced at that church. The corrupt touch of tangible evil.'

Arnold felt cold. He stared at the man facing him. Brandling's eyes had taken on a glazed effect; the dim lighting of the restaurant seemed to hollow his lean cheeks and give him a cadaverous appearance. Arnold shivered. 'This evil you're talking about—'

'I've already told you. It might have started as an older, practised evil. But it changed, and flourished . . . perhaps flourishes still, at Kentside. The cult of Simon de Vieux Pont.'

4

Rafferty Hall was a monstrosity.

It had been built with execrable taste by an expatriate Irishman who had fled Tipperary in the 1820s, obtained a tract of land by cheating at cards, and discovered coal at the northern end of the property. He had ploughed most of his profits into the construction of the Hall, which he saw as a monument. It was a jumble of styles: each time he had gone abroad he came back with new ideas and added them to his growing pile. Consequently, the fifteen-bedroom house which had begun as Gothic in style had, over a period of twelve years, taken on in addition something of the Byzantine, Moorish, Mediterranean, Frankish, Carolingian and Ottonian influences. It boasted flying buttresses where none were required and the east wing roof was so cantilevered that it had fallen in by 1850, to be replaced with a flat roof that let in the rain. The conservatory at the rear was supposed to have been a miniature replica of the Crystal Palace but had collapsed in 1982. The massive stone-pillared entrance had been copied from St Paul's Cathedral and merely served to emphasize the incongruity of the whole structure.

Conservationists tended to regard it with that degree of affection they reserved for the utterly impractical and had fought over the years to keep it in being. It was now owned by the county council since it was far too expensive for an individual to maintain, and was used — or at least, that part of it which was habitable — by Outward Bound or Duke of Edinburgh Award aspirants on weekend forays into the wilds beyond the Common.

It did possess one advantage: a magnificently proportioned main hall adorned with plaster cherubs flying along the tops of the windows, plaster flowers amassed along the ceiling, and plaster satyrs grinning lasciviously down from the corners of the room.

It could seat two hundred people. Arnold did not expect that many to turn up for the Rafferty Common meeting but he arrived early that afternoon, to make sure there was enough seating arranged, just in case the whole of the village and the gipsy encampment turned out for verbal battle.

He had no doubt that it would turn out to be a battle.

The meeting was scheduled for seven that evening. After he had checked with the caretakers and made sure all was ready for the Senior Planning Officer and the Chairman of the Planning Committee — a raised dais so the Chairman could be seen in all his plump and sweating glory; a decanter and separate glass for the Senior Planning Officer to sip delicately as he nerved himself to face his audience — Arnold had time on his hands.

He walked out into the gardens beyond the terrace. The council had made a half-hearted attempt to bring some order to the chaos of the garden Rafferty had planned, but since the property was never going to fall into the stately home league and, therefore, would attract no large number of visitors, the garden had been mainly laid out to grass and desultory landscaping. A clump of trees at the foot of the gentle slope to one side of the house provided a windbreak — there was a cool breeze blowing from the east — and Arnold found an old stone seat there where he could sit in the fading sun and be relatively sheltered from the wind.

He sat there, waiting for the first of the antagonists to arrive, and his thoughts drifted away from the unpleasantness that was to come, to the conversation he had had with Elliott Brandling.

As the evening had advanced and Brandling had become steadily more intoxicated — though his speech showed little sign of it — he had become more expansive in his exposition of the cult of de Vieux Pont.

'Whatever might have happened in ancient times at the Kentside site,' he announced, 'pagan rites, worship of the Devil, Baal, Beelzebub, all that sort of thing, you have to remember the culture in which the Raging Wolf thing began.'

'Irreverent, bloody and bawdy,' Arnold offered sententiously.

'Absolutely right!' There was triumph in Brandling's tones, as though he felt he had made the point. 'Mediaeval life was mirrored, you know, on its stage. It was a time when drama, once used by the Church for liturgical reasons, had left the Church and taken to the street. The subject-matter remained religious but the treatment was secular. The shepherds who watched by night became sheep stealers, sex was celebrated in the rape of Dinah and the peeping of the Elders at Susanna, and sadism in the varieties of torn flesh of the martyrs. Guilty passions, faithless spouses, frail nuns and pregnant abbesses, adulterous queens . . . *Schadenfreude* was certainly not peculiar to the Middle Ages, my friend, but it was a dark variety, believe me.'

'I imagine,' Arnold suggested, 'it was all partly due to the incidence of plague and other calamities.'

'Apocalypse was never far from the mediaeval mind,' Brandling agreed. 'It was enacted in the Day of Judgement and the Harrowing of Hell. Herod appeared with a black beard and Saracen's robes, devils and demons in grisly masks with horns, forked tails and body suits covered in horsehair ran through the audience, pinching and frightening the spectators. Evil was power, in the mediaeval mind.'

'And it was in this atmosphere that the cult came to flourish?'

'The time was right. Apocalypse was in the air. Under the influence of the seemingly malign and capricious events of the time — plague, schism in the Church, constant war, overwrought minds turned to magic and the supernatural. Sorcery and its links to demonology took on new life. And remember, this was not heresy. Demonology and the black arts are the opposite of heresy — not more pious than the Church but impious, seeking communion with the Devil.'

'But hey-ho, the Devil is dead,' Arnold said and took another sip of wine.

'Hah! That's one old song you can't believe — and it certainly wasn't the case in the Middle Ages. A pact with the Devil offered pleasure without penitence, the enjoyment of sexuality, riches and earthly ambitions. It didn't matter a damn if the price was eternal hellfire.'

'Why not?'

'Because the Church told them that's what they could expect at the Day of Judgement anyway! So what was there to lose?'

Arnold grimaced, affecting sobriety. 'I hadn't looked at it like that.'

Brandling called for another brandy and some more coffee to wash it down, and returned to the conversation. 'Women were often central to it, of course — they turned to sorcery for the same reason that they turned to mysticism.'

'But the burnings at the stake were based on confessions wrung from them by torture.'

'Agreed. And the confessions were merely reflections of the inquisitors' own diabolic imaginings. But forget that: simply remember that the times were full of stories of pacts with Beelzebub, flights through the night to copulate with the Devil in the shape of a monstrous black cat, or a goat with flaming eyes, or a gigantic man with coal-black skin, a huge phallus and eyes like flame. The Devil was Gothic, a cloven-hoofed satyr with sharp teeth and claws and a sulphurous smell. So how would men regard someone in the Devil's image: powerful, ruthless, uninhibited, a raper of women and a destroyer of men, whose cruelty had become a byword? It's only a short step from believing in the Devil to seeing him in the flesh, and worshipping the flesh. Even if it's been dead and corrupted for a hundred years.'

'That's how the cult started,' Arnold murmured.

'Oh, there may well have been other reasons. A lust for power; a desire for women; the twisted aberrations of a sick mind coupled with the ability to conjure up images in the minds of fearful and gullible men. But the Raging Wolf was a symbol and a powerful one; the cult grew, and was practised, and borrowed from the Templars, and the whole thing became confused and hazy — but was always based on bloodlust, and a craze for power over other men's minds and bodies.'

'You'd have thought that science, and religion, would have put such matters to flight.'

Brandling shook his head vigorously, spilling some brandy from his glass. It darkened the red stain that lay in front of him on the tablecloth, earlier signs of his passionate exposition. 'Not at all. The reality and power of demons was accepted: the University of Paris held a conclave to outlaw black arts, not disprove their existence; sorcery was always recognized by the Church. It flourished then, and it still exists.'

'But at *Kentside*?'

'I can't be certain, of course . . . but you've felt the evil in that place. I found some references in a newspaper of 1739: diabolic practices were certainly occurring in the vicinity of the village at that time. A priest was unfrocked in 1832: there is some evidence printed in the *Gentleman's Magazine* concerning the disturbances and the Satanic rites practised there. And let's not forget, the dangerous men who practise these arts have always chosen to do so in defiance of the established Church — and that's why they have deliberately used Church property.'

'From what you're saying, Kentside has had a reputation for many years.'

Brandling nodded. 'And I have a feeling it's still used.'

‘I found something there,’ Arnold admitted.

There was a short silence. Arnold looked up. Brandling was staring at him, the dim light hollowing his eyes, emphasizing the leanness of his jawline. ‘What do you mean, you *found* something?’

There was an intensity in the question that confused Arnold. The wine had got to his head now, for he was not an experienced drinker, and he was finding difficulty in ordering his thoughts. He shook his head slowly, trying to clear his brain. ‘Something . . . I’m not sure . . .’

Brandling reached across the table and grasped Arnold’s wrist. His fingers were fierce, biting on the wrist bones, and it was clear that alcohol was also affecting Brandling now, as he seemed to overreact to Arnold’s confusion. ‘You found something, you said. Damn you, Landon, what was it?’

‘I was up at the church . . . I was trying to get its proportions right, as I drew them for you, and explained . . . I stepped back to get a better view, up near the hedge . . . There was a smell . . .’

‘Yes? Go on, for God’s sake . . . what was it?’

‘The rose hedge . . . there was something under the rose hedge. I poked at it with a stick.’ The bile was rising in Arnold’s throat again, as the memory of the odour assailed his senses once more and he felt a return of the sensation, the yielding, putrescent flesh under the prodding of the dead branch. ‘It was something dead . . . decaying . . .’

‘Something?’

‘I don’t know.’ Arnold shook his head, and tried to withdraw his wrist from Brandling’s fierce grip. After a moment the grip relaxed, Brandling seemed more in control of himself, and Arnold said, ‘I got the impression it was something big . . . heavy . . . but it had been under the hedge for some time. An animal maybe.’

‘Quite possibly.’ Brandling suddenly seemed to have lost interest in the conversation and in Arnold himself. He was staring at his brandy glass as though all the problems he might find in the world would be solved there.

Perhaps, Arnold considered, that was what Brandling believed.

* * *

The first straggle of villagers arrived at Rafferty Hall fifteen minutes before the meeting was due to begin. The caretaker showed them into the hall; Arnold waited near the door and at five minutes before the appointed time the Senior Planning Officer's Rover appeared in the drive, bearing the Chairman of the Planning Committee as a passenger.

Tom Lansbury was in his late sixties now and inclined to droopy eyelids in long enquiries; he claimed a distant family relationship with a Labour politician of yesteryear but his own political inclinations were High Tory. He was known for the rose he regularly sported in his buttonhole and the nattiness of his suiting, complete with waistcoat with the last button undone. He was plump, good-natured, sleepy, and utterly unsuited to this kind of planning confrontation. It accounted for the slightly nervous air with which he entered the meeting hall; it was as though he expected to be met with flour bombs or something worse.

Arnold led him and the Senior Planning Officer to the dais. As they settled down Arnold looked back to see Marcus Gullick taking his place in the third row in front of the dais. He sat there squarely, nodding to a few acquaintances around him, before turning his glance to the dais. His thick-lipped mouth was set in a hard line and his badly cropped hair seemed to sprout fiercely from his head, looking for trouble. His arms were folded massively over his chest; he seemed tense, and ready for war.

Tom Lansbury dragged himself to his feet, reluctantly. 'We'd better make a start, ladies and gentlemen. I'm Chairman of the Planning Committee; this is the Senior Planning Officer, and we're here tonight to discuss the situation with regard to Rafferty Common. I'll begin by explaining the present position as I see it, and then any technical questions can be answered by the Senior Planning Officer, or his assistant . . .'

As he spoke, there was a noise at the back of the hall.

Arnold turned his head. The hall was by now perhaps one-third full, but the latest entrants filing in at the back were all from the gipsy encampment. They walked in, dark-visaged, heads low, as though they felt uneasy in this gathering, and some of them seemed to have made some effort to spruce themselves up for the occasion. Among them was Joe Connor; unlike some of his companions, he held his head high, defiance glittering in his dark eyes. While the others took seats at the back of the hall he remained standing, staring down towards the dais, announcing his presence silently, but making it clear to everyone there that he was nobody's butt and was afraid of no one present. After a few seconds, as though he had made his point, he sat down.

The Chairman droned on heavily, explaining that the county was aware local people were disturbed by the presence of gipsies on Rafferty Common, but he had to point out that travelling folk had been coming there for many years. In the past, matters had carried on amicably enough, and it was a pity that recent events seemed to have placed individuals in a more ugly frame of mind. But the fact was that the county had a duty to make provision for sites for travelling folk—

'But it doesn't have to be Rafferty Common!'

It was Marcus Gullick who spoke out loudly. There was a rustle of movement, sounds of support, and the Chairman raised his hand. 'Please. Let me finish. The gipsy families have to be sited somewhere. They are at the Common, and wish to be there.'

'The hell with that! They were served with an order!'

'Yes, but . . .' Tom Lansbury paused helplessly. 'I . . . I think the Senior Planning Officer had better explain the legal position.'

Arnold, in the next few minutes, was forced to admire the Senior Planning Officer. He had never thought the man had it in him. The Senior Planning Officer rose and addressed his audience, explaining the legal position with regard to the site, and when the shouts began he simply ignored them. He went over the points one by one: the issuing of the order, the challenge by the gipsies to the legality of that order, the hearing which had decided that the order had not been properly served, the consequent right of the travelling people to remain on the site pending the result of the county's appeal against the judgement, and the overall duty placed upon the council by the 1968 Act. By the time he came to the end of his peroration, delivered in a steady monotone, the shouts from the front part of the hall had grown to a crescendo, tempers were raised, abuse was being hurled at the platform, but it was as though the Senior Planning Officer had not heard a single sound.

And when he sat down, Arnold realized that was precisely the situation. He had not heard a sound. Once he started speaking, it was clear he had heard only his own voice. The Senior Planning Officer had the capacity to shut out the outside world when he spoke. He was indifferent to his audience, and indifferent to the impact he had upon them.

It was a marvellous quality, but it had infuriated the people in front of them.

Pandemonium had broken loose. Marcus Gullick was on his feet, vying with others of like persuasion to argue that the county officers and members were lily-livered parasites. 'You sit on your backsides in your damned council chambers and you lot take your salaries, and you come out here and tell us how we got to run our lives, just to please scum like them at the back of the hall! We've had enough, and we're all of the same mind here!'

'That's right!' a stout, empurpled farmer just behind him was shouting. 'We're sick of having those scruffy kids running all over our property, thieving, causing damage—'

'I lost three sheep last month! You're not going to tell me it was foxes! They don't cook their catches over open fires!'

'How come my hens have suddenly started producing so few eggs? And how come half a dozen pullets seem to have disappeared in the last few weeks?'

'My wife got scared half to death ten days ago, with those bloody dirty gipsy women coming around, selling useless wooden clothes-pegs and baskets, and threatening her with curses when she showed them the gate! I'm damned if I'm going to have them coming around intimidating the womenfolk when I'm out at work!'

'And what about the way they use the fields and the stream? It's bloody insanitary!'

'Gentlemen, please! Gentlemen!' The Chairman's attempts to impose his authority were ineffectual. He stood there, sweating, portly, his chubby cheeks glistening with anxiety, his hands extended, palms down, making little pressing movements as though to settle recalcitrant children. But they were not children, their tempers were inflamed, and Arnold was of the opinion that if something wasn't done soon to calm them down the Chairman would have a riot on his hands. He recalled Ned Keeton's prophecy that feelings were running so high over Rafferty Common that trouble could erupt.

It was about to erupt — unless he, or someone else in the official party, managed to bring some order to the proceedings.

Next moment matters were taken out of their hands.

From the back of the room there was a sudden, frightening explosion. For just one second everyone stood stock-still, then a woman screamed and half of the audience crouched down amid the crashing of overturned chairs, terrified as though expecting further assaults. Arnold stared wildly towards the back of the hall and in the following silence he saw Gipsy Joe Connor standing there; when the gipsies had entered earlier, they must have smuggled in a shotgun and Connor now stood with legs braced apart, the butt of the shotgun placed arrogantly on his hip, the twin barrels pointing in the air. In the silence there was a further scraping of chairs as people cowered down into their seats and a piece of a cherub's leg dropped to shatter on the floor. Marcus Gullick was still standing, glaring back towards the defiant gipsy. 'Are you crazy?' he roared. 'There're women here!'

'On Rafferty Common there're women *and* children,' Connor shouted back, his dark features set and determined. 'I thought I might need this. There's one barrel been let off into the wall, Marcus Gullick, but if you or any of your friends want the other you're welcome to it!'

'You can't get away with this intimidation!' Gullick bawled, red-faced, his heavy hands clenching at his sides. 'We'll get the law out here to sort you out—'

'The law's on my side,' Connor insisted. 'That's what you people don't seem to understand. We're on Rafferty Common and we're going to stay there as long as we want and all the noise in the world isn't going to make us shift — not planning noise, not village noise, not councillor noise! But the reason I brought this shotgun with me is to make a point. You might get tempted, some of you big men, tempted to do something other than talk and make noise. Well, let it be clear to you. If you want a fight you can have one. The Romanies have never been scared of taking on soft-bellied wimps like you lot. The day you decide to stop talking and do something, we'll be waiting.' He lifted the shotgun, hefting the butt high and thrusting the weapon forward in a belligerent gesture.

'We'll give as good as we get — and more!'

The Chairman was gasping, his mouth opening and shutting like a stranded fish. 'The man's crazy,' he was muttering. 'Out of his mind . . .'

Gullick was still standing, glaring at Gipsy Joe Connor. There was a short silence, and when he spoke his voice had dropped. He was no longer shouting, and his tone was the more menacing for it. 'You're making a bad mistake, Connor. I won't forget this.'

'You're not meant to!'

'You got the gun today. Next time, you'll be the one at the wrong end of the barrels!'

Contemptuously, Gipsy Joe Connor lowered the shotgun until the barrels were pointing directly at Marcus Gullick. To his credit, after an involuntary movement, the farmer stood his ground. There was a long, tense silence, then Connor raised the gun again and pulled the trigger. The second barrel was discharged, the shot crashing into the plaster ceiling after the first.

Criminal assault, Arnold thought helplessly, just in pointing the loaded shotgun at Gullick, and now criminal damage. And yet he had the feeling Gullick would not be the man to press charges — he would want to take his own way to revenge. As for the council and its view of damage to property under its control . . .

Connor had broken the shotgun over his arm. He was grinning wolfishly at Gullick. 'Just to make it clear to you, farmer,' he sneered. 'Any time you want to come to me, I don't need a shotgun to back me up.'

He turned on his heel and marched out of the meeting hall. The dark-visaged men filed quietly out behind him. Their heads were raised now, more confident than when they had come in. Gipsy Joe Connor had made a statement for them; they were with him.

A babble of excited, nervous voices swept around the hall after the door crashed to behind the gipsies. Arnold watched Marcus Gullick. The man had paled. He was silent, ignoring the people around him, several of whom seemed to want to explain how they had been ready to storm the armed gipsy if only he had stayed there a moment longer, armed or not. Their valour seemed to increase the longer the hall was empty of the Romanies, and they thrust forward towards the dais and the unhappy Chairman with demands that the police be called and the Common be swept clear of the pestilence of the travellers at once.

Gullick took no part in the disturbance. He was walking towards the back of the hall, and the doorway. His shoulders were back, his gait stiff-legged with injured pride, and his fingers still clenched at his side. There was a fierce determination about him that was further emphasized by his silence and his refusal to have anything to do with the outcry about him. Arnold could guess at the farmer's thoughts: he was taking Connor's stance personally; it had been directed at him, Marcus Gullick, he had been challenged and his pride was scarred. He intended to do something about it.

It was a bad business.

The Chairman was still trying to fend off the angry villagers. Outside there was the sound of starting cars, as those who had decided they'd had enough excitement for the evening made their departures. Arnold walked to the door; the sun had gone and dusk was beginning to fall, and the glow of the car headlights lanced across the fields towards the village and Rafferty Common.

He went back into Rafferty Hall, and after a while saw the Senior Planning Officer rescue his chairman from the last of the grumbling locals. The Senior Planning Officer caught Arnold's glance and beckoned him forward. 'The Chairman needs a drink. Is there a pub nearby?'

The Plough and Horses at the village would be the last place to take Tom Lansbury: there were bound to be further arguments if they went there and found themselves in the company of villagers stoking up the fires of their resentment. 'We can cross the valley,' Arnold suggested. 'There's a place there called the Three Bells and it's not too far out of the road back to Morpeth.'

The Senior Planning Officer nodded. For a moment Arnold thought he was going to suggest that Arnold took the Chairman home, leaving the Senior Planning Officer free to escape, but then duty overrode inclination and he told Arnold that if he led the way, the pair of them would follow in the Rover. 'You'll be there first,' the Senior Planning Officer said brusquely. 'The Chairman will need a stiff whisky. I'll have a sweet sherry.'

Somehow the choice of drink did not surprise Arnold.

* * *

They reached the Three Bells some fifteen minutes later, having crossed the valley in the gathering dusk and leaving behind them the remnants of the motorcade returning to the village for further heated discussions in the Plough and Horses. Arnold fervently hoped there would be no hotheads out tonight, causing trouble — either from the village on to Rafferty Common, or from the gipsies themselves, who had clearly been in the mood to take the law into their own hands.

It was a night of anxiety all around. Arnold had the drinks waiting for his superior officer and the Chairman by the time they entered the lounge bar of the pub. Lansbury downed his whisky in one gulp and immediately ordered another. 'Getting too old for this game,' he muttered. Arnold wasn't sure whether he was referring to his committee chairmanship or his alcoholic intake.

The Senior Planning Officer sipped his sherry. 'They behaved like animals,' he intoned. 'Can't imagine what set them off.'

Insensitivity, thought Arnold, but refrained from making the comment. He sipped his half of lager and sat on the edge of the conversation as Lansbury expounded on the view that things had been more civilized in politics when he had been a young man. The Senior Planning Officer agreed. Arnold thought back to Marcus Gullick's grandfather with his shotgun and three dogs and wondered where the difference really lay. Miserably, he stayed on with the two men, not wanting to be there, vaguely depressed, and aware that across the other side of the valley war might already have broken out.

As the evening wore on he made a pretext to go outside to his car; the night was cool, the breeze had dropped and a full moon bathed the car park with a pale light. There were no flames across at Rafferty Common; they would have stained the night sky with their glow had there been a conflagration, so the villagers hadn't set fire to the camp at least. Somewhat relieved, Arnold went back in to join the others.

They seemed to have got over their upset; the Chairman was absolutely affable, and even the Senior Planning Officer seemed to have relaxed under the influence of three sweet sherries. Arnold was persuaded to another half of lager but he could find no answering chords of relaxation in himself: he was still anxious, in a way he could neither express nor understand. He had a sense of foreboding, which Tom Lansbury's long-winded political anecdotes did nothing to dispel.

The Chairman finally decided to call it a day at ten-thirty. Arnold saw the pair stumble to the Rover and watched the Senior Planning Officer manoeuvre an unsteady course out of the car park: he was clearly not accustomed to so many sweet sherries.

When the roar of the Rover had faded down the lane leading back towards the main road, Arnold went to his own car. He sat in the driver's seat for a while, still gnawed by a vague anxiety he seemed unable to dispel. The meeting had upset him; the scarred relationship between Gullick and Gipsy Joe Connor could have bad repercussions. It would certainly make his life more difficult, since he still had the responsibility for the Rafferty Common file, and would be concerned with resolution of the dispute. He knew that what had happened tonight was not the last confrontation he could expect.

The car park emptied and the lights in the Three Bells went out. He was on top of a ridge here, with no buildings around: the country inn was fairly isolated, some three-quarters of a mile from the next village, and from where he sat in the car park he could see the distant glow of lights across the valley, and the dark, humped shapes of the hills to the north and west. Their edges were silvered in the moonlight, and in a little while he heard the call of a barn owl, hunting in the darkness, as his kind had hunted for a thousand years. It was an eerie, lonely sound, and in some peculiar manner it turned his mind to Elliott Brandling.

Ben Gibson had suggested the man was lonely. Arnold himself thought he detected uncertainties in the university professor. Yet he had made a reputation in his own field, and his interests were wide-ranging — even to an understanding of why the occult had taken such a fierce grip in the Middle Ages.

Arnold thought back over the conversation in the Fisherman's Wharf. Arnold had suffered for that evening: the following morning he had woken with a groan because of the splitting head occasioned by an unaccustomed amount of alcohol. There had been at least three bottles of red wine, after the Sancerre, and Brandling had also taken at least two brandies. The man must be near alcoholism, Arnold thought — but metabolisms differed. The Senior Planning Officer, for instance: three sweet sherries and he was almost incapable. The thought made Arnold smile, but the smile soon faded. He was depressed, nervous; his fingertips seemed to tingle, and he felt unsettled.

He started the engine and turned the car back towards Rafferty Common. Then he stopped. He had no desire to go through the village: he did not wish to witness any trouble that might have occurred. There might still be street discussion groups or bands of wandering, marauding, gin-soaked gipsies abroad.

He turned the car, aware that he was being fanciful, and headed in the opposite direction. It would mean a considerable detour, but he was not tired, and the driving might take his mind off his nervousness.

The lane was narrow and his headlights danced against the dark hedgerows, picking out occasional points of light, the reflection of eyes in the darkness. A rabbit leaped out of the hedge and bobbed white-tailed in his lights for some fifty yards along the road before it scurried sideways into the undergrowth. Then the road widened, he reached a junction and he looked up at the signpost.

It stated Morpeth in one direction, Kentside in the other.

Almost without thinking, he turned in the direction of Kentside.

As he drove he tried to rationalize his quick decision, but was unable to do so. It was as though he was drawn by some morbid fascination towards the place. He had experienced unpleasant emotions on the last occasion he had gone there, and he could still taste the disgust on his tongue at the thought of the putrescent thing under the rose hedge.

And yet he was returning.

Perhaps it was the story Elliott Brandling had related to him, the developing cult of evil building upon a base that had existed there for centuries, beyond de Vieux Pont perhaps to an older, pagan time when blood sacrifice had been a blinder, less calculating attempt to gain the support of the ancient gods.

Perhaps it was his own innate scepticism, the disbelief of modern man, the refusal to believe old wives' tales, and the need to demonstrate to himself that the emotions raised in his last visit had been irrational, the mood of the night, and ill-founded.

But even as he drove he was cold, and he shivered.

The moon was high now, and the road ahead of him straight and pale, glowing under the moon. He met no other vehicles, and when he passed the stand of oak and crossed the hill there were no lights to be seen ahead, in the semi-deserted village of Kentside. It was as though all had bolted themselves indoors, waiting for the dawn.

He stopped on the ridge, waited for a while with the engine turned off. The night was still; no owls hunted here.

It was as though he were entirely alone in a dark wilderness, nothing stirring, and he sat and listened and all he could hear was the thunder in his own chest.

Arnold drove down into the village. There were no lights. The car rumbled down the street, the echoes of the engine reverberating against the cold walls of the deserted cottages as he passed, to turn into the narrow lane that led to the church. Arnold pulled the car in at the west side of the church wall and killed the engine. He got out, locked the car door, and then stood irresolute for a few minutes.

Nothing stirred.

Slowly he walked towards the old gate in the church wall. Strangely, as he opened it on this occasion it made no squealing sound and yet he could not imagine anyone would have taken the trouble to lubricate its rusty hinges.

His footsteps crunched on the gravel of the pathway. He looked up to the church itself and it seemed to hang above him, dark and oddly menacing, as though it had long lost the capacity to create love and life in a man's mind and had consigned itself to the darkness that surrounded its history.

Arnold shook his head. He must rid himself of such morbid thoughts. He was here to exorcize the demons of his own imagination, not indulge them.

He walked around the front of the church, past the porch at the barred door, and noted almost as an afterthought that a second view of the church only served to confirm his impression that it had been built on an old, axial plan.

A light wind suddenly got up, cold on the back of his neck and face and he moved on, turning the corner of the church to face the graveyard at the rear, fronting against the rose hedge in the far corner. It lay pale under the moonlight, the dilapidated tombstones glowing white, leaning like drunken men after a wild party, uncaring and uncared for.

He stood there for several seconds, not wanting to walk forward to the rose hedge to confront again the disgusting thing that lay there, and he looked up to the bright, deep blue sky and the face of the moon. Then he walked forward.

Twenty feet from the hedge, he stopped. There was a wide, flat tombstone to his right, half hidden by rank grass and weeds. Something dark lay sprawled and huddled on the stone. Arnold's skin was suddenly sensitive and tingling, cold, prickling under the light breeze and he did not want to walk forward, but he did so under a compulsion he could neither resist nor understand.

At first he thought it was a pile of old clothing, but then he knew that the violence at Rafferty Hall had found its echoes here at St Michael's Church.

The man lay on his back. His eyes were wide open, glittering under the moon, but lifeless, and sightless. His arms were thrown wide as though in final supplication and as Arnold stood over him he knew the man was dead.

He was not a young man; the hair was grizzled, the face seamed and lined, and his clothing was dark and ragged. His jacket and shirt had been torn open as though ripped by ravening claws.

The dark stain of blood lay along his savaged chest.

CHAPTER FOUR

1

This was not the first time that Arnold had met Detective Inspector Culpeper.

The policeman was in his mid-fifties; his shoulders were broad and his waist had thickened and experience had added a certain wistfulness to his mouth, as though he wished mankind were better behaved — in Northumberland, at least. The wrinkles around his pouched, friendly eyes gave him an avuncular air, but Arnold had seen those soft, autumn-brown eyes harden, and there could be a narrowing calculation in his glance that emphasized Culpeper was no bucolic, thick-witted bumpkin in spite of his Northumberland accent. His straight, grey hair was neatly parted as always, and when he seated himself in front of Arnold in the interview room he sighed, and nodded to the constable standing just inside the door.

'That'll do, Jenkins. I'll take over from here. But a cup of tea wouldn't be amiss, Mr Landon?'

Inadvertently Arnold glanced at his watch.

It was almost four o'clock and outside dawn would be lightening the dark-blue sky. He nodded. 'Yes, please. But no sugar.' The last cup he had received, some two hours ago, had been so thick with sugar that he had been unable to drink it. The constable had looked offended when he had removed the barely touched cup.

'Well, Mr Landon. Trouble again, hey?'

'Seems so,' Arnold replied miserably. He thought briefly of the shudder that would go through the Senior Planning Officer's frame when he heard, as he undoubtedly would on arrival at his desk in the Planning Department, that Arnold was in Morpeth police station 'helping with inquiries'.

'You've already been questioned, and made a statement, I know,' Culpeper said. 'But I've only just been hauled in out of my warm bed, and when I read some things in your statement I got a bit confused. From our last acquaintance, I was not of the opinion that you were troubled by a lack of . . . logic, or consistency.'

'I'm not sure what you mean.'

Culpeper's wise eyes regarded him with a professional compassion. 'It must be the lateness of the hour . . . the emotions of the moment . . . the churchyard, all that sort of thing.'

'I'm not sure—'

'*Satanism*, Mr Landon?'

Arnold took a deep breath. He should not have mentioned it. When the detective constable had questioned him here in the station, after he had rung 999 and the blue lights had come flashing all around the village and most of the houses had remained resolutely barred, nevertheless, and Arnold had been whisked off to Morpeth for questioning, he had let some of his nervousness be communicated to the sceptical young policeman. When asked why he had gone to St Michael's Church in the first instance he had tried to explain the confusion of his emotions, and his reasons for being there had become jumbled with the pressures of the evening and the meeting at Rafferty Hall.

Culpeper was regarding him owlishly. 'Did they breathalyse you, Mr Landon, when you were brought in here?'

It had been humiliating. Arnold nodded. 'It was a negative result.'

'Just slightly below the limit?'

'I believe so.' Arnold hesitated. 'I did have a few drinks, but not much.'

'Your colleague was less fortunate.'

'Colleague?'

'I believe he claimed to be the Senior Planning Officer. He was in a collision late last night near Morpeth. Both he and his passenger were breathalysed: both were positive. The car's still here: your colleague's gone home, now — we took him and Councillor Lansbury in a police car. Your senior officer will be up before the magistrates in due course.'

He'll die, Arnold thought. He'll shoot himself rather than face the humiliation of a court appearance. Unless he managed to get Tom Lansbury on the bench, facing him. Now that would be an interesting situation. The thought caused a bubble of amusement to effervesce in Arnold's mind.

'Of course,' Culpeper was saying, 'the fact you weren't over the limit isn't the important point here. What I'm trying to suggest is that maybe the effects of alcohol . . . I don't believe you're a heavy drinker, no? Right. Well, maybe the alcohol had some effect upon your thought processes, your perceptions . . .'

'The thing under the rose hedge was real enough and that was why—'

'Yes.' Culpeper stared hard at Arnold. 'We're going to look into that. But I'd like to hear a little more about your . . . theories . . . I mean, to begin with, you'd attended this meeting, which got a bit noisy.'

'That's right. A meeting to discuss the gipsies on Rafferty Common.'

'Good. And you all felt you . . . needed a drink thereafter. Somewhere away from where the villagers might meet.'

'That's right.'

'Did any of the gipsies go to the same pub as you?'

'Where we were? I saw none,' Arnold replied after a moment's thought.

'Would they have normally gone to the pub in the village nearby?'

'I really wouldn't know.'

Culpeper sighed, and nodded. He took a pipe out of his pocket and stared at it gloomily for a few seconds. He stuck it in his mouth and sucked at it but made no attempt to fill it with tobacco. 'So you then drove to Kentside.'

'Yes.'

'Why?' The word was put gently, almost caressingly.

Arnold shook his head. 'I can't entirely explain. A combination of . . . reasons. Mainly, I didn't want to go through the village. The Senior Planning Officer had gone . . . I was heading for Morpeth, and when I saw the Kentside sign, maybe I made a mistake, took the wrong road—'

'That wasn't what you said earlier,' Culpeper admonished quietly.

'I . . . I think I was confused . . . upset at finding the body . . .'

'You said you drove to Kentside deliberately,' Culpeper insisted. 'You had a reason to go there. To exorcize ghosts.'

'Well, not quite that,' Arnold said desperately. 'I mean, last time I was there I was affected by certain . . . feelings.'

'You felt the presence of . . . *evil*.'

There was no hint of sarcasm in Culpeper's voice, and yet Arnold wriggled uncomfortably. 'Well, yes . . . and no . . . I mean, the fact is I was affected . . . maybe it was auto-suggestion—'

'Whose?'

'What do you mean?'

'Auto-suggestion . . . it means thoughts had been planted in your mind. By a supernatural presence? Surely not that,' Culpeper said heavily, a little despondently as though he was disappointed in Arnold.

'No, of course not. It was Professor Brandling.'

There was a short silence. 'Ah,' Culpeper said, and sucked on his pipe ruminatively. 'And just who is Professor Brandling?'

Arnold's spirits dropped. This was only going to get worse. 'Professor Brandling is an expert on monasticism; he told me a story about a cult . . . he has a theory that the cult practices . . . unpleasant rites in St Michael's Church.'

'And that's why you went there?'

Arnold shook his head. 'In the first place, no, I went to check out the church itself . . . to help the Professor in his research. But while I was there . . . that's when I found the body under the rose hedge . . .'

'Yes,' Culpeper said, nodding sagely. 'The other body. And you went back to see if it was still there?'

'Yes. No . . . I don't know. I . . . felt . . .'

'The presence of evil,' Culpeper repeated.

His voice had lowered atone, matching his disappointment. He stared at Arnold and the soft brown eyes held a hint of saddened disbelief. 'Mr Landon, you're under no obligation to stay here, of course. But it is quite a drive to your home, there are further questions we'd like to ask you, and we don't really want to be driving all over the county all the time. The best plan would be if you were to stay in the cells now: they're not uncomfortable. It is quite late, and we'd better have a word with this Mr . . . Professor Brandling? After we've spoken to him, maybe we'll need to have another word with you. So it's best you stay here . . . try to get some sleep . We'll be able to talk again later . . .'

* * *

It was one thing suggesting Arnold should get some rest; it was quite another actually getting to sleep. Arnold lay still on the cot in the dismal police cell and closed his eyes but sleep would not come. The smell of the room was offensive, the graffiti on the wall unpleasant, and he felt a certain claustrophobia as he lay there but he gritted his teeth, kept still and made no move when they looked in at him from time to time. The morning wore on, and at midday a constable came in and asked him if he'd like to go down to the canteen for something to eat.

Arnold thought it best to do so, but was unable to do anything other than pick at the damp haddock and chips that was provided. The tea was heavily sweetened again; this time he drank it, despondently.

It was four in the afternoon before Culpeper came back to see him. Arnold had managed to snatch a few hours' sleep after lunch, but when Culpeper came in he seemed tired, and there were deep lines scored around his mouth, lines Arnold had not noticed before.

'All right, Mr Landon, I've had a session with Professor Brandling now. I have your statement here. Please read it. Is there anything you wish to add, or change?'

His tone did not seem threatening, but Arnold read the statement over carefully, just in case he was being led into some kind of trap. The statement was a fair enough record of what he had said, and even though he felt he could have been less . . . emotional when he made it, nevertheless, it was a fair record . . .

'No,' he said. 'It can stand.'

Culpeper stared at the statement, and shook his head slightly as though he was sorry Arnold was making a fool of himself in this way. He rose heavily and stood looking down at Arnold. 'All right, Mr Landon, you can go now. We may well want to talk to you again, once we have the forensic reports in . . .' He paused. 'I wouldn't advise talking to the press.'

It was the kind of advice the Senior Planning Officer would have appreciated. Arnold nodded, and rose. Culpeper led the way out of the interview room.

When Arnold emerged from the police station he narrowed his eyes against the glare of the bright afternoon sunshine. He felt tired, he needed a shave and a bath, and his stomach was fluttering nervously, in a most peculiar manner. His car had been taken into the police car park; he went there now to collect it, but as he did so he heard someone call his name. He turned to see a slim young man hastening towards him, hand raised. It was Cy Robinson.

'Mr Landon — I have Professor Brandling with me. He'd like to talk to you.'

Arnold groaned inwardly. He followed Robinson across to a car at the entrance to the car park. Elliott Brandling was sitting in the passenger seat.

His skin was grey, his eyes red, and his mouth hung slackly, marked with a loose anger. He looked tired, and emotionally drained, and Arnold knew immediately that the man was suffering from a huge hangover. He glanced at Cy Robinson; the young man shrugged. 'I drove the Professor in . . . When the police called, he called me.'

Brandling fixed his bleary glance on Arnold. 'What the hell's been going on?' He almost snarled the words. Arnold hesitated. 'I . . . I was disturbed—'

'What the hell do you mean by dragging *me* into it?'

The belligerence was barely controlled, and Arnold flushed. He glanced at Cy Robinson, and the young research student seemed somewhat shamefaced. 'Professor Brandling—' he began, but the man's voice cut across his.

'Landon, we need to talk. You got your car here?'

'Yes, it's just across there and—'

'Right. Cy, get in and drive me home. Landon, you follow. We can talk at my place.'

The prospect did not appeal to Arnold. He felt scruffy and tired, and the last thing he wanted was a long, strained conversation with Brandling in his present frame of mind. Perhaps something of his thoughts was communicated to Brandling, for the Professor stared at him and said, 'You look a mess.'

Arnold almost replied that the Professor was in no position to criticize, but bit his tongue. 'I'd really like to get home and freshen up. Maybe—'

'You can do it at my place. I want to talk to you. I can't afford this kind of bloody scandal. There are people who would be only too pleased to put a knife in and gut my career. You can have a meal and a bath at my place, Landon. Cy — get in. Landon — you follow.'

He was brooking no argument.

Cy Robinson looked at Arnold, almost pleadingly. Arnold was left with the impression that Robinson was not over-enthusiastic about taking the Professor home alone, in the man's present mood. Arnold shrugged, and walked to his car. As Cy Robinson drove out of the car park and headed south, Arnold followed closely behind.

2

Professor Brandling's home was, Arnold discovered, beautifully located. It comprised the lower part of a large early-Victorian detached house built on the banks of the Wear; the sloping garden to the south of the house dropped down for some thirty yards to a steep bank from which a view of Durham castle and the university was available; the Wear itself could be glimpsed as it wound around the steep sides of the hill on which the castle stood. In the late afternoon, now, the trees cast long shadows across the close-cropped lawn, and Brandling stood framed in the open doors of the French windows that led out to the garden.

'Beautiful,' Arnold murmured, looking towards the castle.

Brandling turned and stared at him for a moment, his eyes still glinting hard, but the comment seemed to mollify him and calm him somewhat. 'Cy,' he called to his young research student, 'get Landon a drink—'

'No, really—'

'Yes, of course, first things first,' Brandling agreed. 'Cy, the guest-room. Take Mr Landon up, get him some clean towels from the airing cupboard, and show him the bathroom. Landon, get a good soak — you'll find some new razors in the bathroom. Freshen up. We need to talk, but perhaps we could both sensibly get in a proper frame of mind. It's been a long night for you, and a rough morning for me.'

Arnold felt too weary to argue, and the prospect of a hot bath was attractive. He allowed Cy Robinson to take him through to the guest-room.

'I'm sorry,' Robinson apologized. 'But when the Professor is like this — well, frankly—'

'He was drinking heavily last night?'

Robinson frowned uncertainly. 'Usually, he can take it. Once in a while, if he's worried, or down . . . Anyway, I'm sure you'll be comfortable here. The bathroom is across the hallway.' He hesitated. 'Er . . . do you mind if I use the extension phone in your room?'

Arnold shook his head, somewhat surprised, and left the room to go to the bathroom while Robinson placed his call. He found some cheap throwaway razors in a packet on the shelf. As he started to shave he could hear the low murmur of the young man's voice on the phone; by the time he started to run a bath Robinson had finished, and Arnold heard him close the bedroom door and return to the sitting-room.

Somewhat bloody-mindedly, Arnold deliberately took his time over his bath, soaking in the hot water and drifting into a semi-comatose state in which the anxieties and pressures of the night before began to fade. No doubt Brandling would be expecting him soon, but this had been the Professor's idea, dragging him down to Durham, so he could now damned well wait.

To his credit, Brandling made no attempt to hurry Arnold along, and consequently it was six o'clock before Arnold finally emerged, cleaner, more refreshed and certainly more relaxed than he had been when he arrived at the Professor's home.

Brandling was sitting at ease in a leather armchair. He had a glass of pale liquid on the small table beside him. Arnold doubted that it was a soft drink but he could not make out what it was. Near the record-player Cy Robinson was sprawled; he too had a drink — a lager — and he was clearly enjoying the Bartok that emanated from the record-player beside him. He rose as Arnold entered, though Brandling made no attempt to do so. Instead, the Professor grunted, 'Whisky?' and when Arnold assented, he grunted again. His mood had improved, but not by much: he still wanted to have something out with Arnold.

It was not long in coming.

'I'll make no secret of the fact that I had a heavy night last night,' Brandling announced. 'And I'm staying off the bloody brandy for a while; changing my drink. Anyway, it means I was in no sort of temper this morning. But it certainly wasn't improved by a visit from the police. What the hell do you mean by it, Landon, dragging me into this sordid damned business?'

Arnold shook his head. 'I'm sorry, it wasn't my intention to involve you in anything. I merely told the facts as I saw them.'

'Facts? What bloody facts?'

Arnold spent the next few minutes attempting to explain. He sketched in an account of the incidents at Rafferty Hall, described his visit to the pub, and went on to draw attention to his feelings, how they had been affected by his first visit to Kentside, and how he had felt drawn there when he had seen the signpost. He was relieved to see Brandling nodding thoughtfully. Some of the anger had been dissipated and the Professor seemed to be in a more reasonable mood. It could have been the explanation; it might have been the effects of the pale drink that Robinson obtained for him during Arnold's narrative. He might have had a rough night the previous evening, but he was not inhibited from partaking in a hair of the dog, even if its colour was different.

Cy Robinson sat silent as Arnold completed his story. Brandling nodded. 'All right,' he agreed reluctantly, 'maybe you had no choice. But it caused me severe embarrassment. You've got to understand my position . . . Did you know this gipsy person?'

'Gipsy?'

Brandling stared at Arnold. 'That's what I said. The corpse you found in the churchyard was a gipsy — an old man.'

'How do you know that?'

Testily, Brandling replied, 'I was interviewed by Culpeper today, do you remember? He'd been put on to me by you; he wanted to know about my interest in Kentside — and he asked me if I'd had any connections with the gipsies up at Rafferty Common. That's when he let slip it was an old Romany who got murdered.'

Arnold took a stiff draught of his whisky.

Brandling stared at him, then gestured towards Cy Robinson. The young man got up and replenished Arnold's glass. Arnold stared at it uncomprehendingly. An old gipsy . . . murdered after the argument at Rafferty Hall. He thought back, trying to picture who it might have been, but all he could recall were the dark faces of young Romanies, and then that image was blocked out by the picture presented by the stiff walk of Marcus Gullick, angrily leaving the hall, bent on giving an answer to Connor's contemptuous violence.

Maybe the answer had been given, in St Michael's Church, Kentside.

'Culpeper wanted to know about this Satanism thing you mentioned,' Brandling said. 'I told him it wasn't Satanism . . . it was a cult of violence based upon de Vieux Pont.'

Dazedly, Arnold said, 'I didn't really give him details.'

'No, you just mentioned my bloody name!' Brandling was silent for a while, nervously glaring at his glass while the Bartok filtered through the room about them. 'He wanted to know what it was I'd told you. Or as he put it, what I'd filled your head with!'

'It wasn't like that—'

'Ah, man, I'm accustomed to having people scoff at theories they don't understand, or appreciate. In the university . . . but no matter.' He cocked a wary eye in Arnold's direction. 'The thing is, first time you went to Kentside you felt something, didn't you?' Arnold was unable to deny it. He nodded. 'And maybe that . . . feeling drew you back? Hah! I thought so. You know, it doesn't matter in the end what stupid plodding policemen think . . . The fact is, like me, you have certain sensitivities they can't understand. Because I've felt it too.'

'Culpeper would have wanted more than feelings,' Arnold remarked unhappily.

'Yes. Precisely.' Brandling watched Arnold carefully for a few seconds, before saying, 'I gave him some facts, of course.'

'Facts?' Arnold raised his head, aware as he did so of Robinson squirming in his seat, glancing back towards the clock on the wall as though to check the time. Brandling also caught the movement.

'You eager to go somewhere, Cy?' Brandling asked.

The young research student ducked his head in a slight, embarrassed movement. 'When you rang me this morning, asked me to drive you to Morpeth, I had arranged . . . well. I hope you didn't mind, but a little while ago, since I couldn't get to see her this lunchtime, I just rang . . . rang Andrea. From the guest-room. She . . . she's coming to pick me up shortly. You won't be needing me now, I guess . . .'

Brandling was quiet for a few moments. 'No, that's right, lad. I won't need you any more this evening. And I haven't thanked you adequately for your assistance today. Not exactly in the line of duty; something extra. I'm grateful. But you know how this whole thing upset me.'

Robinson bobbed his head.

'You see, Landon,' Brandling went on, still staring at his young researcher, 'it's common enough knowledge that I have a certain problem at the university. It's the fruit of success, in a sense. I wrote a book called *The Scribe of Odilo*: it was a financial success. Colleagues in the university took a view about it: it's all right to publish dusty, boring tomes that no one wants to read, but once you write something that sells in thousands . . . the fact is they didn't care for such success. Jealousy abounds . . . Moreover, this bloody government is determined to abolish tenure. You're aware of that? There are those in the university who'd love to see me out, and with abolition of tenure . . .'

His glance slid towards Arnold, and he sipped at his glass thoughtfully. 'The last thing I can afford is scandal,' he said. 'I've worked hard for my place at this university. My background wasn't of the best — did you know I was raised in an end-terrace house in the back streets of Sunderland? It's not easy, struggling up to a chair in a highly respected university, not when the cards are stacked against you socially. But I made it, and I earned it, and it's important to me and I don't want to lose it. Scandal could lose it for me. That's why I was so angry this morning . . . getting in any way linked to a murder investigation. It could crucify me, Landon.'

He paused again, stared at Cy Robinson. 'Cy knows what I mean,' he added softly. 'Scandal can blow a man's world apart. Cy knows that.'

Robinson shifted uncomfortably in his seat and took a long pull at his lager. A blackbird began to sing lustily in the garden, and all three men were silent for a few minutes as the bird competed with Bartok and the dying sun sent long shadows over the wine-red carpet of the sitting-room.

'What time is she coming, Cy?' Brandling asked at last.

'In about ten minutes.'

Brandling nodded, and was silent.

'You said something about facts,' Arnold remarked, after a little while.

'Facts?' Brandling frowned, as though befuddled, then nodded. 'Oh yes.' He paused, deep in thought, and then cocked an eye in Robinson's direction. 'Cy, before Andrea calls for you would you mind ringing the Cock of the North? Book a table for two, seven thirty. Mr Landon and I will need to eat before he drives north again.'

'I'll do it now,' Robinson said eagerly, and finished his drink before walking out to the phone in the hallway.

'Facts,' Brandling repeated, almost to himself. 'Have you ever come across anyone called Santana . . . Zeke Santana?'

Arnold stared at the Professor. 'Why, the name is familiar . . . the surname, at least. He's been involved in a planning application recently . . .'

Brandling's mouth twisted unpleasantly. 'You must tell me about it sometime. All right, facts, you said. I told you I noted that St Michael's Church had a bad reputation . . . scandals connected with it over a hundred years ago, and hints in the seventeenth century of Black Mass being celebrated in the area — though not necessarily on the site, I admit.'

'I remember you telling me,' Arnold said. 'But what proof did you have to support your supposition regarding the Raging Wolf cult, and a connection with St Michael's?'

'I'm coming to that. It was some three years ago when I was working as usual on my monastic research that I first came across the cult of de Vieux Pont in the records. I started checking on it all, as a matter of course — in the university libraries, and elsewhere. Then I had a visit from Mr Santana.'

'What did he want?' Arnold asked, after a short silence.

Brandling rose, walked across to the drinks cabinet and poured himself another stiff measure. Arnold caught sight of the bottle label. Vodka. The mystery was solved.

'He had misunderstood my interest. Whereas I was interested merely in monastic history, he thought I was checking up on de Vieux Pont for reasons connected with the occult.' Brandling hesitated. 'Maybe I was . . . well, a bit unfair. I was curious . . . I led him on a little. Anyway, the upshot of it was that he intimated to me that he was involved with a little . . . group. And they had certain nights when they . . . indulged themselves. Now he never actually admitted anything, but I was left with the very clear impression that he was more than interested, with his companions, in the cult of the Raging Wolf — and he was inviting me to join their little fun party.'

Arnold stared at the Professor. 'Did you join them?'

'I declined the invitation. But I did get some very broad hints that it was in the Kentside area that they met. From that I made my own deductions. There is something evil about that damned church. And I'm certain that's where they carry out their gory rites.'

'Gory?'

'It's a violent cult,' Brandling said shortly, and sprawled in the chair. 'All right, I called it a "fun party" a moment ago. But their real interest is blood. Just like de Vieux Pont.'

Cy Robinson entered, coughing slightly. 'I'll be going now, Professor. I've made the call; the table's booked.'

'Is she here?'

'She's waiting in the car outside. I . . . I'll see you on Friday, Professor.'

Brandling nodded, and Cy Robinson said goodbye to Arnold, then left. After the door banged shut behind him there was a long silence in the room. Elliott Brandling stared at the carpet, brooding thoughtfully. He shook his head, glanced up at Arnold and frowned. 'He's making a bad mistake.'

Arnold was confused. 'Santana?'

'No, dammit, *Cy*! He's got a fine career ahead of him. His research work is meticulous . . . a bit too careful, if the truth be known, and he tends to range too widely. I try to keep him on the straight path.' Brandling paused, biting nervously at his lip. 'He just doesn't seem to appreciate . . . I know how tough it is to get established in a good university. It's important to me, the most important thing in my life, and I have a feeling it's the same for him. And yet he's prepared to throw it all away.'

'I don't understand,' Arnold said.

'The woman who's picking him up,' Brandling said sourly. 'She's a married woman. He's besotted with her. A bloody librarian, for God's sake! She's older than he is, and they've become completely indiscreet.'

'Does she live with her husband?'

'Separated. But that's not the point. If the university authorities get a scandal shoved in their faces they'll react like wild bulls — *sophisticated* wild bulls, of course, but the effect will be the same. He'll be ruined. And scandal is the stuff of life as far as some of my colleagues are concerned. They love the kind of gossip that will ruin a man. I've warned young Robinson, but he won't listen. He's heading for disaster. Besides . . .'

Arnold waited. The Professor hesitated, and took another long sip at his drink. 'Hell, why shouldn't you know? Fact is, Andrea Sutcliffe — that's her name — she's got one hell of a jealous husband. Separated they may be, but the boy needs to be careful, or one dark night . . .'

Arnold suddenly had a mental picture of the car park in Morpeth, Cy Robinson being driven out with Arnold following behind. And standing on the pavement a man with cold eyes, heavy-browed, angered . . .

'But we were talking about Santana,' Brandling reminded him. 'You said he's been involved with a planning application?'

'That's right. I'm not sure how far . . . In the first instance, it was a man called Edward Chaunter, whose application was turned down. He wanted to set up a religious centre. Then, when he returned, it was to say he was no longer proceeding with that, but was clearing with us a purchase of a Methodist chapel.'

'For the same purpose?'

'That's right. I told him there shouldn't be any problems.'

'Chaunter.' Brandling frowned. 'I fancy I've heard the name . . . But how does Santana fit into this?'

'He was with Chaunter, the second time he came. Santana, and someone called Daniels.' Brandling shook his head doubtfully. 'They seem to be members of some religious cult,' Arnold said slowly. 'They call themselves the Vicars of Jehovah. It was Chaunter . . . he seemed to be the leader. The others, they tended to follow him, if you know what I mean.'

'Zeke Santana never seemed to me to be a leader,' Brandling mused, almost to himself.

After a short silence, Arnold said, 'I don't really see what this has to do with the death of the gipsy in the churchyard, anyway.'

'Don't you?' Brandling shrugged. 'No, maybe not. But you say you found something under the hedge . . . and then this killing . . . and the Raging Wolf cult . . . It could all be coincidental. Ah, the hell with it. I've got other things to worry about, anyway. And that young man, Robinson.' He glared fiercely at Arnold for a moment. 'He's a bloody fool, you see that? I regard him almost as a son, you know, and I can't see him throwing himself away like this, worthlessly.'

'I can understand that.'

'Can you? Are you married, Landon?'

'No.'

'Never had the inclination?'

Arnold felt uncomfortable. 'I've . . . never found someone who—'

'I've never married. There were a couple of women . . . but my work was more important. Getting a chair was more important. That doesn't mean I never wanted a son . . . Were you close to your father, Landon?'

'Yes.'

'I never knew mine.'

The statement came out almost brutally. Arnold sat and watched the Professor as he seemed to turn inward to himself, inspecting his innermost thoughts, seeking solutions.

Arnold felt sorry for him suddenly: he had the image of a man driven by ambition who was now realizing he had missed something in life. A man who could see in his young assistant the possibility of another generation — not of his own flesh, but of his inclinations and in his own academic mould. And Arnold could understand the hurt the man would feel at the thought that his young protégé would be risking university scandal, throwing away his chance for an academic career.

For someone's else's wife.

Brandling looked up suddenly, glared at Arnold, his glance ripping into him, as though probing for his thoughts. 'Don't feel sorry for me, Landon,' he said, almost snarling the words.

'No,' Arnold replied gently. 'No, I won't do that . . . But the table's booked at the Cock of the North. Do you think we'd better start making a move to go and eat?'

3

Arnold had expected to hear no more about the murder at Kentside — since he had nothing more to impart — so he was surprised three days later, when Detective Inspector Culpeper chose to call on Arnold at his office.

Arnold was not pleased. He had already had a difficult interview with the Senior Planning Officer. The man's temper had begun to surface: after a period when he had avoided unpleasantness like the plague, and seen fit to spend no time whatsoever in confrontations with his colleagues, he seemed now to have been badly affected by his arrest and breathalysing. It was, of course, a matter of common gossip in the office that Arnold had discovered a body at St Michael's Church, but it was, Arnold felt, a little unfair that the Senior Planning Officer should have used the event to try to damp down the sensation caused by his own arrest. He had given Arnold a dressing-down, implying that further such discoveries would call his career into question. Arnold had tried to protest that he did not actively seek out corpses as a matter of entertainment, but the Senior Planning Officer ignored the irony and had his say.

The visit of Detective Inspector Culpeper could well serve to heighten the Senior Planning Officer's displeasure, so Arnold was not pleased by the visit.

'Well,' Culpeper said as he sank his bulk into the chair facing Arnold. 'How are you?'

'As well as can be expected,' Arnold replied stiffly, 'when confronted by unexpected visits from the police.'

'Aye, well, I was just passing.'

Arnold wished he hadn't stopped. He said nothing, however, and waited.

'I thought I'd better call in to check a few things with you, with regard to the statement you made,' Culpeper went on. 'I take it there's nothing you want to add to that statement . . . no new thoughts you've had?'

'Nothing.'

'Aye, right. Well, I've had the early reports from Forensic now, and we've gone over the churchyard with a fine-tooth comb, and we've dragged that thing out from under the hedge . . .' He paused, and eyed Arnold speculatively.

After a short silence, his mouth surprisingly dry, Arnold asked, 'What was it?'

Culpeper smiled bleakly. 'It turned out to be the remains of a large, decomposed dog.' There was another short silence.

Arnold asked slowly, 'Had it been killed in the same manner as the old gipsy?'

Culpeper looked up in surprise. 'How did you know it was an old gipsy that had been murdered? You told us you didn't inspect the body, after that first glance.'

Arnold groaned inwardly. 'It was Professor Brandling. He told me.'

'Brandling? Oh, aye.' Culpeper's face darkened at the thought that he might have given more away during his interview with the Professor than perhaps he should have done. 'All right . . . The fact is, we can't quite establish the way in which the dog was killed because rats had got at the body, gnawed and tugged at the flesh, that sort of thing. The Forensic people also haven't given the matter a high degree of priority . . . I mean, a dead dog . . . It's possible that the dog was gutted like the old man was, but in any case, your story of Satanic rites and all that rubbish, well, it really doesn't stand up.'

'Why?'

'First of all, we've had no reports from locals about such goings-on. And locals tend to notice such things.'

Or not talk about them. Arnold remembered the resolutely barred doors in the village the nights he had been there. It was possible superstitious villagers, with a long folk history of black arts being practised in the village, would not easily open their doors at night.

'Second, the old man's murder had nothing to do with Satanic rites. We're sure of that.'

'He was killed ritually, wasn't he?'

'What makes you say that?'

'He'd been knifed, seemed to me. A huge wound in his chest.'

'What's ritual about that? He'd been gutted, yes. And the knife was a big, broad-bladed one. It was twisted before it was dragged out, it seems, but that could have been because of a struggle. The old man was a bit frail, but he was wiry and he could have put up a bit of a battle.'

'The dog—'

'Is irrelevant. I would guess it was unwanted, or sick, was killed by an uncaring owner, could have been run down, tortured by vicious kids. Who knows, or cares, really?' Culpeper's tone was dismissive, and his eyes angry as though he resented Arnold's attempt to bring in the supernatural. 'Look, the fact is, the dog was thrown over the wall, dragged under the hedge by rats, lay there stinking for weeks. It's got nothing to do with Satanism, and it's got nothing to do with the death of the old man.'

'How can you be so sure?'

'Because there's only one thing in common between the incidents.'

'What's that?'

'St Michael's Church. It's a convenient dumping ground, near a semi-deserted village.'

'Dumping ground?'

Culpeper nodded. 'That's it. You see, the early suppositions emerging from Forensic relate to time of death, and to the state of the clothing. First, it looks as though the old man had been dead for a good twenty-four hours before you found him in the churchyard.'

'He'd been lying there all that time? That's impossible! Surely, someone walking through—'

'Few people walk through that churchyard. It's possible the corpse could have been lying there for some time. On the other hand . . .' Culpeper paused thoughtfully. 'Forensic suggest that it's more likely the old man was killed elsewhere — and brought to the site, dumped, like the dog before him. As I said, a convenient disposal site. The thing is, Mr Landon, that effectively gets rid of your wild ideas about Satanic practices, I reckon, don't you? I mean, even if the dog was killed by nutters in black robes in the churchyard, the old man wasn't. He was probably knocked off elsewhere, and brought to the churchyard.'

Arnold was puzzled. The assumptions he had made were now difficult to dislodge.

Culpeper shook his head. 'Anyway, it's not for you to worry about. Just don't go around setting up stories about Black Masses and all that sort of rubbish. It's something the newspapers will delight in — and we'll get in on the end of it all, and be made to look fools. So no more talk of Satanism, Mr Landon, OK?'

Arnold shrugged. 'I was asked to make a statement. I made one. But I'll not be talking outside, out of turn.' He hesitated. 'But if it wasn't anything to do with . . . the cult . . . you agree it's an old gipsy who was murdered. And if the time schedule is as you suggest, it would seem that the murder had nothing to do with the Rafferty Hall fracas.'

'I didn't say it did, Mr Landon,' Culpeper said quietly, 'and I didn't say it didn't. But perhaps you'd favour me with your views.'

Arnold ignored the heavy irony. 'I thought maybe . . . well, it wouldn't be possible if the old man had been killed twenty-four hours earlier. The trouble at Rafferty Hall occurred about three or four hours before I found the dead man, so it couldn't have been . . .'

His voice died away. 'Who?' Culpeper probed gently. 'Couldn't have been who?'

Reluctantly Arnold said, 'There was a lot of noise, shouting, tempers raised—'

'And a shotgun discharged in a threatening manner,' Culpeper added.

'You've heard.'

'I've already spoken to Councillor Lansbury. I intend on interviewing your Senior Planning Officer. But now I'm here to check with you. Can you confirm who fired the shotgun?'

Arnold shrugged. 'A man . . . a gipsy called Connor.'

'How did other parties react?'

Arnold described the scene, the noise, the excitement. And he agreed that Marcus Gullick seemed to have taken a very central role in the affair, standing up to face the threats of the gipsy. 'But as you say, all that could have had nothing to do with the murder of the old man. Marcus Gullick stormed out of the meeting hours after the old gipsy had already been murdered.'

'So it would seem. But do remember, Mr Landon, Forensic could be wrong . . . and they haven't yet put in a final report. Moreover, that scene could perhaps have been the result of the death or disappearance of the old gipsy, don't you think? Or it could have had nothing to do with it at all. Who can tell? At this stage, who can tell?'

Arnold was confused. Culpeper seemed to have no clear leads at all, and no clear purpose to his questions.

Almost casually, Culpeper asked, 'Have you been along to the Rafferty Common site at all?'

Arnold nodded. 'I made an on-site investigation. I have responsibility for the file at the moment.'

'Did you come across this Joe Connor there?'

'I did. We had . . . words.'

'He seems to be a somewhat violent man.'

'He has a sense of wrong. He considers the gipsies are unfairly treated. He has . . . positive views as to how they should respond.'

'Like firing off shotguns.'

'I think,' Arnold said, 'he was making a point, before an audience he regarded as hostile. And making it in front of a local politician.'

'And committing a criminal offence,' Culpeper remarked almost sweetly. 'Do you sympathize with these people, these Romanies?'

Arnold hesitated. 'The council has a duty. The gipsies have . . . an argument. I'm just a planning officer.'

'Hmmm.' Culpeper smiled cynically. 'Careful, aren't you? All right. Now while you were up at Rafferty Common, did you talk to any of the other gipsies there?'

'No.'

'There were some on site?'

'Of course.'

'No contact?'

'No, just with Connor.'

'Was he in a group, or alone, or what?'

'He was alone.' Arnold hesitated. 'He wasn't happy at my being on the site. We had . . . a discussion, in which he made his feelings quite plain. But no one else approached me. They ignored me, rather. It was only when I was leaving that anyone else came forward.'

'To speak to you?'

'No. To speak to Connor.'

Culpeper stared at Arnold, his autumn-brown eyes suddenly hardening as he detected a swift shadow pass over Arnold's features, his confidence sagging at a sudden thought. 'What is it?' he demanded.

'It's nothing. I . . .'

'Something just occurred to you.'

'No. That is, it probably has nothing to do with . . .'

'Out with it, man! How the hell do you know whether it's important, or not?'

Arnold shook his head helplessly. 'I don't know. That's why I'm reluctant—'

'Landon!' warned Culpeper. 'If you're holding anything back . . .'

'It's not that. It's merely that I imagine it's unimportant, but as I was driving away someone approached Connor. They seemed to be having a discussion.'

'Discussion?'

'Argument,' Arnold admitted lamely. Culpeper made a note in his diary, and stared at it for several seconds. 'And this would have been after you'd spoken to Marcus Gullick at his farm, I think.'

'You *have* been checking.'

'It's my business, Mr Landon.' Culpeper turned a blank visage towards Arnold, his eyes giving nothing away. 'Now think hard, please. When this . . . argument was going on, was there anyone else involved?'

'No. Just the two.'

'No one on the fringe of it?'

'No. Except . . .' Arnold had a brief mental flash, an image of a handsome young girl, dark skin, long brown legs.

'Go on.'

'There was a girl. At one of the vans. When the argument started, I was just driving away, but she was leaving the van. She was walking forward, to join them. It's probably of no significance—'

'Probably not, probably not.' But there was a slight, self-satisfied smile on Culpeper's face. 'Just one last question. You say Connor was having an argument with someone. Another gipsy. Was it a man or a woman?'

'It was a man,' Arnold replied.

In the dark churchyard of St Michael's the body had lain in the long grass, with the horrific stain along the length of his chest. Arnold gritted his teeth.

'It was an old man,' he added slowly.

CHAPTER FIVE

1

To spend a Saturday evening with Ben Gibson was a guarantee of tranquillity and a return to a measured consideration of the real values in life. It helped, additionally, that the antiquarian bookseller maintained a cellar of quality wines.

It had been a bad week for Arnold.

Culpeper had not returned, clearly being happy to pursue his inquiries elsewhere. The newspapers had, naturally enough, attempted to obtain 'statements' from Arnold but he had successfully resisted them, not without some degree of annoyance and disruption to the normal pattern of his existence. The Senior Planning Officer seemed to have used his political contacts to ensure a low profile was maintained over his drink-driving offence but he had made it clear to all in the office that he was displeased with his junior officer: Arnold Landon was not his favourite colleague.

For that reason, among others, Arnold was delighted to escape to Ben Gibson's Quayside house on the Saturday evening. He had been feeling guilty about the last visit he had made, when he had left Ben to visit a restaurant with Elliott Brandling; his old friend now seemed genuinely pleased to have his company at dinner, and produced first a fine hock, and secondly a superior burgundy to make the evening flow along happily.

Gibson also laid claim to being something of a culinary genius — 'Not original, of course, but I do have some very old, and very lavish cookbooks' — and if the torpor that settled upon them after dinner was witness to the excellence of the fare, it was an argument Arnold would not dispute. He half reclined in the deep leather armchair in Ben's sitting-room and listened to the vague roar of the traffic over the Tyne Bridge, and most of his troubles washed away.

'I believe Cy Robinson wants a chat with you sometime, Arnold,' Ben remarked as they sat with their glasses of port and the river mists crept silkily along the darkening Quayside, to add an eerie quality to the distant hooting of the freighters downstream.

'What about?' Arnold asked lazily, and with no degree of urgency.

'His research, I imagine. You seem to have become something of a hero to him. Possibly because you've been able to help his *main* hero.'

'Brandling.'

'Correct.'

'Don't know I've helped the Professor that much. The Jarrow site—'

'Have you written up your findings?' Gibson interrupted.

'Last weekend. Had to take my mind off things. So I worked on the papers he gave me, did some digging at the Newcastle Library, and tied up the whole thing as well as I could.'

'You're convinced there was a Cluniac foundation there?'

'As good as. But I just work in stone—'

'Facts.'

Arnold smiled indulgently, and waved his glass in salutation to his host. 'All right, facts. But they still need evidence — documentary evidence — to make them convincing. Otherwise, it's just the subjective mumblings of a humble planning officer.'

'Who's more than likely right. When will you give the results to Brandling?'

'Next few days. When I have the chance. Truth is, that damned Kentside thing . . . I feel, somehow, that Brandling's own subjective musings have landed me into trouble of the kind I could well do without. Culpeper certainly thinks it's all hogwash, and at a distance I have to agree. Anyway, what exactly does Cy Robinson want from me?'

'Exactly? I don't know,' Ben Gibson replied. 'I got that book for him, and it seems to have taken him along his road beautifully. But then he rang me, said he wanted to talk to you—'

'I've been staying out of the office as much as possible,' Arnold admitted. 'The Senior Planning Officer, and this Kentside thing, and the gossip—'

'I understand. Anyway, I told him you were coming around, and I said I'd mention it to you.'

'He's not calling tonight, is he?'

Ben Gibson shook his heavy head and smiled. 'No, no, this is old friends' night. Besides, he'll be elsewhere . . . I'm worried about that young man, Arnold.'

'How do you mean?' Arnold replied, already half guessing at the answer.

Ben Gibson frowned, held his glass against the light and admired the deep colour in the dark liquid. 'As far as I can make out, from hints I've picked up, he's got himself tied up in a difficult relationship. And it's affecting his commitment to his work.'

'You mean his girlfriend?' Arnold asked.

'Mmm.' Ben sipped the port and grimaced in satisfaction. 'He's a young man with a hero, and the chance to work with his hero and develop his own thesis, and at the same time he's got emotional problems with this girl . . .' The old man seemed to struggle for a name.

'Andrea Sutcliffe.'

'Ah. You know of her.'

'Elliott Brandling told me.'

'I've even had a visit,' Ben Gibson said.

Arnold stared at his friend, and put down his glass. 'A visit? From Mrs Sutcliffe?'

'No. From *Mister* Sutcliffe.' Ben Gibson finished his port with a sigh. 'I challenged him, actually. He came into my shop. At my age, and with my experience, you get a feeling about people. He wasn't interested in books. He wanted something else. I challenged him, he told me his name was Jack Sutcliffe, and he wanted to know why his wife had visited this shop.'

'Has she?'

'Only to pick up Cy Robinson.'

'She seems to spend half her life picking up that young man in her car.'

Ben Gibson grinned. 'Young love. It seems to me that though they're separated, she and Sutcliffe, she still tries to avoid trouble. Their assignations tend to be brief — and conducted away from her cottage. She and Cy want to be together, and they grab every chance. Her husband seems to follow her around, keeping a jealous eye on her. I get the impression she's terrified of him — with good cause, if you want my view. He terrifies me.'

Arnold frowned. He thought back to his last visit to Ben's shop, when Cy Robinson had been there. When Arnold had left, he had gained the impression someone was watching him. A cold finger touched his spine. 'I hope you sent the man away with a flea in his ear.'

'His business, not mine,' Ben Gibson said. 'I told him so. But he's a dangerous man, Arnold, and I'm a bit worried about Cy Robinson. A nice young man, he's in deeper water than he realizes. That man Sutcliffe — he's dangerous. Jealousy can be such a violent emotion. And it's affecting Robinson's work. I've seen it. He's worried about it; maybe his lack of progress, or something, it bothers him. And his relationship with Brandling is also concerning him. It's as though he feels he'll be letting the Professor down if his thesis doesn't work out.'

'We all have our crosses,' Arnold suggested.

'And yours is Rafferty Common,' Gibson agreed.

Arnold had already told Ben Gibson about the affair at Rafferty Hall. He had explained to him his early thought that the murder of the old gipsy had been the consequence of the bad blood between Gullick and Connor in some revengeful way, only for that thought to be overturned by Culpeper's information regarding time of death. Both men had agreed, nevertheless, that Rafferty Common remained a flashpoint and Gullick might yet wish to take the law into his own hands, to get his revenge on Connor for the humiliation he had suffered.

'At least Culpeper has it right, in my view,' Ben Gibson suggested. 'You should walk away from this cult theory.'

'You've never been to St Michael's Church,' Arnold said feelingly.

'Even so . . . Brandling's theorizing is something else. I warned you . . . he's a lonely man, and loneliness can lead to obsession. So don't try to make events fit theories — there's no connection between the murder and the cult of de Vieux Pont. The police believe it; so should you.'

* * *

It was easier said than done, nevertheless.

During the next few days Arnold found his thoughts returning to the cult and its relationship to St Michael's, Kentside. He realized it was partly bound up with the fact that he spent two evenings refining his thoughts and findings on the Cluniac foundations at Jarrow, before posting off the material in typescript form to Elliott Brandling. As he worked on that material it was perhaps inevitable that his mind wandered towards de Vieux Pont. But there was also the memory of Brandling's own comments concerning Zeke Santana and the attempt to recruit the Professor into Santana's group. Brandling had linked it to the cult; all Arnold knew was that Santana had some connection with Edward Chaunter and the Vicars of Jehovah.

It seemed, therefore, almost more than coincidental that the Senior Planning Officer sent a note to his office suggesting he call in at the Methodist chapel, now purchased by Chaunter, to ensure that no planning regulations were likely to be broken. Arnold was not a fatalist, but he was certainly ready to believe that sometimes coincidences could be happy. He could fulfil the wishes of the Senior Planning Officer, and at the same time indulge himself, hopefully relieving himself of the burden of the dark thoughts he harboured about the Vicars of Jehovah and the Satanic cult of Simon de Vieux Pont.

The road to Denton Gap wound along the river valley and started to climb along a bluff some seven miles north of Morpeth. The village itself nestled in a hollow, with clumps of ash, and some lonely elm trees to mark the village boundary. It was mid-morning when Arnold had set out, and he had left word in the office where he was going: the Senior Planning Officer had become more careful of his colleagues' activities during the last week, as though he thought clamping down on their diaries was a sign of strength. Even so, Arnold was inclined to dawdle: he saw no reason to rush through the countryside on such a pleasant morning.

He arrived at Denton Gap at midday.

Rather than proceed straight to business he wandered around the village, looking in the shops — it was his lunch-hour after all, and he eventually ended up in a rather twee tea-shop that catered for the meagre walking tourist trade and had a soggy Cornish pasty that was clearly out of place in Northumberland.

It was one-thirty before he made his way along the village street, through the narrow mediaeval alleyway of the Wiend and past the tiny cottage that fronted the Methodist chapel.

It was stark, as many such chapels were, but fairly well built and solid in appearance. A cluttered driveway lay to one end of the gabled structure; some builders' materials were scattered on the site. A Ford Granada was parked near the doorway, which was of solid oak and, Arnold guessed, predated the chapel itself. Arnold placed his own car just to one side of the Granada. He locked the car, and looked at the chapel. The door was open.

Arnold walked in.

The chapel presented a dim interior, cool, unconcerned, dark-panelled and confident after the many resonant voices that had echoed around its walls in the last hundred years. A balustraded mezzanine floor ran the length of one side of the chapel, and Arnold could make out the pine pews that graced it; clearly, the chapel had run out of funds after buying the magnificent oak door. The floor of the chapel was already being gutted: The seating had been removed, some concreting was being undertaken at the far end of the chapel and the walls themselves seemed to have been stripped of the meagre decoration they had enjoyed, to expose bare plaster of a dirty-grey hue. Altogether, not particularly prepossessing.

Like its owner, Arnold thought, as the voice boomed behind him.

'Mr Landon. Not a social visit, I imagine.'

The irony was lost on Arnold. He managed a vague smile as he watched Edward Chaunter come forward, dressed in a clerical grey suit and sporting the severe mouth of an owner surprised. 'Hello, Mr Chaunter. No, just a brief visit to see that all is going well.'

'In planning terms, of course.'

Chaunter's tone was as cold as his eyes.

Arnold retained the vague smile and said, 'There are building materials outside.'

'But the work is inside,' Chaunter ground out. 'As far as I recall, you suggested that since this is not a listed building, and since we have no intention of carrying out external changes, what we do is a matter for us and not for you.'

'That more or less summarizes the situation,' Arnold agreed.

'So your presence is redundant.'

Arnold's smile faded. Chaunter seemed nervous in spite of the arrogance he injected into his tone. It was as though he resented Arnold's presence, but was also unnerved by it.

As though he had something to hide.

'What exactly is it you intend on changing in here?' Arnold asked, turning slowly and inspecting the work that had already been done in the stripping of the interior.

'A simplification, I assure you. A removal of the trappings of Methodism and a return to the simple, direct view of religion, stripped down to its essentials: the relationship between Man and the powers that guide him.'

'I've never seen Methodism as an ornate religion,' Arnold suggested.

'The contorted convolutions of faith and the mediaeval mind—'

'Is that what you're interested in,' Arnold interrupted. 'The mediaeval mind?'

The question seemed to give Edward Chaunter pause. His eyes narrowed and he hesitated, as though reluctant to answer immediately, afraid of saying something that should remain unsaid. Arnold's own soreness and irritation over the events of the last week suddenly made him press on, probing. 'This thing at Kentside, for instance. There's one theory that the church there has odd connections with the mediaeval period. For instance, your own cult—'

'Movement!' snapped Chaunter.

'The Vicars of Jehovah. What do they believe in?' Arnold pressed.

'Simplicity,' Chaunter rejoined, saying nothing, and aware of it.

'And that's what you'll be doing in here. Preparing a simple shrine and worshipping place. To what, Mr Chaunter? For what?'

Chaunter had recovered his composure. 'Become a follower of our movement, Mr Landon, and all will be revealed. But I suspect your presence betrays no real interest in our movement. What is it you want?'

'Just the chance to look around,' Arnold said. 'Just to check that—'

'That nothing untoward is occurring,' Chaunter interrupted. Arnold suspected the sarcasm in the remark: Chaunter was throwing his own suspicions back in his face. That denoted confidence, that there was nothing to be seen in the chapel — nothing incriminating about the cult, or what it stood for.

Arnold allowed himself to be taken on a brief tour, nevertheless. At some stage in the proceedings, almost silently, Zeke Santana joined them, tall, gaunt, holding in his nervous energy with barely contained effort. He seemed to want to challenge Arnold but he said nothing, merely attaching himself to the tour, but Arnold was uncomfortably aware of his presence. He shadowed Chaunter, but the two men did not speak to each other. There was a soft menace in the man's presence that disturbed Arnold.

When he had looked briefly around, and walked up the iron spiral staircase to the balcony above, Arnold pronounced himself satisfied and prepared to leave.

'I'll have to move my car,' Santana said, speaking for the first time. He smiled, but it was without warmth. 'I've blocked you in.'

They emerged into the driveway. There was now a dark-red Citroen parked behind Arnold, and behind that a lorry. Santana glanced at Arnold. 'We'll have to move the lorry, as well. You may be delayed.' He appeared in no manner distressed by the possibility.

It was some ten minutes before the young, short-sleeved lorry-driver was persuaded to make his appearance. During that time Arnold was left to his own devices. He sat on the wall, waiting, realizing this was merely a petty triumph for Chaunter and Santana, a method of obtaining revenge for the slights they deemed they had suffered in the past at the hands of the Planning Department.

When the lorry-driver came out to move the vehicle blocking Santana, Arnold was aware of a telephone ringing, somewhere inside the chapel. He watched the lorry reverse in a cloud of blue exhaust fumes and park down the road, and saw Santana get into his car. Chaunter suddenly appeared in the doorway of the chapel. He seemed displeased.

'Landon. The call's for you!'

'*Me*?'

Arnold was taken aback. The only people who knew he was here were the clerks in the office. He hurried inside. In a small room to the left of the spiral staircase he was shown a telephone.

'Hello?'

'Landon?' It was the Senior Planning Officer. 'There's trouble. Up at Rafferty Common. The police have been called. You'd better get up there at once.'

The urgency in his tone convinced Arnold no argument was possible.

He hurried out into the yard. Santana was edging backwards, reversing into the main road. He was moving perilously close to the wall and the stone gatepost, and Arnold moved forward instinctively to warn him, see him out safely. Before he could reach the driveway there was a grating sound, Santana wound down his window and cursed vehemently, and Arnold realized the wing of the red Citroen had been dented badly.

'All right, take it forward slowly,' Arnold called out.

Santana was not the best of drivers. There was a screech of gears, the car lurched forward almost out of control, and it took another three locks of the steering wheel to get Santana safely out into the road.

Arnold got into his own car thoughtfully.

His heart was pounding and there was a weakness in his upper arms that emphasized the tension that now gripped him. He was sweating lightly as he reversed with an exaggerated care out into the main road.

He pulled out, almost alongside Santana.

The man was glaring at him. Then Santana turned, glanced back over his shoulder, and leaned over in the seat to twitch back into place the car rug that had been displaced in the lurching of his reversing from the chapel yard.

Arnold engaged gear and drove slowly through the village, heading for Rafferty Common. But his mind was no longer on what might be lying ahead, by way of trouble.

He could not erase the image of the sharp, glinting blade that had been exposed when the rug had fallen aside in Santana's car: the honed, chased blade of a short ceremonial sword.

2

Arnold was still a half-mile from Rafferty Common when he realized that there was no chance of reaching it by car. The lane ahead of him was blocked: two police cars, blue roof lights flashing impotently, were pulled in under the trees while a dumper truck was parked in front of them. It had been deliberately driven, it seemed to Arnold, so that it lay athwart the narrow lane, effectively blocking off any progress. The driver was nowhere to be seen, and the uniformed driver of one police car was standing beside his door, urgently speaking into his radio microphone while his companions clustered helplessly around the dumper truck.

Beyond them, over the hill towards Rafferty Common, there was a muted roaring, the sound of vehicles, and shouting.

Arnold reversed a short way down the lane, thinking hard. He found a lay-by near the stream, a place where people would be accustomed to pull in to relax and enjoy the meadows. He got out, locked his car, and hurried across the field, crossed the stream and began to climb the hill. He was breathing hard as he made his way through the trees that clumped on the hill, and was in a light sweat, but it was occasioned as much by a sense of foreboding as exertion.

At the top of the hill the trees thinned. Arnold thrust his way through bracken and alder until he had a view over the Common. He sucked in his breath.

Marcus Gullick and the other farmers had decided to take the law into their own hands.

Four Land Rovers were drawn up almost in military formation just beyond the narrow bridge that led on to the Common. Beyond them was a menacing row of three large tractors and two JCBs, towering, poised with their shovels raised high, advancing towards the gipsy encampment like some horrific dream of science-fiction violence. In front of the advancing line was a small group of men, waving their hands and yelling, while behind them, at the caravans, there was a mad scurrying of the elderly, women and children, grabbing up possessions from static vans, while three of the more modern vehicles had started up but managed to collide with each other in the confusion. A number of ponies were galloping around the field, excited and terrified by the noise and clamour, while a knot of men and women chased after them, trying desperately to harness them to drag some of the older vans out of the path of the roaring, menacing JCBs.

Marcus Gullick had clearly decided enough was enough and the insults at Rafferty Hall had pushed him over the edge. He had called together his supporters and they were going to clear Rafferty Common by force, by cutting a swathe through the vans, destroying them as they went.

It could still be bluff, Arnold thought frantically, as he began to run down the hill. But he doubted it, and certainly, if he had been one of the gipsies, he wouldn't have been inclined to call Gullick's bluff. The sight of the advancing monsters had terrified the women and children: Arnold could hear their screams as they scrambled frantically out of the path of the advance; the heavy machines trundled forward, inexorably, almost dinosaur-like in their slow advance, but the more menacing for all that.

Arnold now understood why the dumper truck had been drawn across the lane on the other side of the hill. Gullick had planned this attack with precision: he had gathered with his friends and their vehicles, and left one, the dumper truck, in the lane to prevent the police from interfering with his plan to move the gipsies off the Common. There was to be no more discussion, and no more compromise. When the police finally broke through, there would be no opportunity for argument because the location would have been destroyed. Arnold could guess what was going to happen: a few vehicles — those that lay in the way — would be destroyed. Then the shovels would drop, and great swathes of earth would be thrown up on the Common, closing it off, rendering it impossible for vans to stay, or return. Gullick would, no doubt, leave one method of egress, and then the lane would be cleared on the other side of the hill and the gipsies forced off the Common, retreating into the lane.

Those that would still be capable of movement.

And there was nothing the police could do about it.

Arnold was still not sure why he himself was running down the hill. The Senior Planning Officer must have had early warning of the attempt to destroy the gipsy encampment — perhaps a phone call from someone at the village had alerted County Hall, and by phoning Arnold the Senior Planning Officer knew he would have a colleague at the scene quickly, since Arnold's visit to the Methodist chapel left him close to the scene. But what exactly he expected Arnold to do when he got to the Common was another matter. Remonstrate with Gullick? There was enough remonstration already going on, with men and women screaming and waving their arms, but Gullick was undeterred. As he ran forward, Arnold could fancy that he made out the man himself, in one of the JCBs, determinedly bearing down on the first line of vans.

Arnold reached the Common. He slowed, gasping for breath, as a small knot of children, dark-eyed and panic-stricken, ran past him, then stopped and regrouped to stand in a huddle and stare back, chattering excitedly at the thought of the coming devastation. There were no farmers standing by: all were ensconced safely in the cabs of the JCBs or on the seats of the tractors, and there was much revving of engines and emission of blue exhaust, as though they themselves were somewhat nervous and wanted to make as much menacing noise as possible to prevent retaliation from the beleaguered gipsies.

There was no doubt in Arnold's mind that the gipsies would make some sort of stand. Most of them might run around and scream, but there would be some of like mind to Joe Connor: Arnold had seen them in Rafferty Hall.

He stood there, helplessly, behind the line of the slowly advancing machinery, and looked around in vain for police uniforms. The police could have climbed the hill as he had and avoided the road block, but either it had not occurred to them to do so, or else they were still concerned with removing the dumper truck first, and then advancing towards the Common.

Perhaps they were even unaware of the true seriousness of the situation on the Common itself.

Even as the thought crossed his mind, Arnold became aware that the position was turning more ugly up ahead. He heard shouting, and then above the roar of the engines, the sound of a shotgun, discharged above the trucks. He hurried to one side, where he could get a better view ahead, and at the first line of vans he could see a small group of men. They were standing in a line, as though challenging the JCBs to run them down. Three of the men held shotguns: all were trained on the one vehicle.

Arnold could guess who would be driving that vehicle; he could also guess that a raised shotgun would not stop Marcus Gullick now he had committed himself to this wildness.

In the centre of the group Arnold could make out Gipsy Joe Connor. His mouth was open; he was shouting something but Arnold could not make out the words. Their import was clear enough. If Gullick advanced any further, all three shotguns would be used in defence of the gipsy homes.

The tractors belched huge gusts of blue exhaust as they slowed, two of them slewing to one side to avoid collision with the JCBs. Arnold realized that uncertainty had set in with the JCB drivers: the shotguns had unnerved them. The line was wavering, breaking in formation as the leader himself — Marcus Gullick — paused, and the others ground to a halt. There was a long drawn-out few moments when all seemed in the balance with Joe Connor bawling wildly, waving his shotgun, yelling threats, and then the shovel of the leading JCB rose and dropped, positioning itself so that it offered protection for the driver in the cab, and the JCB began to lurch forward again, alone, but determined.

The other drivers hung back, yet uncommitted, but Marcus Gullick was driving his JCB directly at the group, calling their bluff as they were trying to call his. The nerve of the defending Romanies broke; they scattered, running, but Connor was made of sterner stuff. He was dancing to one side, trying to get a glimpse of Gullick in the cab, so he could let loose a shot at him. But Gullick dragged on the stick, lurching the shovel across the gipsy's line of vision, as he moved nearer the first line of vans. Connor tried to get closer, red in the face and still shouting obscenities, but the next moment there was the grinding, tearing scream of metal as the shovel struck the first of the vans, toppling it sideways and crushing its roof as the JCB advanced.

Horrified, Arnold stared as Connor leaped for safety, then, as the JCB ground past him, scrambled up on to the stricken van, clambering to get a foothold, elevating himself some six feet above the ground, till he was able to obtain a sight on the JCB driver. Then he levelled the shotgun, aiming directly into the cab of the JCB.

In all the roaring and gusting of exhausts, and shouting and screaming of women, there seemed to be a sudden silence, an eye in the storm where all was still, half frozen with expectation, a holding of the breath. It was a moment only, and yet it seemed a lifetime.

Then the explosion came, Connor dropped back from the van, losing his balance as the shotgun kicked under the discharge of both barrels, and the JCE lurched, swung sideways with a wild roaring sound, its shovel arm dropping to thunder on the roof of the second van in the line.

But the JCB had stopped its advance, and behind Arnold there was a new sound: the wailing of police sirens as the cars came lurching and bumping over the grass.

The cavalry's arrived, Arnold thought angrily, but too bloody late to save this situation.

* * *

The confusion seemed to become worse. As the line of tractors and JCBs was broken and began to scatter, some of the farmers now suddenly no longer wanted to be part of a situation where someone had been shot. The gipsies began to surge forward, yelling, complaining, aware that the arrival of the police meant that they had the opportunity to wreak their own form of violence on the men who had attacked them.

All was pandemonium. Arnold found himself pushed and shoved to one side by some burly uniformed policemen, and he became aware that the police themselves seemed uncertain about how to handle the situation. They had gone charging in with their cars towards the JCBs, then swung to a skidding halt in showers of grass and dirt. Some nine policemen had clambered out of the cars and three of them were trying to persuade the angry gesticulating gipsies to move back towards the encampment, while the others were yelling at the farmers, bawling orders at them which they appeared to misunderstand in their own panic to get away from the carnage of the two wrecked vans. Two policemen were clambering up on to the JCB, one hauling at Joe Connor, still flourishing the shotgun as he attempted to beat his way into the cab; the other was elbowing shattered glass from the cab window, and Arnold could see blood on the face of the man slumped in the cab. He was fairly certain it was Marcus Gullick, but he could not be sure whether the farmer had been hit by flying glass or by the discharge of the shotgun itself.

In unblocking the road beyond the hill the police had made the mistake of not sealing it again, and there was a steady stream of people from the village now coming on to the site to observe excitedly the aftermath of the violence of Rafferty Common. Another two police cars were surging through the mob, waving arms ineffectually attempting to dissuade them from adding to the confusion.

Arnold heard his own name called and turned, expecting someone from the Planning Office, but was surprised to see Cy Robinson. The young researcher was wild-eyed, his mouth open as he stared around him. 'Mr Landon! What on earth's happening here?'

Arnold was in no mood to waste time explaining. He was more than ever questioning what he himself was doing there, but thought he ought to try to help, make contact with the police, find out if he could be of any assistance. He turned away, tried to edge forward through the jostling crowd of Romanies and villagers, some of whom were beginning to argue violently among themselves, seemingly anxious to start their own flare-ups, perhaps with a view to settling old scores.

'Mr Landon! I heard that—'

It was Robinson again, at Arnold's elbow. Irritated, Arnold glared at him. 'What the hell are you doing here? This isn't an entertainment! People have been hurt—'

'No, I wanted to have a word with you, and I'd gone to your office when I heard there was trouble up here and they said you were coming so I drove up and—'

His young face was strained and anxious, and he was grabbing at Arnold's arm almost as though he wanted to protect him, but Arnold was angry, pulling away at the inconsequentiality of the man's words when trouble was still looming all about them.

The last police car to arrive was edging its way forward through the crowd, horn blaring. Arnold stared at it in surprise. Sticking his head out of the passenger window and shouting angrily was Detective Inspector Culpeper. He was waving a fist, shouting for people to get out of the way, and as the car moved past Arnold he caught a glimpse of a woman in the back seat, huddled beside a police constable.

It was the brown-legged gipsy girl Arnold had seen on his last visit to the encampment. Perhaps she had escaped from the site, he thought, gone to fetch help. Like others, it had come too late.

Up ahead, Connor had finally been dragged from the cab of the JCB, and a burly policeman had him by shoulder and elbow, pushing him back against one of the overturned vans. The shotgun had been dropped in the struggle, but it was not in the possession of the police: Arnold guessed one of the gipsy supporters would have spirited it away by now. The police might charge Gipsy Joe Connor with shooting, but they'd never find the gun — and who then knew what the law would say?

Marcus Gullick was being helped down from the cab of the JCB as the crowd was intermittently forced back by the small knot of angry policemen. Gullick was bleeding profusely, and his hands were clutching his face, but he could walk, and Arnold guessed his wounds were superficial. It would have probably been the flying glass: he'd be badly cut, but he'd survive. From the way the burly policeman was thrusting Connor against the side of the van, on the other hand, Arnold suspected the gipsy would be lucky to survive, intact, a night in the police cells while charges were brought.

Culpeper had got out of his car. He was shouting something at one of the uniformed policemen, and the two began to thrust their way through the thinning crowd towards Connor and the restraining policeman. Connor watched them coming sullenly; it was as though the fight had largely gone out of him now that he had fired at Gullick. He had meant to kill, in his anger; perhaps his failure to do so had drained him, and his head was down as his supporters, still yelling abuse and waving their fists, were pushed back. The police were few, but this was a job they had done before — crowd control.

Cy Robinson was tugging at Arnold's sleeve again. 'Mr Landon—'

'For God's sake,' Arnold snapped. 'Leave it for a moment, will you?'

Culpeper had reached Connor. He was saying something to him and the gipsy looked up. He seemed surprised, then alarmed, and he looked past Culpeper to the police car that had brought the detective inspector. He caught a glimpse of the girl in the back and suddenly the anger had returned to his face. He swung around, glared at Culpeper and shouted madly, and then surged forward with a wild heave of his body.

Taken by surprise, the policeman holding him was knocked off balance, struck his head against the side of the van and sank to his knees. Culpeper shouted, tried to grab at Connor but the gipsy sidestepped his charge, and then swung a fist at the detective inspector's head. Culpeper staggered sideways, blood streaming from his nose, and Connor was jumping forward, thrusting into the crowd of gipsies. There was a confused flurry, a whirling of bodies, and then the crowd thinned, scattering, not protecting Connor but moving away from him in panic.

Arnold saw him, isolated, and he saw the dull glint of the knife in his hand.

Everything seemed to stand still for one long second as the crowd waited, staring, and the police were equally frozen, immobile with shock. Then a constable stepped forward, and Connor made a wild slash with the knife, the blade whistling through the air. The policeman stopped, white-faced, there was a babble of shouting and screaming, the crowd thinned further and Connor lurched forward in a shambling run.

He was headed straight for Arnold. Arnold was unable to move. Gipsy Joe Connor was running, the knife waving wildly in front of him as he ran. His mouth was slack and loose, as though he was shouting, but there was no sound. His eyes were dark with the worst kind of fury, anger mingled with panic, and Arnold knew the man was desperate, almost crazed, but he was unable to move out of his path as the gipsy ran towards him through the screaming, scattering crowd.

When he was some ten yards from Arnold, Connor saw him, recognized him. The look in his eyes changed, his head came up, and he seemed to make a sudden decision. He was still stabbing at the air with his right hand, knife raised, but his left hand came up now as though he was reaching for Arnold, to grab him by the jacket. He thundered forward and at the last moment Arnold turned, to get out of his way. He lurched backwards, cannoning into Cy Robinson, and then he fell, rolling on the ground as Connor's feet stumbled over him.

The gipsy half fell, and now he was shouting wild, obscene words, but Arnold was on the ground and Connor was standing over him, ignoring him. Instead, he had grasped the sweater of Cy Robinson, was dragging the terrified young man towards him and the point of the knife was at Robinson's throat. Connor's voice came out as a thin-pitched scream.

'Stay clear of me, or I'll gut this bastard!' The noise levels dropped, the shouting died. There was a vague murmuring, like gathering swarms of bees, but then that died also and a vast silence swept in with even the car engines silent. Everyone within thirty yards of the tableau stood still, shocked, and Arnold himself, prostrate at Cy Robinson's feet, was unable to bring himself to move.

'I mean what I said,' Connor was yelling. 'I'll get this bastard if anyone makes a move to stop me!'

His voice was harsh and strained, and when Arnold looked up he could see that the man's eyes were pouched with panic, swollen with an unreasoning fear. Then Connor was stepping away, dragging the frightened researcher with him, and the crowd fell back, blue-uniformed policemen standing with arms held wide, as though trying to stop the rush of a mad dog.

A moment later Arnold realized where Connor was heading.

The Land Rovers had brought up the rear line of the attacking motorcade of the farmers. Two of them had already swung out of line and had careered across to the left when Connor had first appeared with the shotgun. Two remained, one askew and empty, the other idle, with a gaping driver staring down panic-stricken at the advancing gipsy. Then he too realized Connor's intention. His reaction was immediate. He opened the passenger door, clambered out and fled into the crowd. Next moment Connor was shoving the luckless researcher into the driver's seat and was clambering up beside him, the knife still menacing Robinson's throat. He snarled something at the young man, and the engine thundered into life. The driver, in his panic, had left the keys in the ignition.

'Now get the hell out of the way, or he's a dead man!'

The crowd was easily persuaded. Two policemen pounded after the Land Rover as it lurched forward over the grass, clutching at the rear of the vehicle, but the chase was hopeless as the Land Rover gathered speed, bouncing over the hummocky grass, crashing down the bank into the stream and roaring wildly as it climbed out on the other side.

He was not making for the road: Connor was astute enough to realize even in his panic that he could be blocked down there. He was taking to the fields, and the hill, and as his intentions became apparent the police cars also started up, sirens wailing agonizingly, wailing their distress as they slithered across the grass, lurching and bouncing, stalling as they hit the bank of the stream. Men were yelling and waving their arms, ordering vehicles out of the road, but the confusion was total. A Land Rover was commandeered but already it was too late: Connor's vehicle, with Cy Robinson at the wheel, trying to keep the knife from his throat, was climbing the hill towards the trees and a few moments later breasted the rise and was lost to sight.

Arnold saw Culpeper running back towards the car. The gipsy girl was struggling to get out of the police vehicle. She was screaming something and the constable with her was trying to hold on to her, arms grasped around her waist.

Culpeper was beside himself with rage. 'The idiots are letting the bastard get away,' he was shouting at the top of his voice. 'Radio to headquarters — the murdering bastard's on the loose!'

3

There were numerous arrests. Sporadic fighting continued at Rafferty Common over the next hour; extra police were drafted in, and the running battles at the fringe of the Common were ignored at first while the police attempted to maintain general order, but finally those young men who persisted in their vendettas were bundled into one or the other of the Black Marias that appeared on the scene.

A statement was taken from Arnold but he was allowed to leave Rafferty Common after a while. He was thankful to escape: this was an occasion where the Senior Planning Officer would have to take the blame for Arnold's involvement, so there was that to be grateful for, at least.

He went straight home. He felt mentally and physically bruised, and in some odd way responsible for the predicament in which Cy Robinson had been landed. An account of the fracas on Rafferty Common was given on the television news, but there was a certain coyness about the manner in which the announcer referred to the police hunt: clearly, not much information had yet been released to the media, and the one shot of police activity was of an angry-faced Culpeper hurrying into Morpeth police station, refusing to answer reporters' questions and bundling in with him a girl with a coat draped over her head. Arnold's guess was that it was the young gipsy girl, but he could not guess why her presence was still required at Morpeth, nor what she had to do with Connor's escape.

An hour or so after the telecast the phone rang. It was Elliott Brandling.

'Landon? Have you heard the news?'

Arnold hesitated. 'About Rafferty Common?'

'Well, yes, but really about Cy Robinson! He was grabbed at the battle, apparently, and forced to drive someone away. Have you heard nothing about it?'

'I . . . I was there, in fact,' Arnold said lamely.

There was a short silence. Arnold could hear Elliott Brandling breathing; it had an irregular sound. Brandling was clearly moved by the thought of his young researcher in danger. 'What exactly happened up there, Landon?'

After an initial hesitation, Arnold explained. There seemed little point in not doing so. Brandling was clearly concerned, and in a little while, no doubt, the newspapers, radio and television would have all the details anyway.

'And the police have no idea where he's taken Cy?'

'I think Connor just grabbed him as a hostage, and set out to get away as quickly as possible. He could have gone anywhere. My guess is he'll have headed inland, maybe into the forested areas, until he's had time to cool down and think about what he does next. It seems a bit extreme, acting like that. I'm sure Gullick's injuries won't turn out to be all that serious . . . though the damage and violence at Rafferty Common was pretty bad. And the shotgun . . . But still, it was Gullick and his friends who caused the flash point.'

'But what the hell was Cy doing up there anyway?' Brandling asked, in an irritated tone.

'I don't know. I gather he'd gone to my office to see me about something. I've no idea what. Then he heard, when the news came in about trouble at the gipsy site, that I'd be up there. He must have thought he'd like to see the fun. Only it wasn't fun. And certainly not now.'

There was a short silence. Brandling sounded strained. 'Do you think he'll come to any harm?'

'I wouldn't think so,' Arnold replied reassuringly. 'He'll have the sense to do as he's told. My guess is, given the chance to calm down, Connor will turn him out, to make good his own escape. Even that is a pretty futile thing to do. I can't imagine what's driving Connor. Unless . . .'

'Yes?'

A thought had struck Arnold. It was not one he wanted to discuss over the phone with Brandling. 'Nothing. Anyway, if I hear anything I'll get in touch. You'll do the same?'

'I will. As soon as I hear anything,' Brandling replied, and rang off.

Neither radio nor television had any further news to impart that evening but the following morning the newspapers were carrying an item which confirmed Arnold's own suspicion.

Gipsy Joe Connor was being hunted not merely for the part he had played in the battle of Rafferty Common. He was being sought for questioning in connection with the murder of the old gipsy whose body Arnold had found in St Michael's Church, Kentside.

But for the next three days, of the whereabouts of Cy Robinson or Gipsy Joe Connor there was no news. It was as though they had vanished into the air of the Northumberland hills.

* * *

Arnold was called in to the station at Morpeth on the third day. He was a little surprised that it had taken them so long to get around to interviewing him. The discussion was not a long one, nevertheless. It was Culpeper again, looking tired and strained.

'All right, Landon, it's simple enough. We're trying to fill in some of the background to all this. We understand Robinson came to see you at Morpeth, before he chased up to Rafferty Common.'

'That's right.'

'Did he come to see you about the gipsies?'

'I don't know.'

'Or about Connor in particular?'

'I really don't know. He tried to speak to me at Rafferty Common but there wasn't the chance in the confusion . . . And then everything happened so quickly.'

'But why did Connor grab Robinson, in particular?' Culpeper demanded.

'I . . . I think it was an accident . . . I think he came running forward, recognized me . . . and decided to grab me as a hostage. But I fell . . .'

Culpeper was frowning. 'Why you?' Arnold shrugged. 'I think it was a spur-of-the-moment decision. We had had words, before. Maybe he saw me, thought about how the whole question of planning had in a way brought about this battle on the Common, and decided to grab me. I thought afterwards he was over-reacting but . . . I understand you want him for other offences.'

Culpeper ground his teeth. 'He's a murderous bastard. The shotgun at Rafferty Hall, we've heard about that. Then the Common. And his running confirms it. I went up there to bring him in for questioning. That old gipsy that was killed: he was grandfather to one of the young girls at the encampment. He'd warned Connor off her several times. I think he warned him once too often. That's who stuck the knife in the old Romany — Gipsy Joe Connor.'

And now he'd been holding a knife at the throat of Cy Robinson for the last three days, Arnold thought miserably.

Culpeper asked him to write out a statement and Arnold did so. Culpeper read it through and was asking him to sign it when there was a tap on the door and a police constable looked in.

'A word, sir?'

Arnold was left alone in the interview room for twenty minutes. He was getting rather impatient by the time Culpeper returned. Any thought of remonstration died on his lips, however, when he saw the expression on Culpeper's face.

'We've just had some news,' Culpeper said slowly.

'Of Connor?'

Culpeper shook his head. 'No, of Cyril Robinson.'

Arnold waited. Culpeper sat down and stared hard at Arnold. There was an odd hardness in the autumn-brown eyes, a confusion stained with anger. 'I don't think you've told us all you know, Mr Landon.'

'I don't understand,' Arnold faltered. 'Just what the hell is going on?' Culpeper snarled, a rasping tone entering his voice. 'Detective Inspector—'

'We've just been informed that Cy Robinson has been found. Or rather . . . his body's been found.'

Arnold went cold. 'He's dead?'

'Knifed. But that's not all.' Culpeper leaned forward. 'What the hell *is* going on, Landon?'

'I've no idea what you're getting at—'

'They found the body with a knife wound in the chest at what seems to be one of your haunts, Landon,' Culpeper said coldly. 'In the churchyard at St Michael's, Kentside.'

CHAPTER SIX

1

Elliott Brandling had been drinking.

Arnold was well aware of the man's predilections and capacities but it was clear that Cy Robinson's murder had badly affected him. As soon as he had left Morpeth Arnold, unable to satisfy Detective Inspector Culpeper by giving him the answers he seemed convinced Arnold could provide, had rung Brandling. He was not at the University, and when Arnold rang the Professor's home there was no answer.

Concerned, Arnold had rung several times, with no response. He recalled how Ben Gibson had described the man as lonely and obsessive; he could remember the impression he had gained from Brandling, how the man regarded Cy Robinson as a son. Their closeness was obvious; if Brandling found out that Robinson was dead the effect could be devastating. Arnold felt it incumbent upon himself to break the news — but he was unable to raise the man on the phone. As the late afternoon lengthened into early evening he decided he could wait no longer: he drove to Durham, and found the Professor sitting in the darkening garden, a half-empty bottle of vodka by his side. Arnold suspected, from Brandling's demeanour, that it was not the first bottle that had been attacked.

He sat down beside him and said quietly, 'When did you hear?'

Brandling turned a tired face towards Arnold. His eyes were hooded, as though he had been overcome by a great weariness; his mouth was slack, disappointment lining his features, and his skin had a greyish hue. He looked ten years older, and his elegance had deserted him. After a long silence, he replied, 'This afternoon. Someone phoned this afternoon, at the University. And then it was on the news, on the radio.'

Arnold felt the need, suddenly, for a drink himself. Brandling must have divined the thought for he waved a negligent hand towards the house. 'There's a glass inside. Help yourself.'

Arnold returned with a glass of whisky. He sat down beside the Professor. 'Are you all right?' he asked inanely, after a short silence.

Brandling nodded vaguely, and inspected his drink. He shook his head then, in a slow, indeterminate movement. 'He had a brilliant future ahead of him, you know. Such a waste.'

There was nothing Arnold could think of to say. At last, he offered his condolences, awkwardly, and with diffidence.

'When did *you* hear?' Brandling queried, staring at the pale liquid in his glass.

'Morpeth police told me.'

'Do they have any idea who did it?'

Arnold stared at him, surprised. 'They . . . well, they're still looking for Connor.'

'The gipsy? Dammit, yes, the gipsy, I must be losing my senses.' Brandling put his head back and stared at the louring sky. 'But why would the man kill Cy?'

'I don't know. Panicked, maybe.' Arnold hesitated. 'He's on the run. Maybe he was afraid Cy would give him away. Maybe there was a fight.'

'That doesn't explain the churchyard,' Brandling said slowly, and hiccupped. 'And why did the bastard gipsy run anyway?'

'The police wanted to question him over the murder of the old Romany. Apparently, there was bad blood between the pair of them — something to do with Connor's seduction of the old man's granddaughter.'

Elliott Brandling began to laugh. It was an odd sound in the quiet garden; lacking humour, it seemed almost an echo of dry autumn leaves, whispering in the walled recesses of the old house. 'So what's with this gipsy, then, that he keeps dumping bodies in St Michael's Church?'

'That's something the police were questioning me about,' Arnold said.

'You? What the hell can you tell them?' Brandling asked sharply.

'Nothing. But they didn't like me saying so. But the only theory they — and I — can come up with is that having killed the old man and successfully dumped him without being seen in the churchyard, Gipsy Joe Connor simply repeated himself . . . apparently, as many murderers do.'

Elliott Brandling shook his head. 'I can't go along with that.'

'What other solution can there be?'

Brandling was silent for a while. He leaned forward and poured himself another vodka. Arnold moved to stop him, but then kept his counsel. It was perhaps better that the man drank himself into oblivion on this occasion. Tomorrow would come soon enough . . . and with it the realization that his young protégé was truly dead, unable to fulfil his early promise. And Elliott Brandling would have to face a loneliness made more hollow by the echoes of a relationship that was now ended.

The two men sat quietly in the garden as the skies darkened. They said nothing, and Arnold finished his drink, but made no attempt to get another as Brandling, seemingly forgetful of his presence, sat on, drinking steadily into the twilight.

It was nine o'clock, and the moon had risen, fat and creamy and full, seeming to glow in the night sky, when Elliott

Brandling suddenly raised his head to stare at it. After a short silence, he said, 'They're wrong.'

'Wrong?'

'The police.'

'I don't understand.'

'There's another solution. I'm not convinced about this man Connor. He could have let Cy go; he could have released him. And maybe Connor didn't kill the old gipsy either. The fact that Connor and the old man had a quarrel could be irrelevant. What about Andrea?'

'His girlfriend? You're surely not suggesting—'

'Not that Andrea Sutcliffe would want Cy dead. But even then . . .' Brandling shook his head irritably. 'No, it's not that either. We . . . they're just ignoring the real key to it all.'

'What key?'

'St Michael's Church.'

Arnold was silent, but the hairs on the back of his neck began to rise as he realized this was a thought that had been plaguing him ever since the questioning by Culpeper: the illogicality of St Michael's Church in the plans and actions of a man seeking to evade justice. Of course, Culpeper had suggested Connor could have gone back there to dump Robinson's body on the supposition that it would be the last place the police would look — and maybe the gipsy was now still hiding out somewhere in that vicinity. But the argument had not rung true in Culpeper's tones, and they had not rung true in Arnold's mind.

'St Michael's Church . . .' he repeated slowly.

'The cult of the Raging Wolf.'

'Brandling—'

'Hear me out,' the Professor said in a tone that was almost dreamlike. 'If we ignore the facts relating to Rafferty Common, and Connor's trouble with the old man, isn't there another picture we could project? The cult exists . . . I'm sure of it. It uses — or has used — St Michael's Church. So let's think about that. You found that thing under the rose hedge—'

'It was just a dog—'

'It was a ritual sacrifice. Perhaps the first in a while . . . perhaps the very first. But a bloodlust had begun with that animal. Maybe there were others. Maybe even human beings. Who knows? The cult of de Vieux Pont was always based on bloodlust.'

'Yes, but—'

'So what if the Master, one night, was seeking something more than was usual? What if he wanted human blood?' Brandling's head was thrown back, staring at the cold, expressionless face of the moon. 'What if he came across an old man, a gipsy, wandering late at night, walking back from the pub, perhaps, or even, for that matter, seeking his granddaughter, wanting to know who she was with?'

Arnold shook his head. 'There's no evidence—'

'What if he struck the old man down, brought him to the church, and conducted the blood ritual with his group? And what if that lust then becomes so exciting, so insatiable, that things are not the same unless there is another killing?'

'You can't be serious, Brandling!'

'Am I not?' Brandling laughed shortly. 'Such a scenario is no wilder than that of the police. If Connor did release Cy . . . did Culpeper suggest anyone had rung in?'

'No, but—'

'What if Cy went to the wrong people for help?' Brandling demanded. 'What if they stumbled upon him, maybe bleeding and unconscious from an attack by Connor? There are several possibilities. The one incontrovertible fact is that his body was found in St Michael's Church. And it's there that the cult of the Raging Wolf is practised!'

'But probably no more,' Arnold said slowly, as he became intoxicated by the seeping logic of the argument and the whisky.

'No more?' Brandling's lean features were suddenly turned in his direction. 'What do you mean by that?'

'You told me Zeke Santana approached you to be a member of the cult.'

'That's so.'

'Santana is a follower of Edward Chaunter and his Vicars of Jehovah. They've bought a disused Methodist chapel; they're gutting it, refurbishing it, for their own purposes.'

Brandling was quiet, his breathing steady, but there was a sudden tension in his body now that was communicated to Arnold.

'So?' Brandling asked, almost menacingly.

'I was at the chapel. I saw Santana. He had an accident with his car . . . hit the wall. There was a rug on the back seat, and it got disturbed. I saw what was under the rug.'

'What?' Brandling almost snarled the sound.

'It was a ceremonial sword of some kind.'

'A ritual sword,' Brandling whispered. 'A sword to deliver the kiss of death.'

He inspected the glass in his hand, held it up against the light of the moon and then drained it. He leaned over and picked up the bottle, and for a moment Arnold thought he was about to drink what remained. Instead he turned it upside down and watched it drain, slurping into the grass at his feet. He rose, unsteadily, and looked at Arnold.

'I think it is time we went to take a look at this chapel, together.'

* * *

The sky was now bright, with high scudding clouds chasing across the face of the moon. The two men drove in separate cars. Arnold had argued for several minutes with Brandling about the wisdom of the Professor's driving after drinking so much, but Brandling had been insistent that he was perfectly capable of handling the car. Nor, indeed, did he seem to have damaged his faculties by the drinking: there was no slur to his speech, his hands and walk were steady, and he was quietly insistent in his argument with Arnold.

Whatever depression might have been affecting him on Arnold's arrival was also now dissipated. It was as though the prospect of doing something positive in relation to the death of his young friend had given him a surge of adrenalin which brightened his eye and straightened his back. There was a new determination about his bearing; the confidence that had seemed to have deserted him earlier had now returned.

Arnold led the way.

They headed north on the motorway, cruised over the Tyne Bridge and past the city centre, noisy and glittering to their left, and drove on into the quietness of the Northumberland countryside, leaving the main roads and climbing the winding lanes leading west of Morpeth towards Denton Gap. Elliott Brandling kept pace with Arnold, a regulation fifty yards behind, his headlights seeming to lift and fall, as though flashing signals of reassurance to Arnold as the road wound and dipped and lifted over the rising hills.

There was surprisingly little traffic about, and they made good time even after they left the main roads. The hills ahead were silver-rimmed under the bright moon and as they got closer to Denton Gap Arnold felt a vague excitement beginning to shiver in his bones and his body began to ache nervously, anticipating unknown and indescribable events lying ahead of them.

The village itself was quiet; the evening was not over for some, still drinking in the village pub, and there was a scattering of vehicles in the car park but there was no one in the main street itself, and Arnold drove up to the village grocery store and parked outside. As he killed his lights Elliott Brandling pulled in behind him.

'The chapel is about three hundred yards ahead,' Arnold said quietly, as Brandling locked his car. 'If we park here, we can walk up to the chapel and remain unobserved.'

'If anyone is looking out,' Brandling said almost savagely. 'Maybe they'll be too high from their recent vicious rituals to even think about security.'

Arnold stared at him. He was tall in the moonlight, and his cheeks were hollowed, dark circles around his eyes seeming to emphasize features that had become cadaverous with the pain of the last few hours. There was something in his words that disturbed Arnold: Brandling seemed to be making judgements ahead of the facts. What was it Cy Robinson had said about him, about the Professor's research methods? Capable of making a quantum leap . . . the kind of leap that other researchers doubted in terms of validity, the kind of leap that had brought criticism within his own university. Such thinking was out of place here, when the night was bright with moonlight, and a cool chill breeze blew, and the village was silent and dark.

Arnold shivered inexplicably. He had the kind of sudden premonition that he despised: events could not be foretold or anticipated in such a way, it was merely a physical response to one's surroundings. And yet there had been that feeling of evil in the churchyard of St Michael's at Kentside . . .

'Down this way,' he said quietly, and Elliott Brandling fell into step beside him as they walked down the street, their shoes making little sound on the pavement, and their shadows splitting and dividing under the combined effect of the sharp moonlight and the vague street lamps above their heads.

They came to the end of the street and turned to make their way past the turning leading down to the chapel itself. The building loomed up ahead of them; there were no lights to be seen in the chapel itself, but Arnold could make out a dark mass parked in the driveway, where he had earlier seen the builders' rubble. As they moved quietly forward Arnold realized it was a lorry, left there overnight, but seemingly having nothing to do with the builders. The sign along its side proclaimed it was used for drinks haulage.

'It looks as though there'll be no representatives of the Vicars of Jehovah here tonight,' Arnold said.

'Why do you say that?'

'A lorry-driver isn't likely to leave his vehicle parked like this, casually, unless he's aware the building is rarely used at night. And if he isn't parked casually, but with permission, the cult is hardly likely to be doing anything odd, when people might be around.'

Brandling grunted, unconvinced.

They moved towards the porch. Brandling stepped up to the door and tried it gently, but it was locked. Arnold stood back, surveying the building overall, and could see that no external work was being undertaken, as Chaunter had said. He walked along the driveway, passed the lorry and stood in the area at the rear of the property. Something rustled in the deep grass at the far end, near the wall, and there was a fluttering noise as though he had disturbed some large bird. Next moment he caught a glimpse of a barn owl, heavy in flight, crossing silently from the lime tree above the wall, disturbed in its night hunting by their arrival.

Brandling was standing just behind him.

Arnold's nerves jumped at the realization of the man's presence; he had not heard him arrive.

'Anything to be seen?' Brandling queried.

'Nothing,' Arnold replied. But then, what had they been expecting? He glanced at Brandling uncertainly; this visit had been the Professor's idea, kindled by a desire to seek out those whom he believed had killed Cy Robinson, but Arnold felt unable to raise any great enthusiasm for the project. Even if Brandling was right, and the Vicars of Jehovah were one and the same with the cult of de Vieux Pont, the connection with Cy's murder had not been made, and he could not see what was to be gained by standing in the moonlight, at the back of the rubble-strewn yard of the chapel in Denton Gap.

'Hush! Listen!'

Arnold caught his breath involuntarily at the urgency in Brandling's tones. He stood stock-still, controlling his breathing, listening for the sounds that must have caught Brandling's attention. But there was nothing apart from the soft soughing of the breeze in the long grass, distant vague sounds of humanity from the pub across the village and occasional indeterminate rustling, the nocturnal passage of life in the undergrowth.

'Did you hear nothing?'

'No,' Arnold admitted.

'But you can feel it, can't you, you can feel it, just like the other place?' Brandling hissed.

The man's arm touched Arnold's; it seemed to be trembling. Arnold remained still, and his mind drifted back to the church at St Michael's, when his own dark insecurities had surfaced and he had felt the touch of evil and corruption in the churchyard. Brandling was trembling, and the breeze was cool on their faces but Arnold's heart was not racing the way it had done at St Michael's, and he could hear only the natural sounds of the night, could feel no overhanging menace.

'Can't you feel it?' Brandling insisted, and he gripped Arnold's elbow. The fingers were fierce, digging into Arnold's arm, and Arnold began to wonder whether alcohol had begun to affect Brandling's nerves, causing him to imagine things that Arnold himself was not experiencing.

The fingers relaxed, abruptly. A car was driving slowly down the street, seeming to pause at the turning to the chapel, idling, as though the driver was looking towards the building, checking. Then it moved slowly on, and drove into the main street. As the sound of its engine faded Brandling expelled his breath in a ragged sound, as though he had been holding it expectantly, watching, expecting one of the cult to emerge from the darkness.

'I think we'd better go home,' Arnold said shortly.

Brandling stared at him. The Professor's face was pale in the moonlight, but Arnold could not see his eyes. 'You think there is nothing here?' Brandling asked in a hoarse voice.

'There's no one here,' Arnold replied carefully.

'But I feel His presence,' Brandling insisted. 'The Evil One, the Master . . . he may not be here in body, but the corruption of his soul has left its mark here. Landon, I know these people . . . they approached me, remember. They've used the church at Kentside, and they've left their horror there, but now they need a new site, and it's here, I feel it, I know that they'll move their blood worship here, inside, where they will be unseen . . .'

'Come on. I think we should go now,' Arnold said, after a short silence.

Brandling made no reply. He was clearly reluctant to leave and he stood staring about him as though attempting to search out and identify the evil he had described. Arnold hesitated, touched his arm gently, and stepped away, back towards the driveway. After a moment Elliott Brandling followed him, stumbling over the rough ground in the darkness, disappointed, it seemed, that Arnold had failed to experience the same emotions that he had, here in the chapel grounds.

They walked back down the quiet street.

There seemed to be nothing they could say to each other. They reached the cars and stood there for several seconds; up the main street a car engine coughed into life, headlights flicked up, illuminating them, and a car drove slowly past. Arnold could not make out the driver's face in the dim interior of the car.

'Are you going to be all right?' Arnold asked.

'Driving back?' Brandling responded, and gave a short laugh. 'Driving's no problem. Thinking . . . that's another matter. How do you control the churning inside your skull, Landon?'

Arnold made no answer. After a short while Brandling unlocked the car door and got in. He wound down his window as though wishing to speak to Arnold but he made no remark. He reversed the car, turned in the road, and did not look back to Arnold as he drove away, back towards Durham. Arnold felt sorry for him. The cottage on the banks of the Wear would be a lonely place, holding only thoughts for company.

He got into his own car, and headed for home. Some stragglers were emerging from the pub, getting into their cars, and a small exodus took place as he was driving past. One or two of the cars behind him were eager to overtake so he drove slowly, encouraging them. Eventually, he had the winding lanes to himself with the exception of the odd car behind him, headlights appearing and disappearing in his wing mirror.

He took the Morpeth turning and as the road widened he was no longer virtually alone, with home-goers from local pubs and from Newcastle cinemas making their way north.

He was not certain he was looking forward to a lonely night at his bungalow himself, but he was tired, emotionally drained, and upset at the thought of the murder of Cy Robinson. A nightcap, perhaps, and then he would sleep.

When he reached the lane leading towards his own home he saw a strange car parked a little way down, against the hedge, but paid little attention to it. In the lane there were several bungalows, with their own parking areas, but the lane itself was clear. He pulled into his driveway and killed the engine. As he did so he thought he heard the sound of a car door slamming, further down the lane.

Arnold walked to the doorway, selecting the key that would open his front door. He inserted the key, and heard footsteps half running in the dark lane. He paused, looked back, and his nerve ends began to tingle. Whatever he had not felt in the chapel yard he was beginning to feel now. He was at his own home, there could be no real danger, but the eerie sound of footsteps running in the lane made the hairs rise on the back of his neck and his skin tingle with cold anticipation.

He had left no lights on inside the bungalow. He opened the door, stepped inside, fumbled for the switch and as light flooded the porch and front garden he turned, realizing the footsteps had turned into his own driveway. He had his hand on the door, ready to slam it shut when he saw who it was running into his drive, scrambling past his car parked there. It was a young woman, blonde hair shining in the light from his hall. Her face was ashen, her eyes wide and frightened. And she was calling his name.

* * *

It was obvious she needed a drink, and before he tried to make sense of her hysterical outpourings he needed to calm her down. She was distraught and dishevelled; she wore no make-up and her hair was uncombed, her eyes red-rimmed and swollen. But he knew who she was, almost instinctively — he had seen her briefly picking up Cy Robinson, but it was her appearance here in this condition that made him realize immediately who she was.

'You're Andrea Sutcliffe.'

'Mr Landon. I must speak to you. I have to tell you—'

He ushered her inside, slammed the door behind them, made her sit down in the sitting-room and went to pour her a drink. He gave it to her and she took a long draught immediately. He sat down opposite her, feeling immensely sorry for her, knowing what she must be going through.

'You've . . . you've heard about Cy,' she muttered, and the tears were in her eyes again.

'I've heard. I'm desperately sorry.'

She stared at him as though she had barely heard him, then she cocked her head on one side, in an oddly childish gesture, as though she were questioning his good faith, or listening for something.

'I saw him . . . the morning before he went looking for you. It was I who told him he ought to talk to you . . . he seemed to think you were a . . . sympathetic person, someone he could discuss things with.'

Arnold frowned, puzzled. 'Well, that's . . . that's fine, but what did he want to talk to me about?'

'He was worried . . .' She hesitated again, then gave a jerk as though she was startled, and she looked around her, eyes wide and scared. 'You . . . you know I'm married . . . separated?'

'I have been told,' Arnold admitted. 'But I don't see that it was any of my business or—'

'No. He was worried . . . he needed to tell you, try to get your help because it was something he couldn't deal with himself, it would raise too many problems, too many hurts—'

The doorbell rang, startling them both.

Andrea Sutcliffe jerked again, like a marionette, and in a jagged voice said, 'Put out the lights!'

‘Please.’ Arnold stretched out a hand, touched her arm. ‘It’s all right.’ It was absurd to douse the lights simply because someone had rung the doorbell. The woman was frightened and upset by her lover’s death, but that was no reason for over-reaction on Arnold’s part. He patted her on the arm. ‘One moment,’ he said.

She tried to detain him, grabbing at his hand. ‘Please, I’m scared. Don’t answer the door. When I heard Cy had been taken away at knife-point at the Common I didn’t know what to think, or do, because he said it was so important, that it was so central to his life . . . please, I’m scared, and now that Cy’s dead . . .’

In spite of himself Arnold felt a flash of irritation. The woman was almost hysterical, little of what she said made sense, he had already been subjected to the over-emotional reactions of Elliott Brandling and the useless drive out to the Methodist chapel and he was in no mood to be influenced by this outburst of panic. He detached himself from her grasp. ‘I’ll be back in a moment, Mrs Sutcliffe.’

He walked to the door. The bell rang again, insistently. Through the glass panel in the upper part of the door he could make out the vague shape of a man’s head. He reached out, slipped the catch, and the next moment the door exploded in on him, knocking him back against the wall.

Arnold stumbled, cannoned backwards, losing his balance and falling to the ground, sending the telephone table crashing over.

He was aware of a scream from the sitting-room, Andrea Sutcliffe panicked by the noise, but he was trying to rise to his feet as the door yawned on its hinges from the powerful kick that had smashed it open in his face. He was rising, crouching, when the dark form of the assailant came thrusting in. A shoe took him in the lower stomach, and Arnold doubled over, retching, as flashes of light illuminated the blackness that was already engulfing his brain. He took a blow behind the left ear, and then he heard the dull sound, rhythmic, painful, that signified the kicks delivered to his ribs.

He lost consciousness briefly, to return in a little while to hear more thudding, throbbing sounds, and a woman's voice screaming.

Then he subsided once more into a velvet encompassing darkness.

CHAPTER SEVEN

1

Fully dressed, Arnold felt rather better, and at least the headaches were gone even if he still remained very much aware of his bruises. He was still careful about his breathing, although the sharp stabbing pains from his cracked ribs would ease, the hospital doctors had assured him, and he would shortly be able to remove the strapping from around his chest.

The morning was bright and sunny. He had been in the General Hospital for three days now, under observation, and Ben Gibson had visited him a couple of times, as well as Ned Keeton and one or two others from the Morpeth office. Now Arnold was due for discharge — although he had been advised he should not start work for another week — and Ben Gibson had arranged to pick him up and take him home to the bungalow.

It was Ben who had also seen to the repairs necessary to the bungalow: a new front door and some redecoration in the hall. Arnold frowned. He could still remember very little about the attack, after those first few horrifying seconds. As he sat in his chair near the window and enjoyed the warmth of the sunshine he could have imagined it had all been a horrible dream, except for the sharp pains in his chest, and the discolouration of the bruises on his face and body.

'You could have been killed,' the doctor had said. 'If the kicks had splintered your ribcage and pierced a lung—'

'What about Andrea Sutcliffe?' Arnold had asked.

The doctor's young features were noncommittal. 'She's still in a coma. She was badly hurt . . .'

Arnold heard the door open behind him. He turned his head and saw the young nurse standing there, smiling at him. 'Mr Landon . . . there's someone to see you.'

It would be Ben Gibson. Arnold nodded, and began to rise carefully from his chair as the nurse stepped aside to make way for the man entering the room. He sank back again as he realized it was not the antiquarian bookseller. It was Detective Inspector Culpeper.

The policeman came into the room as though he were treading on eggs. He was almost on tiptoe, surprisingly affected by the atmosphere of the hospital, far different from the bustle of the Morpeth police station. He seemed ill at ease, diffident, and almost apologetic. He summoned up a vague smile as he advanced towards Arnold. 'Mr Landon. How are you?'

'I think the phrase is . . . as well as can be expected. I'm going home today.'

'So I understand.'

'Ben Gibson is coming to fetch me.'

'I know. He's along the corridor. We arrived more or less together. I asked him to wait.'

'Why?'

Culpeper glanced uneasily around the room and then with a self-conscious air perched himself on the edge of the bed. He frowned at Arnold and pursed his lips. 'I did have a . . . conversation with you, couple of days ago.'

'I'm sorry I couldn't be very helpful,' Arnold apologized.

'Well, you were in some pain . . . and a bit hazy. I just wonder now whether there's anything more you can remember.'

Arnold shook his head. 'I don't think so. I remember you coming, of course. But I think I told you all I could remember then. It was all so quick, so confusing. And once

I'd been knocked down, and he started kicking me—' Arnold shrugged — 'it all got a bit . . . dark.'

'You can't offer a description of the man?' Arnold shook his head again.

Culpeper was silent for a short while, staring thoughtfully at Arnold's bruised face. 'Mrs Sutcliffe's still in a coma. She took a bad beating. The suspicion is that the assailant was really after her, rather than you. He certainly made a thorough job over her . . . but he didn't kill her. Got close to it, mind, but . . .' Culpeper glowered at Arnold, and chewed at his lip. 'What the hell is all this about, Landon?'

'What do you mean?' Arnold asked in surprise at Culpeper's tone.

'I got a feeling about this,' Culpeper announced. 'Suddenly I've got a minor crime wave on my hands. All right, we're used to having the dogs out when the pubs close on a Saturday night, and there's always the odd knifing or traffic accident to keep us lively, but this is different. I got two murders, a riot and now a criminal assault and battery with GBH to deal with. And somehow or other you seem to be floating around at the edges of all of them.'

The stabbing pain in his chest could hardly justify, in Arnold's view, the argument that he had been floating at the edge of the situation, but he said nothing.

After a few moments, Culpeper went on. 'Let's take these things one by one. You just happen to be in the vicinity of the Common when the riot takes place—'

'It's my job,' Arnold protested. 'The Senior Planning Officer asked me to go up there!'

'An acquaintance of yours then gets abducted and subsequently murdered, presumably by this wild gipsy—'

'Cy Robinson was hardly even an acquaintance, just someone whom I'd come across as a research assistant for Professor Brandling at—'

'But you said to us you got the impression he was up there at Rafferty Common to see you. He'd first called at your office, and then came running up to the gipsy encampment.'

'Even so—'

'And then there's the dead gipsy. You just happen to find him, and by way of explanation you come up with some ridiculous story about Satanism, which sounds very much to me like some red herring you've been cooking, and you give me some guff about the presence of evil . . .'

Arnold found his attention wandering. Did red herrings actually get cooked? Desperately he tried to concentrate. 'All I told you then, Detective Inspector, was what I felt . . . experienced . . .'

'But what's it all about, Landon? And how come it all seems to circle around you?'

Arnold stared at the policeman foolishly. He could hardly credit what he was hearing. He was being given the impression that Culpeper was in some way almost holding Arnold responsible for these events. 'You can't think that I—'

'I won't tell you what I think,' Culpeper said heavily. 'But I will tell you what I've got. I've got you and Mrs Sutcliffe knocked about. I've got one dead old man and one dead young man. The old gipsy, well, we can trace some of his movements on the night he died. Not unusually, he'd been to a pub not far from Rafferty Common. He was seen to leave unsteadily, walk down the road, singing. Then he disappeared. We think he was clubbed to death, taken to the churchyard where you found him, and savaged with a knife.'

'The evil I spoke of—'

'Never mind that for a moment,' Culpeper interrupted. 'Young Robinson gets grabbed as a hostage by Gipsy Joe Connor, and later turns up very dead, when he's no longer of any use to Connor. It's likely Connor used him until he found a safe place — then was afraid Robinson could lead us to him. Or maybe the young man tried to put up a fight, or escape. Connor knifed him and dumped him in the churchyard at Kentside. But again, what's with this churchyard?'

'I've already tried to explain—'

'But then what happens? You yourself get clobbered . . . and after you'd been chasing after this damned cult you're fixated upon.'

'I'm not—'

'We've spoken to Professor Brandling. He tells me you were both sussing out the Methodist chapel earlier, before you went home. And he tells me he had the impression someone was driving around in the village, maybe watching the pair of you.'

'That could be true,' Arnold admitted. 'There was a car—'

'Which makes me ask, against my better inclinations,' Culpeper said heavily, 'if you'll be prepared to help me.'

'How?'

Culpeper sighed audibly. 'Mr Gibson is waiting to take you home. But he's agreed to come to Morpeth police station first, and drive you home from there, if you agree to cooperate.'

'What do you want me to do?'

'I want you to take a look at a few people in a line-up, to see if you can identify any of them as your attacker when you and Andrea Sutcliffe were beaten in your bungalow.'

* * *

There had seemed little point in refusing. After Arnold's initial protestations that he could remember nothing of his attacker, Culpeper had stressed that although he might well have seen nothing, there was the possibility that something might happen at the line-up which would make him recall details that would be of assistance in the police investigations.

'After all,' Culpeper had added, 'we're sort of in limbo at the moment. We got Gullick on ice after the riot at Rafferty Common: he spent a couple of nights in jail, and then we released him on bail pending the drawing up of charges of criminal assault and malicious damage. We know where he is, and I don't conceive he's going to do a runner. But

Connor, we still haven't seen hide nor hair of him. There's a lead we're following at the moment in North Yorkshire, but these damn Romanies look after their own and, although we're ploughing through all the camps up here, in the north it's a slow business. We'll get him, but it'll possibly be later rather than sooner. And then there's Sutcliffe.'

'Andrea's husband?'

'You know him?' Culpeper asked.

'No. Although . . .'

'Go on.'

'No, it's nothing,' Arnold insisted. Culpeper stared at him for a moment, and then looked out of the car window as they made their way through the main street in Morpeth. They were nearing police headquarters, and in a few moments they would be turning into the police car park.

'What about Sutcliffe?' Arnold asked as the car came to a stop.

Culpeper's mouth twisted unpleasantly. 'Suddenly, no one wants to talk to the police. He's not available. Looks like *he's* done a runner, too.'

Culpeper unlocked the car door and clambered out heavily. After a moment's hesitation Arnold did likewise, wincing as he felt a stab of pain in his ribcage while twisting his way out of the car. He glanced back: another vehicle was nosing its way into the car park.

The faithful Ben Gibson, following them, and ready to take Arnold home to peace and quiet once this nonsense of the identity parade was over. Arnold looked at Culpeper's back, as the policeman walked ahead of him. 'This man Sutcliffe. You think he might have attacked me and Andrea?'

'Violence,' Culpeper suggested cynically, as he glanced back over his shoulder towards Arnold, 'often begins in the home.'

'But why would Sutcliffe want to attack me?' Arnold asked.

'Are you a ladies' man, Mr Landon?' Culpeper asked wryly.

2

The room was long and narrow and faced with brick. No pictures hung on the walls, which had been recently whitewashed, rather ineffectively, since Arnold could still make out scrawled graffiti under the thin covering.

Culpeper was standing just behind him, in the doorway. They were accompanied by two further policemen and a policewoman of Amazonian proportions. Lined up against the far wall of the room were seven men of varying heights and descriptions; two dressed casually in sweaters and jeans, the others in suits.

'All right,' Culpeper whispered in a low tone. 'You got the drill? You just take your time, walk along the line. Come back, take a second walk if you want to. Then if you recognize the guy who put the boot into you at your house, all you have to do is put out a hand and touch him.' When Arnold glanced back almost inadvertently, Culpeper grinned. 'Don't worry. If you identify your assailant he won't have the chance to do you again. That's why we got the muscle in here with us.' He paused, breathing heavily. 'All right. We're grateful for your assistance, Mr Landon. If you'd now like to take the walk . . .'

Reluctantly, Arnold walked towards the line of men standing with their backs against the wall. Culpeper stayed near the door, but at an angle which allowed him to observe the expression on Arnold's face. The others accompanied Arnold in a threatening phalanx.

The first man in the identity parade was someone Arnold had never consciously seen before; his eyes were fixed on a point above Arnold's head and his jaw jutted angrily. Arnold moved on.

The second man was also unknown to him, but as Arnold stepped sideways along the line to look at him an involuntary movement to the man's left drew his attention. To his surprise, he found himself staring at a man he had met before, in his own office, in the company of Edward Chaunter.

Nick Daniels held himself erect, making himself look as tall as his short frame would allow. His thin moustache was downturned, his mouth drooping with anxiety, soft, weak, and scared. On their first meeting Arnold had been aware of a lurking unease in Daniels's eyes, but now sheer terror glistened glaucously in those eyes as they flickered, unable to remain still, seeking a corner of the room to focus on safety. The strips of grey hair above his ears were dank with perspiration as Arnold stood in front of him, staring. When Arnold moved on, Daniels shivered.

The sixth man in the identity parade was also known to Arnold. Indeed, having seen Daniels in the line-up Arnold was almost expecting to see Zeke Santana. But Santana's attitude was different from that apparent in Daniels's demeanour. Santana was plainly furious, and the coldness of his anger was apparent in the clenching of his fists and the tension of his lean frame. He seemed poised for violent flight, almost leaning forward as though he was about to launch himself against Arnold, or the police guard with him. Arnold opened his mouth to say something, then thought better of it. As he moved on to the last man — a stranger — in the identity parade, he could feel Santana's cold glance boring into the back of his neck.

Culpeper was still standing at the door when Arnold returned. 'Another look?' he asked.

Arnold shook his head.

'You need to be sure,' Culpeper warned.

'I am sure.'

Culpeper nodded, then turned on his heel and marched ahead of the small group until they came to an interview room. He turned on Arnold. 'Well?'

'If by that you mean do I recognize any of those men as the one who attacked me, the answer is no. I don't recognize any of them — but then, I didn't see the man who attacked me, did I?'

'You don't recognize any of them?' Culpeper asked, his eyes narrowing.

'I recognize two of them, of course — Nick Daniels and Zeke Santana,' Arnold said, exasperated. 'But that's because I've had dealings with them. Not because I think either of them was at my bungalow—'

'Dealings? In connection with this churchyard thing?'

'No, not exactly. It was in connection with a planning application for the Methodist chapel and the Vicars of Jehovah.'

Culpeper nodded, but he seemed far from satisfied. He hesitated for a moment, then turned to the other officers who had accompanied them. 'All right, that'll do. This is a waste of time. We'll call it a day: send them all home.' He turned back to Arnold as the door closed behind his colleagues. 'You're not being much help, Landon.'

'I'm doing all I can to help,' Arnold insisted. 'But what the hell are you doing dragging those two into the identity parade? You surely don't believe one of them attacked me?'

Culpeper reddened, and his mouth became sullen. 'Police business is my business, not yours, Landon. It was just put to me that . . . But if not them, who did thump you, hey?'

'I don't know. And I don't even know why. But I don't think there's anything more I can do now . . . so do you think I can go home?' Culpeper nodded sourly. 'Follow me.

Mr Gibson will be out in the main entrance. He'll take you home.'

Culpeper pushed open the door and led the way down the corridor, past the canteen and into the main entrance of the station, nodding to the sergeant on duty as he passed. There were two men seated on the bench facing them, just inside the entrance. One was Ben Gibson. The other was Professor Elliott Brandling.

'You ready to go home, Arnold?' Ben Gibson asked, smiling, and coming forward with his right hand outstretched.

'He's ready,' Culpeper said shortly. His glance was fixed on Brandling, however, and resentment seemed to be simmering in his eyes. 'What are *you* doing here, Professor?'

Brandling hesitated, seeming to want to ask something. Instead, he explained, 'I . . . I thought I'd call to see how Landon was.'

'Yes, I can imagine,' Culpeper said, his voice heavy with irony. 'Well, I guess there'll be no further need for you to hang around here now, will there? Or was there something you wanted to ask me?'

Brandling frowned, conscious of the challenge in the detective inspector's voice, but he made no response to it. Instead, he turned and stood beside Arnold. 'You all right now?'

'I'm looking forward to getting home,' Arnold said.

'You never saw—'

'He never saw who attacked him,' Culpeper interrupted, 'and he didn't pick anyone out at the identity parade. Now we've got plenty to do here, and no time to stand around wasting any more time. I'll say goodbye . . . and thank you, Mr Landon.'

Arnold felt he wished to add . . . for nothing.

Ben Gibson's hand was on his arm and they were headed for the door when someone else came through the swing doors behind them. Arnold glanced back, and saw the first of the men from the identity parade. The group had been released. Arnold stepped out with Ben into the sunshine and Brandling was at his back. They made their way down towards the car park, but Arnold was aware of the footsteps behind them as some of the individuals who had taken part in the line-up walked to the park as they did. And ahead of them, in the car park, there was a tall, thin man standing beside one of the cars.

It was Edward Chaunter, leader of the Vicars of Jehovah.

As Arnold walked with his companions across the car park towards Ben Gibson's car, Brandling was saying, 'I hope you didn't mind my coming along. I felt kind of responsible for what happened.'

'Responsible?' Arnold wondered.

'Well, you and I, we'd been up to that chapel . . . and I had the feeling we were being watched,' Brandling said hesitantly. 'I thought maybe one of the cult had followed you, wanted to silence you—'

'To stop me from saying what?' Arnold asked. 'I don't know anything, except what you've told me about them, and their activities.'

Brandling stared at him, frowning. 'But you felt it yourself . . . the corruption . . . the evil in that churchyard . . .'

'Professor Brandling!'

The men who had been coming out of the police station behind them had now dispersed, with the exception of Nick Daniels and Zeke Santana. They were standing alongside the car belonging to Edward Chaunter, and it was the tall, saturnine leader of the Vicars of Jehovah who had called Brandling's name.

Brandling hesitated for a moment, his eyes narrowing, then he turned to face Chaunter. 'Yes?'

Chaunter's cold eyes were expressionless as he sauntered forward, Daniels and Santana walking just slightly behind him. He stepped up close to the university don and stared at him, as though weighing him up carefully, seeking to balance the strengths in the man against any possible weaknesses that might be exploited. 'I gain the impression it's you who are responsible for that . . . farce.'

Brandling hesitated. His chin came up. 'I don't know what you're talking about.'

'I'm talking about that identity parade. I get the distinct impression it was due to your intervention. It was your suggestion, I understand, that my colleagues should be put through the humiliation of that line-up. I don't know you—'

Brandling began to turn away dismissively. Chaunter's tone changed, his voice coming out in a snarl. 'What the hell have you got against us, Brandling?'

The Professor caught Arnold's glance and hesitated, seemed to be about to turn and speak, but thought better of it. A police car was nosing into the car park, blue light flashing, as Brandling said to Arnold, 'I'll give you a ring, try to get to see you when you're feeling better.'

'*Brandling*!' Chaunter snapped again.

The Professor was moving away, brushing past Arnold, intent on ignoring the man. Chaunter stood stock-still, glaring angrily after Brandling, but the studied insult was too much for one of Chaunter's companions: with a strangled shout Zeke Santana thrust past his leader, grabbed Brandling by the shoulder and swung him around. 'Here's an end to your interference!' he shouted, throwing a punch at Brandling's head with his right hand.

The blow caught Brandling on the temple and he staggered, clutching at Santana's jacket. Santana tried to hit him again as Chaunter moved in, shouting, Ben Gibson attempted to interpose himself between the men, and Arnold lurched back against the side of the car, pain shooting through his chest.

Then pandemonium broke loose. The siren of a police car began to wail as it skidded to a stop in front of the station, tyres squealing; doors opened and banged, a number of burly officers came charging out of the main entrance into the car park, and a man was dragged from the police car, coat thrown hastily over his head, and ushered quickly into the police station while Santana and Brandling threw wild blows at each other, both men enraged and largely ineffective in their anger, with Chaunter trying to take part and Daniels dancing at the edge of the fracas.

Brandling was down on one knee and Santana was trying to club him into submission with his fists. The look on the man's face was murderous, and Arnold could now believe that he was capable of carrying out the attack at his bungalow. He seemed almost crazed with rage and determined to crush the man at his feet. Chaunter was dragging at his arm, trying to pull him away, and Ben Gibson himself fell back, reeling from a stray blow to the cheekbone.

The battle lasted possibly only half a minute, but it seemed longer to Arnold before the burly figure of Detective Inspector Culpeper was among them, thrusting the antagonists apart, with several uniformed policemen in support. After a brief struggle Santana was held in an armlock by a red-faced constable, and Brandling's arms, too, were gripped. The Professor was white-faced, but Arnold was disturbed to see in the man's eyes an echo of the madness that had appeared in Santana.

The police siren was cut off suddenly, and the blue light died. Detective Inspector Culpeper stood in the middle of the hustling, sweating group. Then suddenly he was bawling at the top of his voice, red-necked, eyes bulging with anger and frustration.

'I've had enough of this! Get all these bastards back inside the station!'

3

'I ought to throw the book at you! If you'd been a bunch of yobbos in the Market Place, or yuppies outside the King's Arms, you'd all have been inside cooling your heels overnight in the cells, and maybe facing a magistrate in the morning. But are you crazy or something? You're grown men, and you're brawling in the police car park for God's sake! What the hell was it all about?'

The room was large, and furnished as a lecture room with a series of chairs arranged in rows and a raised dais at the front where Culpeper stood, hands on hips, glowering at them all. Arnold's chest was aching and he tried to keep his breathing shallow, reluctant to face the stab of pain that would surely come from his cracked ribs if he got too excited. He glanced across to Ben Gibson: the old man looked distressed, his face ashen, but beside him Elliott Brandling sat with his jaw tense, fists clenched. If Culpeper was hoping that gathering the group together in this room was going to allow them to cool off he would be mistaken, for Zeke Santana also had not pulled himself together — he continued to shoot angry glances in Brandling's direction and there was clearly no love lost between the two men. Chaunter held himself slightly aloof, lip twisted disdainfully, as though the thought of finding himself in the police station was beneath his dignity, and his friend Daniels was sweating profusely but, like Santana, angrily aware of the presence of Elliott Brandling.

No one spoke.

'So you've got nothing to say to explain that stupidity out there,' Culpeper growled. 'Fine. But there's no way I'm letting you out on the street just yet. You can all stay here and cool down, enjoy each other's company, then I'll get you all escorted from the premises in a little while — separately. That way, hopefully, you won't make fools of yourselves again.'

He glared around at them for a few moments and then motioned to the duty constable to leave the room. 'Right. I've got to see someone who's just seen fit to favour us with his presence. You might have seen him arrive in the police car — or maybe you were too busy scuffling. I'll be back in about ten minutes, so take that time to cool down. If anyone then wants to give me an explanation . . .'

He waited again for a few moments, and then he strode from the room. Arnold felt distinctly uncomfortable. It seemed to him that Culpeper was making a mistake leaving the protagonists in the same room without supervision. It was hardly in accordance with normal police procedure, he imagined.

On the other hand it was hardly a usual occurrence, having a group of respectable men brawling in the police car park. He glanced at Ben Gibson and saw the old man staring at him owlishly. His mouth was twitching, and Arnold himself suddenly felt the urge to laugh. He managed a smile, half suppressed, before he heard Chaunter, clearly seeing nothing funny in the situation, state coldly, 'I regard this as your responsibility, Professor Brandling.'

The Professor straightened in his chair. 'Me? I hardly started the fracas. You people seem addicted to violence,' he responded. 'It's like a drug to you. It's why you keep homicidal maniacs like Santana in your midst!'

'I don't have to take that!' Santana gritted, half rising from his seat. Chaunter put a hand on his arm, gripping him fiercely, as he continued to fix his cold eyes on Brandling.

'You seem to wish to provoke trouble,' Chaunter said. 'The scene in the car park wasn't enough?'

'I didn't start it,' Brandling insisted in a flat tone.

'It depends what you mean by starting,' Daniels complained. 'What the hell you got against us?'

There was a short silence. Ben Gibson shifted uneasily in his chair. Chaunter leaned forward. 'You'll hardly deny this . . . identity parade . . . was your idea, Brandling?'

'I don't control the police.'

'But you'll have placed the suggestion in their minds,' Chaunter insisted.

Elliott Brandling turned his head and stared at Arnold, as though seeking support, before turning back to Chaunter. 'You forget, Chaunter, I know about you. It's not so long since one of your acolytes — Santana there — tried to recruit me into your cult.'

'Clearly, that was a mistake,' Chaunter said in a soft, dangerous voice. 'Your affinity with the religious among us cannot be—'

'If by religion you mean worship of the Devil, that's true!' Brandling interrupted. 'After Santana contacted me I did a bit more research about what your Vicars of Jehovah stand for. And I know that it's just a cloak for the cult of the Raging Wolf. What you're interested in, among your sick little group, is esotericism, the excitement of darkness, the corruption of established Church practices, the twisting of truths and the lascivious use of flesh and blood and pain in your rituals! You don't fool me, Chaunter! The cult of de Vieux Pont was always a crazy, black one, feeding off murder and death and violence and blood. I wouldn't join your damned organization, but I know all about the rituals at St Michael's Church, and I can guess what you want to do at the Methodist chapel. It all got too much, didn't it? You went too far with the old gipsy, and he died. But you couldn't keep your hands clean, you needed the blood. A dog was one thing; a human being was another. The excitement of the ritual was different with human life involved, and you had to do it again with poor Cy. But it's dangerous out there in the open at Kentside, isn't it? You'll be safer, closer, more secret and confined in your own premises, at the old chapel. What changes are you making there, Chaunter? What obscenities are you making arrangements for?'

'This is crazy!' Nick Daniels was shaking. His eyes were bulging and his mouth seemed to have lost the capacity to form words properly; loose and rubbery, it was working ineffectually, so that his disjointed efforts to speak were barely intelligible. 'Madness . . . can't really believe that . . . set up . . . Tell him, Chaunter . . . tell him!'

'Why?' Chaunter demanded, rising to his feet. 'Why are you uttering these slanderous statements about us, Brandling?'

Elliott Brandling rose also. He stood facing Chaunter, eyes glittering dangerously, and Arnold remembered how shaken the man had been by the death of his young research assistant. 'Do you deny it? Do you really deny that your . . . sect . . . is nothing more than a cover for your real activities — the cult of de Vieux Pont?'

Chaunter stood rigid. He touched his lips with his tongue. In the silence, as Daniels and Santana stared at him expectantly, Daniels still shaking with fear, Arnold was aware of the perspiration glistening on Chaunter's forehead, the silent rage inside the man. Chaunter always seemed so ice-cold, but now internal tensions had seized him, and anxiety and fury was making him sweat. 'Deny?' he repeated, and there was a tremor in his voice.

'What will we find at the chapel, if we look?' Brandling sneered. 'Can you deny de Vieux Pont, Chaunter?'

Slowly, Chaunter shook his head. 'No, I won't deny that we . . . we practise ancient rites connected with de Vieux Pont.'

There was an audible sigh from Zeke Santana.

'But what you say,' Chaunter continued, 'is all the product of your own fevered imagination. We've never—'

'Does not blood enter into your rituals?' Brandling demanded. 'Remember, I've read widely, and I was approached by Santana!'

Daniels tried to say something, but Chaunter forestalled him with a magisterial wave of his hand. He was regaining control of himself, and he was watching Elliott Brandling keenly, as though trying to identify the weakness in the man's argument. 'All right, yes, blood does have a place in our rituals.'

'And sacrifice?'

'Edward—!'

Chaunter ignored Santana's interruption. 'Yes, I suppose you could say so. But let's be clear, Brandling. I'm not talking about human sacrifice. A dog, perhaps—'

'And that was only once,' Daniels burst out excitedly. 'For God's sake, it was just a game, a shivery sort of exciting game in the moonlight. We used to have a ritual, and Chaunter would intone, and we even used slabs of meat . . . and then there was a dog once and . . .' His eyes were glistening, and his mouth was wet. Arnold stared at him, not certain whether it was fear that moved him or the recollection of the pathetic excitements the group had indulged in.

Irritably, as though feeling Daniels had denigrated the cult's activities, Chaunter snapped, 'That's enough, Nick! But let's be clear, human sacrifice was never—'

'You're lying!'

'Brandling—'

'It's all part of a pattern!' Brandling insisted violently. 'Slabs of meat in the ritual; a dog; then an old man—'

'You're mad!' Chaunter was almost shouting, suddenly, as the seriousness of what Brandling was saying finally got through to him. 'What the hell's the matter with you, Brandling? Why are you attacking us like this?'

'Because I know you killed Cy Robinson! You murdered him in your obscene rituals! I tried to warn people — I told Landon here. I spoke to the police! All right, I *did* suggest that Culpeper should haul you in for the identity parade. Apparently you, Chaunter, had an alibi for the relevant time—'

'Relevant time? What are you talking about?'

'You can't fool us. Landon and I were up at the chapel, trying to discover what you were up to. We heard a car; we knew we were being watched. And then when Landon was attacked in his home I knew we had you! One of you beat up Landon and the girl — and it's all to cover up—'

The door opened, and Brandling's words were cut off.

Detective Inspector Culpeper stood framed in the doorway. 'Mr Landon?'

Arnold rose, awkwardly. 'Yes?'

'There's someone here who'd like to speak to you.'

* * *

His eyes were hooded and sullen. Half-healed scratches ran down the side of his face, starting just below his dark, beetling eyebrows and ending at his jawline. He held his hands in front of him, left hand clutching the right. The knuckles were bruised and swollen. Culpeper stood just behind him, smiling, clearly enjoying himself. 'We won't bother with a line-up, Mr Landon. Have you ever seen *this* man before?'

Arnold nodded. He remembered: outside his office car park, as he drove away behind Cy Robinson and Andrea Sutcliffe, this man had been standing, staring, with hate in his eyes.

'He has something to say to you, Landon. Contrition, sort of. Mr Sutcliffe, be my guest.'

Andrea Sutcliffe's husband raised his head.

His eyes were still sullen, but his voice was steady. 'Mr Landon, I'm sorry. I just wanted to tell you . . . it was a mistake. You got to realize, I was crazy with jealousy, and she was running around with that Robinson, and I watched . . . I saw that you knew Robinson, saw you at Mr Gibson's shop . . . and after I heard Robinson was dead I thought she might come back to me, but instead, when I followed her, I saw her go to your bungalow, wait for your return, go inside, and I thought . . . I went crazy . . . I beat the door down . . .' He frowned, chewed at his lip. 'I'm sorry. I realized later you couldn't have been . . .'

'Not exactly cut out to take Robinson's place, hey?' Culpeper beamed. 'So, Mr Landon, it's cleared up. Sutcliffe here gave himself up this morning. He's admitted to bashing his wife and attacking you, says he's sorry, but that's easily done, isn't it? All right, my lad, we'll get you booked and then we'll talk—'

'This man's wife,' Chaunter interrupted, 'she was having an affair with Robinson, the man who was killed?'

Culpeper nodded happily. 'And Mr Sutcliffe here thinks he can walk in, confess to thumping her and Landon at the bungalow, and not expect us to ask questions about why he dumped Robinson in the churchyard after he killed him.'

Sutcliffe's head jerked, puppet-like. 'I never laid a hand on that young bastard! I was jealous as hell, and I followed them and watched them, but it was only when I thought she was going to someone else, Mr Landon, that I finally cracked. You can't lay that on me, not the responsibility for Robinson's murder!'

Arnold stared at the man, heard the panic in his voice, but was also aware of something else in his tone — a conviction, and a determination to resist that rang true. He looked at Chaunter, still cold-eyed, but more vulnerable now after the events of the last few minutes; at Brandling, still glaring his hatred at the Vicars of Jehovah; at the shaking Daniels and the vicious Santana.

Somehow, there was something missing, the bond that drew all these men, himself, Ben Gibson, and Andrea Sutcliffe's husband, together.

He frowned, thinking, churning over half-remembered facts. 'Mr Sutcliffe,' he asked suddenly. 'You thought your wife was turning to me after Cy Robinson's death?'

The man shuffled awkwardly, and nodded. 'For what?'

'I don't know. I thought . . . a man . . . companionship . . . I don't know. I was crazy.'

'So you didn't know why she wanted to see me?'

'What's that got to do with anything?' Culpeper growled, and began to turn Sutcliffe towards the door. 'Your private life's your affair, Landon.'

Arnold stared at Culpeper. *Missing piece . . . missing pieces* . . . 'What about Connor?' he asked.

Culpeper turned back. 'The gipsy? We think he's in North Yorkshire. With luck, we'll get our hands on him within twenty-four hours.'

'Then maybe,' Arnold said slowly, deep in thought, 'this is all about the Albigensian heresies.'

4

Edward Chaunter sat down slowly and deliberately. His eyes were fixed on Arnold and his mouth was like a steel trap. Following his example, Santana sat down too, watchful and tense. Chaunter cleared his throat with deliberation. 'I should warn you, Landon. Things have been said here this morning which are slanderous. Brandling has made accusations . . . if you are now going to add to them, in front of witnesses, I warn you I shall take the appropriate action, civil or criminal, and I'll see you ruined!'

'What the hell are the Albigensian heresies?' Culpeper asked, reluctantly. 'What are you getting at, Landon?'

'Missing pieces,' Arnold replied. He looked at Brandling.

'The early Roman Church was not powerful enough to disregard preachers who asserted teachings other than those approved by Mother Church,' Brandling said quietly. 'Any teaching which was . . . different . . . from established practice was regarded as heresy. One such heresy — the Albigensian — flourished in mediaeval France. It was rooted out. It was what the Inquisition was all about; that, and property confiscation, of course. Religion was always about power, and power about land.'

Culpeper glared at the Professor. 'Save me the history lesson. Landon, what are you on about?'

'The reason why Andrea Sutcliffe wanted to see me.'

'I don't see it's important,' Culpeper insisted.

'Forgive me, but I disagree. When she arrived she was distraught, upset. At Cy Robinson's death, of course. But she wanted to tell me something. She was prevented from doing so by the brutal attack from her husband. But I ask myself, what did she want to say? And why me?'

Ben Gibson coughed nervously. His eyes were bright, his brow furrowed. 'I got a book for him, for young Robinson. It upset him, I'm sure of that. He worked on it, then he came to see me, said he wanted to discuss it with Mr Landon.'

'I think that's why he came to my office. He didn't find me there, heard I'd gone to Rafferty Common, and followed me there. But why? Was it to tell me something . . . or to seek my advice?'

'Advice about what?' Elliott Brandling asked in a puzzled tone.

'I'm not sure,' Arnold said wonderingly.

'And I wonder,' Ben Gibson said in a quiet voice, 'what connection there might be between the Albigensian heresy and the cult of de Vieux Pont.'

'They're both heresies,' Brandling snapped viciously, 'both reviled in the mediaeval period, both rooted out at one time, but some foul roots remained as far as the Raging Wolf cult was concerned.'

Chaunter raised a thin, menacing hand. 'I don't know what you're driving at here, but you're not going to get away with tying us to anything to do with Robinson! We know nothing about his death and you'll never prove we were involved.'

Arnold shook his head, frowning. He looked at Brandling and at Ben Gibson, and said, 'Let's approach this from a different angle. Let's put ourselves in Robinson's shoes. He has the book Ben provided; something in it disturbs him. What would he do? In whom would he confide?'

‘His mistress?’ Ben Gibson suggested. Sutcliffe’s head came up angrily at the word. He looked at Culpeper, but the detective was frowning, listening to Arnold.

‘I think maybe that’s why Andrea Sutcliffe came to see me,’ Arnold suggested. ‘She knew what Robinson was upset about; maybe she advised him to see me. And when he died, she decided to see me herself. And she was scared!’

‘Of her husband?’ Brandling asked.

‘Of him . . . but maybe of something else too. After all, Cy Robinson was *dead*.’

There was a short silence. The atmosphere in the room had changed; whereas previously the tension had lain in the verbal battle between Brandling and the Vicars of Jehovah, now there was a palpable electricity in the room, directed towards Arnold. He felt it, was aware of their eyes on him, and he grasped Ben Gibson’s arm as though for support. His breathing was suddenly quick, and knifing pains went through his chest as he spoke. ‘Rafferty Common, of course, was chance. Gipsy Joe Connor grabbed Robinson as a hostage and fled. But why would he kill him?’

‘I don’t think he did,’ Culpeper growled. ‘We’ll find out what happened when I’ve had a few hours with Mr Sutcliffe here!’

‘But if *you* couldn’t find Connor and Robinson, how did Sutcliffe find him to kill him?’ Arnold asked. ‘And isn’t it more likely that Connor released Cy Robinson once he was clear — but left him somewhere isolated, where he wouldn’t be able to get in touch easily with anyone?’

‘He would have walked to a phone,’ Ben Gibson suggested, ‘and called the police.’

‘Or a friend,’ Arnold added.

‘Andrea Sutcliffe?’

‘What if she wasn’t available?’

‘You?’

‘He’d last seen me at Rafferty Common,’ Arnold replied. ‘There’d be someone else he’d turn to then, if not before. A man he admired and respected. A man also to whom he could talk about what was bothering him — the Albigensian heresies. Perhaps the man to whom he should have spoken right at the beginning, instead of worrying himself with Andrea and me. The Albigensian heresies . . .' Arnold shook his head, as half-remembered scraps, comments, unmatched pieces of conversations drifted through his mind. A man long dead, a reputation founded on just a few publications, a writer who had used minor publishing houses . . .

Arnold turned his head to look at the man beside him. 'I've never read *The Scribe of Odilo*,' he said.

5

The battered leather armchair creaked as Culpeper lowered himself into it. He stroked the scarred leather with his hands, gently, admiringly, as though pleased with this concession to his comfort denied to lesser men in the force. A fly buzzed noisily against the warm windowpane and Culpeper watched it thoughtfully for a little while. Then he turned to look at Arnold.

'You'd better tell me what this is all about.'

Arnold felt sick. 'I'm a fool. And I've been used.'

Culpeper glanced at Elliott Brandling and at Ben Gibson, seated beside him. Gibson's head was down as he contemplated his hands. Brandling's features were composed but wooden, lacking any expression.

'That tells me nothing,' Culpeper said.

'There never was anything I could really do for Professor Brandling that he couldn't have undertaken himself. The Jarrow ruins — he already knew what they meant. The church at Kentside . . . it was *that* he wanted me to get interested in, and with a little auto-suggestion I fell in beautifully; naive, stupid . . . and I found the remains of the dog under the hedge. I've no doubt he already knew about that, wanted me to find it, to establish a confirmation of what he wanted.'

'And what was that?' Culpeper asked, puzzled.

'He wanted to establish, independently of himself, the belief that the Vicars of Jehovah, masquerading under that name to hide their true cult — of de Vieux Pont — were a dangerous group of homicidally inclined fantasists. And he succeeded. I believed it. I told you of it. But it was never true, of course. They're just a pathetic bunch of play-actors, pretending with slabs of meat and stray dogs that they're the Lords of Darkness. They're nut cases, twisted, maybe, but they're not homicidal. He's fooled me, used me, ever since we accidentally met that day at the Lit and Phil.'

'No,' Ben Gibson interjected. He seemed vaguely confused at the sound of his own voice, and looked up apologetically to Culpeper. 'I mean . . . it was no accident. Professor Brandling asked . . . asked me to arrange that meeting. I'm sorry, Arnold, I was on the point of telling you several times, but somehow I never got around to it.'

Arnold nodded; it only confirmed his suspicions. Culpeper looked at Brandling but the Professor seemed indifferent to his surroundings; after the fury and the tension of his confrontation with Chaunter, he seemed to have withdrawn. His chin was sunk to his chest and he was staring without expression at the desk in front of him.

'Now why,' Culpeper asked, 'should Professor Brandling . . . use you in this way?'

Arnold hesitated, struggling to find the right words in the maelstrom of doubt and self-recrimination that boiled in his brain. 'I don't know . . . I think . . . my guess is, at some stage in the last few months he had realized there'd come a time when he would have to kill Cy Robinson.'

Ben Gibson's head jerked. He looked at Arnold and his cheeks were pale. The fly buzzed even more noisily against the window and Culpeper contemplated it for a moment with growing irritation. 'We more or less got to that point when we were back there with the others, Landon.' He glanced uneasily at Brandling but there was no response. 'But what reason would he have for killing his own research assistant?'

'I don't know.'

'Landon—' Culpeper warned.

'I don't know, but I can guess,' Arnold admitted hurriedly. 'I think it's to do with *The Scribe of Odilo*. You've got to remember, Inspector, that Brandling came late to the University and has never entirely been accepted there, for his background or his research qualifications. There was jealousy, of course, over the success of *The Scribe of Odilo*, but from what Robinson himself hinted there was criticism of certain "quantum leaps" Brandling seemed to have taken. I think that was jargon for suggesting Brandling hadn't done some essential basic research in presenting his thesis.'

'I'm not interested in university politics,' Culpeper growled.

Arnold steeled himself not to look at Brandling; he was speaking as if the Professor was not present in the room. 'Ben warned me some time ago that Brandling was obsessive. I've seen some evidence of it. He's desperately committed to his position and status in the University, but Robinson — who came to him with agreed research when another professor left — was in some way endangering that position. I think Brandling would never have allowed Robinson to research the Albigensian heresies if he'd had a choice. Robinson consulted him during the research, and Brandling realized the boy would eventually hit on something which would destroy Brandling's own position in the University.'

'What?'

'I don't know.'

'Bloody hell!' Culpeper rose, turned to the window and watched the angry fly for several seconds. He picked up a piece of paper from his desk, pressed it against the struggling fly, and squashed it flat against the windowpane. He slumped back in his chair. The room was strangely silent without the persistent buzzing at the window.

'Landon, it seems to me we're indulging in theories that get us nowhere.'

'But if we make the assumptions I've suggested, the hypotheses—'

'Landon—'

'If we do, look at how it would have happened! Brandling knew of the cult's activities — he'd been asked to join them. He would need to distance himself from the killing of Cy Robinson, if it ever became necessary. So first, he involved me.' Arnold hesitated, sneaking a glance at the silent Brandling. 'But it was also necessary to establish a pattern, to keep that distance. He needed someone else to die, someone weak, unable to struggle, a vagrant, an old down-and-out with whom he'd never be connected. In fact, he found an old gipsy, walking drunkenly back to Rafferty Common. He killed him; made a pretence at savage ritual, and put the body at St Michael's Church.'

'But why—'

'It was the Devil-worshipping cult that would be blamed! Brandling was laying the groundwork — and I went along with it. And he had to move quickly; he was getting desperate, because Ben had told him he'd found Robinson a book printed by an obscure publisher, written by Brandling's own old mentor, now dead . . .'

Arnold's voice died away uncertainly. He stared at Ben for several seconds, but did not see him. He was thinking of an old man who worked on research which he never published, and on tracts which appeared briefly, but in obscure manuals.

'You're telling me he deliberately killed an old man, without motive, just to set up another killing?' Culpeper's tone was grating.

Arnold came out of his reverie. He nodded. 'It was necessary — to throw suspicion towards the Vicars of Jehovah. Things got confusing for him then, because suspicion actually fell upon Gipsy Joe Connor, owing to the feud he had with the old man over the granddaughter.'

'They must have got even more confusing when Connor grabbed Robinson as a hostage,' Ben Gibson suggested.

Arnold nodded. 'But more importantly, it still meant suspicion was diverted even further from Brandling himself. And then his chance came. I think he got a phone call from Robinson, after the abduction.'

Culpeper grunted. 'After Connor dumped him at the wayside.'

'That's right. Robinson had begun to realize what Brandling had feared. He wanted to approach the Professor but was unwilling, scared maybe. He told Andrea Sutcliffe about it; she advised him to talk to me because of my antiquarian interests. Robinson tried to see me, followed me up to Rafferty Common, was abducted . . . and when he was released, maybe he tried to get one of us first, or maybe he thought he ought to contact Brandling, have it out with him, tell him what he'd found. It was a mistake, but understandable. I think Brandling drove out to pick him up, and was forced to do the thing he finally dreaded. He killed him, used a knife again to give it the appearance of ritual, and then dumped the body at St Michael's. The rest of it — our visit to the chapel, the identity parade, the insistence that Chaunter and his friends were dangerous — was merely taking advantage of the confusion, but keeping a finger strongly pointed towards the cult of de Vieux Pont.'

Culpeper was silent. His brows drew together; he stared at his stubby fingers, and slowly shook his head. 'Do you know, there's hardly one shred of evidence in all that, hardly a thing I could put to a court. You tell a great story, Landon, but . . .'

'What will happen when Connor is brought in and tells us where he dropped Robinson, unharmed?' Arnold demanded.

Culpeper shrugged. 'Another supposition.'

'And when Andrea Sutcliffe comes out of her coma and tells us what Robinson discussed with her and what she wanted to see me about?'

Culpeper shrugged again. 'She's likely to recover . . . but are you certain she'll tell us what you think? Besides, in all this . . .' He hesitated, stared at Brandling for a long moment again, but the Professor made no movement. 'In all this you haven't really uncovered the motive for such planned, brutal behaviour.'

'A man's life,' Elliott Brandling said, almost musing.

'What's that?'

'A man's life.' As silence gathered about him in the room Brandling stirred, drew himself together, sat more upright in the chair. His eyes were still clouded, and he was frowning, thinking. 'Mine . . . all I've worked for and earned. And that of David Loxton. He died some years ago. Brilliant scholar. But the kind I could never match. No ambition . . . but brilliant. He wasted his career, and I was there when he died and when I saw his papers — I was his research assistant — I realized how much he had wasted. I decided it was my chance. I took those papers, used the material, published it. The result was *The Scribe of Odilo*. And it made my reputation — I got my chair eventually. But there were things missing . . . things Loxton himself had already published, linking passages I couldn't use without the plagiarism becoming obvious. The game would have been given away. Do you understand?' He looked up at Arnold but his eyes were blank, and weary with a great disappointment and loss.

'It was that which Robinson discovered?' Arnold asked gently. 'A Loxton publication, on which you'd based your own published research?'

'The Albigensian heresies. They'd have known, at the University. I'd have been disgraced. I'd have seen my reputation destroyed; never have got another job. I tried to warn Cy, steer him away, but he was obsessed, even thought he was emulating me. Obsessed . . . as I've been obsessed. In the end . . . I never really thought I'd have to do it. I didn't *want* to do it. At the beginning, I just thought I'd better lay the groundwork, almost like an academic exercise, a piece of research, you know? But then . . . That vicious, stupid cult, prancing around playing silly games . . . And the old man, he was only a gipsy, what did he matter? But Cy . . . that was different. I didn't want to do it. He forced me; he made it inevitable . . . so bloody, unnecessarily inevitable . . .'

* * *

Ben Gibson opened the car door and helped Arnold get in. The sharp pains in his chest had increased with his laboured, excited breathing, but he knew that during the drive home he'd be able to relax, and it would be a week before he'd have to return to work. Then there would be the Rafferty Common thing to sort out, against a background or charges against Gullick, and Connor, when they caught him. The Planning Department would have to look at the Methodist chapel approval again, in view of what Arnold had heard, and he supposed the police would want to bring charges of desecration at St Michael's, though that was none of Arnold's business.

Ben got in behind the steering wheel, started the car and the vehicle lurched its way out of the car park. He was not the most able of drivers. They manoeuvred their way through Morpeth and headed out towards Arnold's bungalow. Ben Gibson was silent for most of the drive, but as they entered the lane leading to the bungalow, he said, 'Is Brandling . . . is he all right?' He hesitated. 'I mean, in spite of what you said, if he . . . if he hadn't spoken up like that, if he'd just kept silent . . . what could Culpeper have done? Why did Brandling behave like that?'

Arnold looked out of the window. He could understand. 'Because it was over,' he said.

'His career? Because of the scandal?'

'Not just that,' Arnold said. 'Don't you remember telling me? He's an obsessive man . . . but a lonely one too.'

And there had been a night on the banks of the Wear, at Elliott Brandling's house, when that loneliness had come through to Arnold in all its intensity. Brandling had seen in Robinson his own future — the son he would never have, the researcher he would never be. He had been forced to make a choice: to allow his own career to be destroyed, or to destroy the threat to that career.

Perhaps there, in Culpeper's room, Brandling had looked at himself and at his actions in the cold light of reason and had decided that in the end he had made the wrong choice.

THE END

ALSO BY ROY LEWIS

ERIC WARD MYSTERIES

Book 1: THE SEDLEIGH HALL MURDER
Book 2: THE FARMING MURDER
Book 3: THE QUAYSIDE MURDER
Book 4: THE DIAMOND MURDER
Book 5: THE GEORDIE MURDER
Book 6: THE SHIPPING MURDER
Book 7: THE CITY OF LONDON MURDER
Book 8: THE APARTMENT MURDER
Book 9: THE SPANISH VILLA MURDER
Book 10: THE MARRIAGE MURDER
Book 11: THE WASTEFUL MURDER
Book 12: THE PHANTOM MURDER
Book 13: THE SLAUGHTERHOUSE MURDER
Book 14: THE TATTOO MURDER
Book 15: THE FOOTBALL MURDER
Book 16: THE TUTANKHAMUN MURDER
Book 17: THE ZODIAC MURDER

INSPECTOR JOHN CROW

Book 1: A LOVER TOO MANY
Book 2: ERROR OF JUDGMENT
Book 3: THE WOODS MURDER
Book 4: MURDER FOR MONEY
Book 5: MURDER IN THE MINE
Book 6: A COTSWOLDS MURDER
Book 7: A FOX HUNTING MURDER
Book 8: A DARTMOOR MURDER

ARNOLD LANDON MYSTERIES

Book 1: MURDER IN THE BARN
Book 2: MURDER IN THE MANOR
Book 3: MURDER IN THE FARMHOUSE
Book 4: MURDER IN THE STABLE YARD
Book 5: MURDER IN THE CHURCH

Thank you for reading this book.

If you enjoyed it please leave feedback on Amazon or Goodreads, and if there is anything we missed or you have a question about, then please get in touch. We appreciate you choosing our book.

Founded in 2014 in Shoreditch, London, we at Joffe Books pride ourselves on our history of innovative publishing. We were thrilled to be shortlisted for Independent Publisher of the Year at the British Book Awards.

www.joffebooks.com

We're very grateful to eagle-eyed readers who take the time to contact us. Please send any errors you find to corrections@joffebooks.com. We'll get them fixed ASAP.

Printed in Great Britain
by Amazon

64171591R10142